# The Bugles Blowing

## NICOLAS FREELING

**VINTAGE BOOKS**
*A Division of Random House*
*New York*

First Vintage Books Edition, February 1980

Copyright © 1975 by Nicolas Freeling

All rights reserved under International and Pan-American Copyright Conventions. Published in the United States by Random House, Inc., New York. Originally published by Harper and Row, Publishers, Inc., New York, in 1975.

The poem, "A Barrack-Room Ballad," is from *Departmental Ditties and Ballads and Barrack-Room Ballads* by Rudyard Kipling, published by Doubleday & Co., New York.

*Library of Congress Cataloging in Publication Data*
Freeling, Nicolas.
The bugles blowing.
Reprint of the 1975 ed. published by Harper & Row, New York.
I. Title.
[PZ4.F854Bu   1980]   [PR6056.R4]   79-23078
ISBN 0-394-74551-5

Manufactured in the United States of America

"What are the bugles blowing for?" said Files-on-Parade.
"To turn you out, to turn you out," the Colour-Sergeant
said. . . .

"What makes the rear-rank breathe so hard?" said Files-
on-Parade.
"It's bitter cold, it's bitter cold," the Colour-Sergeant said.
"What makes that front-rank man fall down?" said Files-
on-Parade.
"A touch of sun, a touch of sun," the Colour-Sergeant
said.
They are hanging Danny Deever, they are marching of
him round,
They have halted Danny Deever by his coffin on the
ground;
And he'll swing in half a minute for a sneaking shooting
hound—
O they're hanging Danny Deever in the morning!
—*"A Barrack-Room Ballad" by Rudyard Kipling*

Kipling's dropped aspirates in his "soldier talk" now
appear dated. Anyway, as George Orwell remarked several years ago, to restore them strengthens. On the other
hand, the sentiments expressed do not date, and need no
strengthening. Such was also the opinion of T. S. Eliot,
an officially approved poet, highly thought of by all civil
servants.

—*N.F.*

# THE BUGLES BLOWING

# 1. The First Magistrate
## Reviews a Dossier

The President of the Republic had had supper with his family, in his flat. He did this once a week, on average, and when he could, which was rarer, he spent the rest of the evening with them. Even if he had official business afterward, he did not discuss it, since, like any trained thinker, he could switch off compartments of his mind. Tonight, though he had made jokes, had eaten simply, as usual—a fish salad—and had drunk a glass or two of his favorite country wine (unpretentious, shipped for him in a barrel from the village and served in a jug), it was evident to those around him that he was not comfortable; this was unusual but nobody had commented.

Now he was walking with his quick nervous stride, for he was a man of scarcely fifty, and liked to correct the deskbound stoop by simple exercise—a thing rarely possible in his good city because of being recognized, and, too, one so rarely had the time. In chilly drizzling autumn rain, most eyes were downcast or masked by umbrellas, and paid no heed to the passer. If they had, and perchance been importunate, there were two secret-service men, one walking a little in front. He must have had eyes in the back of his head, though, for when the President looked at his watch and decided sadly to get on with it, he dropped back at once, and as the car drew up the three men got into it

3

as smoothly, perhaps, as for a scene in a gangster movie.

The President took all this for granted: he was well served. The guards were a burden of his office, and a heavy one, and a daily one. There were other burdens heavier yet, but not, thank heaven, daily. The car whisked through the wet shiny streets, turned in at the gate of the official residence, drew up at the portal; he jumped out, handed his hat and damp raincoat to a valet, went straight to his private office, and switched on his reading lamp and sat down. There was only one file on his desk: here, too, he was well served. The ordinary clothbound files were marked with a simple code showing the department where they originated. Ministry of Justice. This evening the President was not economist, administrator, or diplomat, but magistrate.

To be First Magistrate is in general an empty title, but in this country there is one decision that is taken by the President alone; it is too important to be left to the Minister of the Interior or the Keeper of the Seals. The legal and juridical problems have been examined by those competent to do so. What is left is a human, personal problem, for it is nothing more or less than a man's life. In the case of a man condemned to death for a capital crime by the Assize Court, in the Republic, the prerogative of mercy belongs to the President solely. The death penalty in France still exists, untouched on the statute book. It is rarely demanded by the Public Prosecutor, and still more rarely passed by the court. As for the President, he had never met this problem before. There is a tradition, and a good one, that he takes this particular function very seriously, dating from Vincent Auriol, the first President of the Fourth Republic, and followed by all his successors.

4

The file on the President's desk was a man's personal dossier.

It was unusually thick: this was no banal criminal, no man made brutish by hardship or unbalanced by illness. The lawyers and the doctors were quite clear on this subject. No mental disease, no psychosis or, by any definition, disabling neurosis. No legal or juridical flaw in procedure. No doubt, in fact, anywhere. The authorship of the crime had never even been questioned. And here it all was, neatly typed abstracts of everything, from the preliminary police inquiry down to the Court of Appeals. But there had been—still was —a political element. It had been examined by the political police, considered by the President's personal assistants. Conclusion: nothing there to justify interference with due process of law.

Politics . . . The President was a skilled and adroit politician; he would hardly have been elected otherwise. His mind, his training and formation, his experience as a state servant—all had bent this man toward a habit of seeing things in abstract terms. In religion, philosophy, in political and economic science, he rationalized as far as he could, as far as was consistent, as far as he dared. One could and did consider even such things as his family life, his health, his pleasures and enjoyments as abstract matters. There were limits to this—luckily.

At the end of the dossier were the usual letters. Relatives, the usual requests for personal interviews, the defense counsel, the elderly gentleman who was a judge at the Court of Human Rights, the notable criminal advocate who was the leading pleader against capital punishment. Last there was a letter still sealed, unopened by his secretariat, marked "Uncensored"

5

and the envelope stamped with a prison visa. A plain white envelope of good quality, addressed by hand to "The President of the Republic. Personal." Black ink from a real pen, firm upright handwriting of character and intelligence. No need of a graphologist's report to tell the President that, or the multiple reports of psychiatric experts, all in the dossier, which he had read attentively.

The letter had been respected. One did not fabricate letter bombs from condemned cells. The President reached for his letter knife, part of a simple and very beautiful desk set given him by the People's Republic of China. What form of death penalty did they have in China? It was not, he thought, a problem they allowed to worry them. Did they shoot people? If one admitted the idea at all, a bullet was perhaps as dignified—and honest—a method as any. Talk of barbarity was cant. Whether one broke or severed a neck by traditional methods, or adopted the clumsier techniques of the chemically minded, who imagined that gas, electricity, or a pharmaceutical poison was more hygienic—tidier, as it were—than blood, it was cant; the whole thing was barbaric. One took life: there was an executioner, and a victim. Whether the one be doctor or butcher, the other dressed in formal evening clothes or rags, whether the procedure be public or secret, the fact remained unaltered. The firing squad was, in any case, reserved in this country as a military punishment.

The President permitted himself a formal meditation on death, such as took place when he entered the crypt of the Monument to the Resistance on Fort Mont Valérien—there were also other occasions, some private.

He opened and read the letter. It did not help him much. The man asked, in simple and formal language, to be put to death. That was all. He thought for only a moment or two longer before deciding that his yes or no was not yet ripe. He put the letter back in the envelope and this back in the file, closed it, pushed it to one side, took a sheet of memo paper and uncapped his pen, thought a moment before putting it to the paper, then wrote rapidly.

"I will not pronounce on this matter before an element which in my view is missing has been supplied. Pray instruct that the officer conducting the original police inquiry be brought here and given an interview with me. This will be done immediately." He initialed, attached the half-sheet to the clip outside the file, drank a little Vittel water, and went to bed, where he slept as soundly as the man in the cell.

## 2. The Duty Officer in Hot Weather

Henri Castang was sitting on the base of his spine in a hard wooden chair before an open window of the Police Judiciaire offices on a flaming hot August day —and a Sunday, at that—whistling to himself, drearily enough.

"Memphis in June." Sounded good sung by Mr. Carmichael in that blurry, whisky-laden voice. Even whistled by himself, it had a nice tune, which he could do with one finger on the piano. The words had a pretty irony. Cousin Amanda making a rhubarb pie.

He didn't know much about Memphis, but getting it slung in your eye was nearer the mark at a rough guess.

Half the country was on holiday, and the other half wasn't doing more than it had to, because the thermometer marked thirty degrees, and being the weekend, the working half had gone off to look for the sweet oleander in the surrounding countryside. Castang didn't know about perfume but guessed that the acrid stench of recently doused forest fires would be more like it. There was nobody in the office but him, and a duty agent asleep somewhere, and a switchboard operator doing a crossword puzzle, and this here shady verandah. He nearly split his narrow Frankish face yawning. His face was all of a muddle, like the rest of him. If he saw the back of his head when getting a haircut, it was a Mediterranean bullet, round and Gaulish. The features were not straightforward Slav, the way his wife's were, but were vaguely Bohemian in cast, and the short wiry black hair was going prematurely gray in bits. He wished he were in Memphis, it would make a change.

Probably not much of one. Cities were all the same. If Castang had waked up in Bremen or Palermo, he would have gone to the office just the same, and soon picked up the local accent. This was just a provincial capital. Half a million souls, say, counting the outlying suburbs, counting the Portuguese and the Turks, and the British, and a few Americans, all doubtless in the C.I.A.

As a cop, you'd see no difference. You'd be filling in the same forms in Malmö or Barcelona, with Martin Beck or Van der Valk as a boss instead of Com-

8

missaire Richard, who was less eccentric, but what odds did that make?

Richard wasn't on holiday but he had taken the weekend off. Out somewhere playing golf, Castang supposed. Or something.

You could only express the difference in clichés. In Memphis, he supposed, there'd be more blacks, and here the cops wore képis so you were in France, but in the long run it was all McKeesport, Pennsylvania, and the smell would be just the same.

Work was languid. He'd been there all morning and had caught up on the paper. And now it was midafternoon and hot, even though this old barrack was solidly built with thick walls. Plainclothes cops had a gun problem. Castang was wearing a loose overshirt of rough towel material, which abosorbed sweat and came low enough to conceal the belt holster on his right hip. It gave his stocky body an oddly squat look but he didn't care. What you lost in dignity you gained in comfort.

He looked out at the horse-chestnut trees, in full leaf but rusty already: they didn't much care for their diet of salt in winter and sulphur dioxide in summer. In the branches hung a paper dart. The last duty dogsbody had been engaged in aeronautical research.

The telephone rang while he was in mid-yawn.

"I wish to speak to the Commissaire." It was a peremptory voice, used to prompt obedience.

"Not here at present, I'm afraid."

"Away?"

"Just out. Sunday, you know."

"Ah. Yes, of course."

"Duty officer speaking; can I help you?"

"I require your presence," abruptly.

9

"You'd like to explain your difficulty?"

"I am a murderer." Type with loose screws, further loosened by the heat.

"Yes?" in a deadish voice. "Who of?"

"My wife. My daughter. A man." Brisk and factual, but the nuts often were; they had it all worked out, most detailed and plausible.

"Where?"

"Here. My home, I'm speaking from my home address. Number 7, Rue des Écrivains." Not in Memphis. Here.

"When?"

"Now. Ten—no, roughly twenty minutes ago."

"What with?" These bald questions were the only quick way of detecting a real emergency. The nuts sometimes replied to this one with "An atom bomb," or "The evil eye."

"A gun. My gun. I keep it in the bedside table. It is my legitimate property." This insistence on legitimacy struck Castang: a pointer, too, that he was not dealing with loose screws.

"And your name is?"

"La Touche. Gilbert La Touche." Something, too, familiar about this name; it rang a bell somewhere, but dim. Castang pulled a message pad toward him with the phone tucked in his collarbone, picking up a ball-point and glancing at his watch. Message received 16:37. Dog watch in dog day, while in doldrum, but this might be a squall, for a small black cloud had appeared upon the brassy and boring horizon.

"Right, I'm taking notes. Mr. Gilbert La Touche, 7 Rue des Écrivains, you think you may have killed one or more persons with a pistol; that's all correct? Have you rung a doctor?"

10

"No. No use."

"Or Police Secours?"

"No. I am aware that the criminal police is needed; it was logical to ring you."

Logical . . . legitimate . . . He wrote "appears collected" on the scratch pad, and said, "You've a family doctor?"

"Serves no purpose," with a sort of polite irritability.

"People sometimes look dead and aren't."

"There is no mistake," primly, a man unaccustomed to his judgment being called into question.

"If for no one else, then for you. You may not realize it, but you're suffering from shock."

"Nonsense. In the absence of the Commissaire, nobody is needed but yourself—and talk less, man."

"Are you alone in the house?"

"Yes—the servants . . ."

"Never mind. I'll be with you in a few minutes— about five. Do nothing at all. Don't touch anything— remain where you are."

Pure routine—Castang clicked the receiver bar.

"Switchboard—that was an emergency. Hold and record incoming calls. I'll check back when I know what's in it; may be serious."

The duty agent, a handsome boy from Nice with wavy black hair and pale skin—rather a silly boy— was typing languidly in the outer office.

"Come on," said Castang briefly. "Emergency." The keys of the wagon, a small Renault with no markings. The boy put on his gun belt. Castang slipped and checked his own pistol, leaving it cocked. If the fellow really had a gun . . . maniacs were sometimes unpredictable.

The Rue des Écrivains was in the oldest part of the

11

town, a quarter where streets were medievally narrow and some houses, however patched and repatched, had bones many hundreds of years old. One-way streets, with no parking permitted. Here it was really hot. At the corner was a tiny fountain with a trio of plane trees grouped around it, at which Castang made a face, it looked so fresh and peaceful. They'd have to park on the pavement in the grilling afternoon heat that was funneled and pinned down by these high narrow walls.

### 3. Unmoved Calm of an Inspector of Finance

It came as a surprise. Number 7 was an archway with a coat of arms over it in carved stone, crumbled by time. Double doors stood open, of three-inch oak iron-knopped and barred. They drove through into a little cobbled courtyard: a car was parked, but there was room for a second. It was shady and pleasant, with a vine growing on the sunny wall and boxes of geraniums, and decorated with its original furnishings of wrought iron: things for attaching horses, holding torches, scraping mud off one's boots. Behind, chiseled stone, white plaster, wrought-iron balconies—a small town house of the seventeenth century.

Castang looked at it and said, "Nice house." There wasn't any more to say; homicides can happen anywhere. He did not know, though Vera could have told him, that it was one of the showpieces of the city, a "hôtel particulier" classed as a historic monument. It meant to the police only that the people inside, dead or otherwise, were rich.

More wrought iron, like black lace, with a monogram worked into it. A bell handle, which, when pulled, produced a faint musical jangle like falling water far away. Then complete silence. Siesta time for the rich. A prolonged siesta, a big sleep.

The door opened; a man stood there, a man of fifty, perfectly tranquil. Neatly dressed in a summer suit, Legion of Honor in buttonhole. In no sense disarranged or abnormal, no twitching or grimacing, but the controlled voice of authority that had spoken on the telephone.

"You are the police?"

"Castang. I am an officer of Police Judiciaire, this is Agent Lucciani." A hand invited entry, courteously.

"We'll go upstairs." Floor marble, black-and-white chessboard. Stairs white marble, wrought-iron balustrade. Portraits in gilt frames: florid fat-faced persons in lace and watered silk, men in wigs, women in complicated and unsanitary-looking hairstyles. Landing of pale parquet with geometric patterns of paler marquetry. Doors open to a suite of drawing rooms.

Stairs continuing, narrower. Second landing, like the first, but bedrooms and—a lot more recently— bathrooms. The stairs went on to another story, but in plain wood, to children and servants.

A door stood open. Castang could see part of a bed padded in dull yellow silk. The fresh blood made a color contrast.

As the man said. Three bodies. Unmistakably dead. Two women: one middle-aged, one young. A man: large, massive, hairy. All naked. Flagrant; a crime of passion. The man lay on the floor, on his back; sev-

13

eral entry wounds in the big belly. The women on the bed, each executed with a single shot in the head. A small-caliber pistol: Castang looked for it. It was there on the floor, a little 6.35 Colt. Automatic, six-shot. Now empty; the man had four wounds. Castang picked it up with a ball-point through the trigger-guard. Pretty little gun, walnut-gripped, a woman's-handbag model; the work it had done meant it was no toy after all. He wrapped it in a paper tissue and put it away. The three were very dead indeed, and the man calm and, one would say, perfectly sane. But rules were rules.

"We'll need this doctor."

"As you like," indifferently.

"One who knows you, preferably. Use your phone? You'll show M. Lucciani? Doctor right away, Jacques, then switchboard. Photographer, technicians, and message through to Richard at his home if you can; no hurry for ambulance, dead on arrival; notify the path lab three customers. Official notification to the Proc for a homicide. M. La Touche?"

"Yes." Standing there so tranquil, with a slight smile, as though appreciative of efficiency in others. So much calm was abnormal.

"You told me that you were the author of these deaths. You maintain that? Very well. The doctor is for you; it's a rule. I want you now to understand this clearly. This is a homicide, it has the appearance of a crime. I am an officer of police. Pending the arrival of the Commissaire, or the Procureur, or another legal officer, I assume the responsibility for everything here. I will be bound shortly to put certain questions to you. You are free not to answer them—or, indeed, not to say anything at all—if you think it

14

would incriminate you to do so. Do you understand that?"

"Perfectly. I am neither shocked nor confused, and in complete possession of all my faculties."

"You have no right to say that, and I take no note of it: it is simply untrue. I may not, in any case, question you till the doctor's had a look at you. Till then I want you to stay downstairs with M. Lucciani: he has to keep an eye on you. All right?"

"I understand," still with that slight ironic smile.

"Very well. Don't drink any alcohol."

"I never do," simply.

Castang was alone. There would be the usual thorough technical examination. Everything would be photographed from every angle. It was unnecessary —perhaps. It was obvious what had happened— perhaps. Only one thing was obvious to him at that minute; it was going to be less simple than it looked, if only because inevitably the press was going to jump upon this. It was important in the extreme that all the formalities should be most carefully observed, that it should be cut and dried. There was no margin for error whatever. He wished that Richard were here. He wasn't, and the likelihood was he wouldn't be. Very well, pending the arrival of an officer of the law, which he himself wasn't as a simple police officer, he was going to see that everything was carried out as the law dictated. Which meant no more, really, than having things tidy. The human element came later.

Looked at in this mechanical light, the thing was easy. The man had arrived unexpectedly, unheard. He had taken his wife in flagrant adultery—*and* his daughter. Castang frowned at that. Outside his experience, this detail. And outside most people's, too

15

—no? But there it was. Surprised, the trio had been more or less paralyzed. The man had walked over to the bedside table, taken the pistol he knew to be there —it mattered little whether it was his or his wife's; it was there: the drawer still stood open. The big man, the lover—and a fine big hunk of flesh he had been, even if a little too fat (but all that flesh was grass now)—had tried to react. A mistake: four bullets in that big target. And then, quite coolly, and that was a thing which would have a legal meaning later on, the man had shot the two women, with one well-aimed shot each. So no self-defense, no struggle or accidental discharge. A straightforward assassination.

Two well-made women. A cop felt no emotion of any sort whatever looking at the two still beautiful naked bodies. With a small-size pistol; the bullets had stayed in the heads. No mess. Little blood. Even the features were scarcely distorted. But grass, grass, grass.

A crime of passion by a husband is not, whatever the public believes, a legal argument. But temporary insanity, of course, is. It would not be a difficult affair, if there was no mistake in the preliminary inquiry. And that was his, Henri Castang's, job.

The windows were open but in the hot windless air the smell of perfume, smokeless powder, and fresh blood hung overpoweringly, like honeysuckle. He stared out at a stone-flagged terrace, where the upper classes had been accustomed to drink tea, and a formal walled garden beyond, with box hedge and flowers, box hedge and vegetables, the usual herbs round a sundial and a strip of grass to finish with, and fruit trees espaliered against the walls. Lovingly cared for, probably by some Portuguese footman.

16

The dim memory of why the name La Touche meant something had come swimming back . . . Paper . . . a yearly report of some sort: the fellow was a financier. It hadn't interested Castang, who knew nothing of finance. A bank; an insurance company? No, something governmental—the Accounts Tribunal, that was it: the controlling body on public spending—the fellow was an Inspector of Finance! Absolutely the top of the basket. But he'd killed people just the same as a factory hand at Renault. The difference was that this one would have highly placed friends. No wonder he was calm. Castang's nose twitched as he turned back to the room. The smell, above all, was of money. Not that it bothered him: he'd be off this case in twenty-four hours, as soon as the preliminaries were accomplished.

The doorbell rang.

The doctor was the bloodless secretive kind who thinks a word, let alone a smile, diminishes his capital and amounts to an act of recklessness. And guess where that leads to. He looked at his patient in the study downstairs, was brief about it, rejoined Castang, who was smoking in the hall, with downcast eyes and a nunlike glide that conveyed distaste for the police. Giving any information whatever was a grave infringement of ethics, and it took a struggle.

"If you refuse to answer, I'll have the police doctor go over him, that's all."

"Unnecessary," prim.

"No disabling malady, such as might cause abnormal behavior?"

"Such as what?"

"Like epilepsy"—sighing—"or diabetes or migraine."

17

"No."

"Physical symptoms of nervous trouble, a depression, or overtension?"

"This was a superficial examination," contemptuously.

"Quite. I'm forced to remind you of the legal obligations. He's in possession of his faculties?"

"Meaningless."

"Meaning that he can see, hear, speak, and understand clearly, and is able to return an answer to simple questions."

"You mean bullying." Castang was used to it. Every cop is.

"Doctor," agreeably, "you should commit a murder."

"How dare you?"

"You would discover just how many safeguards there are for a presumed author—neither accused, charged, nor condemned—of a criminal act."

"Do you wish me to complain to your superiors?"

"The Public Prosecutor will be here shortly."

"You are ignoble," signing his name bitterly, tearing sheets off his memo and prescription pads, handing them over with hatred.

"You will be reimbursed by the state, Doctor," making it sound insulting. "Have you given him a sedative or other medicament?"

"Yes. Though there is an aid, prescribed there, for the restoration of neurophysical equilibrium. To withhold it might constitute failure in coming to the aid of a person in danger. A criminal offense—as you are doubtless aware. I would so testify." Snap, as of jaws of crocodile; the man headed for the door. Castang didn't stop him.

"Lucciani—a cop to stand in front of the gate. And find a chemist that's open."

La Touche was sitting in a stiff little armchair maintaining his air of polite indifference.

"How do you feel?" asked Castang.

"Tired. It's nothing. I am quite rational. Able to answer your questions."

"Very few for the present. I should like to have a formal identification of these persons. Your wife?"

"Yes."

"And your daughter?"

"Yes."

"Is the man known to you?"

"Yes."

"There may, you see, be relatives to notify."

"He's a painter. His name is Davids. He lives in Paris. I forget the address. There's probably a card in his wallet."

"Thank you. Has he a wife?"

"I believe so."

Castang did not pursue it.

## 4. Due Process of Law

An ancient prescription in French criminal law is that in grave crimes "the Parquet shall descend" upon the scene. It is jargon for the legal authorities: the Public Prosecutor, known as the Proc, or his substitute, and one of the Judges of Instruction attached to the local tribunal. In former days, these grave gentlemen were obliged to visit in person—accompanied by their clerks

—the theatre of affairs. It was not at all a stupid idea. Lawyers are ridiculously divorced from any sense of reality at all times.

However, nowadays the "visit" has become a formality. A police officer of the rank of commissaire is by definition an officer of justice, and his presence insures that the law has been respected. It is rare nowadays that the Procureur appears in person.

Castang was not a commissaire, though he held a law degree, which is a condition; with a bit more seniority, and by passing an examination, he might expect to become one. He was an officer of police, with several powers conferred by the Code of Criminal Procedure; he could, for example, interrogate witnesses. But there was a lot he couldn't do. He was waiting, in consequence, for a substitute, one of the half-dozen or more bright young men attached, in a major city, to the Prosecutor's office.

It came as a slight shock to see the Procureur in person. Though when Castang thought of it, the surprise lessened. An Inspector of Finance is a highly placed personage. To see the occasion treated as a social call was a foretaste, doubtless, of things to come.

"Hallo, Castang," cordially. "How are you, then?" offering a legal hand, large, dry, and chalky. "Not been on holiday yet? Well, Gilbert"—imperturbable, as though invited for cocktails—"this is a sorry matter. My condolences are nonetheless sincere for my being obliged to undertake a melancholy duty, as you will understand. I heard of this with consternation. Now, Castang, where's Richard?"

"I don't know, sir. He will have been notified, I should hope, by now."

"Well, well, we'll manage without him. Tell me briefly, then."

"M. La Touche himself notified me by telephone of what had happened. I have taken the usual steps. The technicians will be here shortly—here they are, in fact—for verification, though at first sight there is— well, let's say it seems straightforward. M. La Touche has made the necessary identifications, and has been kind enough to give me his complete cooperation." It takes a good deal to embarrass a cop, but Castang did feel a slight oppression at La Touche just standing there in a casual social attitude of someone receiving guests at a large boring party where a lot of people are present just to grease the wheels of business. A bit glassy of eye: "Ah, Mr. Ergh. So good of you to come."

"The doctor has just been," added Castang colorlessly. "M. La Touche feels able to tell me whatever I need to know."

The Proc nodded: it was what he needed to know.

"Would you have the goodness to show me, Gilbert? Castang accompanies us with your permission." The technical squad were holding back politely, waiting for the Proc to pass in front of them. He was a bit like the parish priest, thought Castang irreverently, come to say the rosary at a wake: he walked on heavy feet to the bedroom, looked calmly at the scene offered, came back downstairs with a nod to the photographer to go ahead, slowly drew out a cigarette case, blew out the first puff of smoke with a noisy, stolid heave of the lungs. La Touche might have been showing the house to a prospective buyer. No, no—no damp anywhere.

"Very well, Castang, in Richard's absence you'll continue with your preliminary inquiry. Gilbert."

"Yes?"

"I'll be leaving. This goes forward with no further intervention on my part. A question for form: have you an advocate here in the town with any penal experience?"

"Dieudonné is my usual man of affairs. His practice is commercial. His brains, I suppose, would supply the lack of habit in the Penal Code. I imagine he'd be competent."

"He'll know what to do, at least. I'll get on to him, unless he's away. Jérôme's away. Let's see; Szymanowski will be senior judge in that case—you don't know him personally, do you?"

"No."

"Very well. I'll designate him accordingly to instruct this affair. You'll be all right with Castang here. He's an able chap; he'll see that matters are handled correctly."

"The press will, I suspect, be here very shortly," said Castang.

"Not while I'm here, they won't," said the Proc sharply. It gave him leverage to get his big body moving. "I'm going," abruptly.

Castang watched him go walking heavily through the courtyard, looking neither right nor left. At the gate he was accosted by a familiar, slightly cheap figure. Like dogs, thought Castang; they know it all and understand nothing. They rush wildly, eagerly at anything, perpetually bringing back sticks with an air of vast importance, and when faced by a master figure, they cringe. The Procureur paid no attention to the questions and just rumbled ahead like a tank. There was already a clown there with a microphone.

"Lucciani," said Castang, "press. There'll be more.

Tell them Richard—" No. Useless; they had to be given bones, however bare. No cop can afford to be high-hat with the press. They can be bellowed at, but if you are sulky they bite. "Let them as far as the hall and no further—and make sure of that. Tell them nothing else because of the technicians. . . . M. La Touche"—surprised to find himself so deferent—"you realize your privacy is going to get pretty badly invaded. We'll keep your house guarded but right now it's run the gauntlet. You may as well get it over with. There's paperwork to do, so I have to ferry you down to the office. I don't want to put handcuffs on you but for you just to accompany me in a friendly informal way. Have I your word for that?"

"Certainly," vaguely. "Sorry; I mean yes, of course. I feel rather sleepy, I'm afraid."

"We'll have some coffee—or, to be accurate, Nescafé. Let's move on, shall we?"

"Lucciani," Cástang said, stopping at the bottom of the stairs with an expressionless face for the photoflash, "see that the house remains guarded and that the cop is relayed, and that you in person lock up after the ambulance has been, and that you in person bring me the keys. . . ." He turned to a reporter, saying, "Castang, Inspector, P.J. This is M. La Touche, the owner of the house, who has for the moment nothing to tell you."

"What is this?" a journalist interrupted tartly. "Suicide, homicide, or what?"

"The appearance is homicide. The Procureur has authorized me to make a preliminary inquiry. Since that's all I know, it's all I can tell you."

"This is the suspect?"

"As you can see, he is not handcuffed. He is doing his best to shed light upon the circumstances. The

23

rest remains to be seen. That is why an inquiry has been ordered."

"How many dead are there?"

"Three: two women and a man. Mme. and Mlle. La Touche and a man so far identified only as a M. Davids. All have died as a result of gunshot wounds, whose authorship the technical examination in progress should determine. The Procureur authorizes nothing further at this time, and no photographs in other parts of the house. This evening at the office, M. Richard may be able to make a fuller statement. That's all."

As they got into the car, a movie camera filmed them for that evening's television news. They made their way through the obstacle of some fifty curious onlookers and headed for "the office." Not the administrative office from which he had been called, but the urban police headquarters, an extremely ugly building of the mid-nineteenth century and massive discomfort, but at least cool. The interrogation rooms used by the P.J. were at the back. Castang found a cop and sent him for paper cups of coffee. The result was hot and strong, anyway.

"We have to keep you—you realize? Detention cells here at the back. Tomorrow sometime, you'll be presented as we call it to the instructing judge—you aren't familiar, I imagine, with these procedures. I realize you're tired, but we have some work this evening. Not a great deal. I'm allowed to question you for only so long. There are intervals laid down for rest, meals, and so on. Then a bit more work before bed. Tomorrow with any luck we'll be finished with these preliminaries, and the judge decides what happens further, and your lawyer will be present and it will be explained to you. Sorry about this stuff, it's the best we can do. All set? This is called a verbal process," as though to a child. Castang was repeating a lesson long learned by heart. "It's a typed paraphrase in abbreviation of the question-and-answer process. You have the right to alter and obliterate anything you disagree with before signing it. It serves to give the judge a broad outline, and as basis for further inquiry should that prove necessary."

## 5. The Rights of a Suspect
### Are Safeguarded

La Touche seemed to be waking up a little. Shock wearing off, or the stimulus of Nescafé, a thaw at finding the cops a little less like orangutans than previously supposed—perhaps a little of all three.

Castang was hammering at bureaucracy: date of father's birth.

"Lord—1894, I do believe. Am I accused? I've forgotten this branch of law, I'm afraid."

"You aren't even a suspect. You're a presumed." Inspector of Finance: Master of the Rolls—lawyers loved these antique titles. "Judge makes an act of accusation if he sees fit. It's to be expected that he will. And you are—were—married to Hélène de la . . . That's a mouthful; spell it, would you?" These names of the nobility, as encountered in the births, deaths, and marriages of the *Figaro*—all orthographical death-traps. "Sounds very grand."

"It is," said La Touche. "Like Oriane de Guermantes; all the duchesses are her cousins. Since I admit everything, this statement will be rather bald, despite the imposing preamble. The judge will be disappointed because his dossier will remain meager. I suppose I'll be expected to plead insanity."

"Don't let your mind run ahead. You've two daughters, Charlotte and Victoria. Which is the dead girl?" without inflection.

"Charlotte," likewise. "The younger. Seventeen."

"All right, that's finished with. So now a brief sketch of events. You came home. Unexpectedly?"

When it is all written down, some people become confused. Often they make long rambling explanations to alleviate guilt when it cannot be obviated. They become immensely loquacious. The uneducated may take refuge in stout denial, saying "You lie" to the most unimpeachable fact. The bourgeois, with some training in logic, see every piece of evidence as incontrovertible but they embroider interminably. The professional criminal, of course, is like a politician: when he cannot lie, he equivocates. Experience teaches the investigating officer how to produce a clear and if possible coherent narrative, with helpful remarks ranging from "For God's sake, say something I can believe" down to "I wouldn't put it quite that way if I were you," to a misery who is quite unaware how shatteringly he is incriminating himself. He does this as much in self-defense as in sympathy. He will be accused anyway by a defending counsel of fabricating evidence and extorting admissions by threat, if no worse.

La Touche, befitting a man with legal training, used spare manageable sentences easy to transcribe literally; he thought before he spoke; he weighed his words.

What presented difficulty was that he seemed deliberately to paint himself in as black a light as possible. Castang found himself almost "offering inducements" to make the statement less bald, "behaving improperly" —but there were no tape recorders running.

"Had you remembered that the servants were away? Would it be a thing you would ordinarily recall?"

"It made no difference whether they were there or not. The servants all knew perfectly. They always do."

"Since this painter was making a portrait, there was nothing unusual or striking in his being there that afternoon."

"Davids can't resist any woman." Present tense. Is the man really aware that he has killed these people?

"But there are plenty of women who would find him resistible, who would in fact resist him."

"Not my wife." Which was as bald as you could wish it.

"You suspected, then, infidelities. But it would still come as a violent shock."

"I didn't have to suspect. It was even knowledge I took for granted. She was notorious."

"Come, now."

"If not widely known, then deeply. Thoroughly, if you prefer."

"Were you intent upon stopping scandal?"

"She made no scandal. Well brought up. A sense of what is becoming. Occasionally reckless, but took pains not to compromise me—at work, say. Not that I am in the least a public figure."

You are now, though.

"The presence of your daughter would have been to you a guarantee, wouldn't it?"

"Not in the slightest. Corrupt. Always has been."

"Come—no, all right, leave that. Despite everything, when you stumbled upon this scene—isn't it fair to say you had a violent reaction?"

"By no means."

"Think carefully. Anger, humiliation, even envy. One may act in what appears a calm fashion—or some people can—but there is a violent interior tempest."

"No."

"I am not trying to suggest you were incapacitated. That would be going beyond my brief, which is just to get at facts. Then no emotion at all?"

"I said, M. Castang, no violent emotions. I felt many things, in a controlled fashion. I decided to finish with all that."

The man would be saying in a moment that his act was premeditated! He did. . . .

This won't do, thought Castang. The man can't have forgotten all his penal law. He must surely realize that if he confesses to homicide with premeditation he is technically an assassin, and risks the death penalty. Castang stopped and lit a cigarette, making an affair of searching for a light. He reflected that the psychiatrists would pounce on all this. Rigidity, overwhelming need of tidy patterns, rejection of wounding and disabling images, castration right and left: the shrinks would make hay.

"I can guess," said La Touche amiably, "what is passing through your mind."

Castang changed the subject. "Could we have a brief résumé of your studies and qualifications, and, perhaps in broad outline, your career?"

"Certainly."

Cooperative, conscientious, Castang thought. That

is surely relevant and must be noted. And doesn't it show a sense of remorse? The pill the doctor had prescribed, too, was relevant—it was likely quite a strong sedative. The man had not wished to take it. On being urged, he shrugged, said he'd make no fuss.

Uncanny the way he picked up one's thought.

"I should like to say that I'm aware everyone is going to ask me whether I feel remorse. Down to the President of the Assize Court. I'd better make myself clear right from the start. I'd like you to note it."

The manner of authority comes from the tranquil certainty of being obeyed. A wish is a command. But you haven't—have you?—lived through twenty years of marriage without realizing that family life is played according to different rules.

"That's what I'm here for."

"Pity I feel," said the man accustomed to dictating memos, "and consciousness of an irrevocable action. I have, though, learned to make decisions and to carry them out without useless doubts and scruples after the event. We thus separate the notion of remorse from that of regret or a useless longing that what is should not be. It is done and I did it."

Castang typed obediently, word for word. To feel a sort of moral superiority in the man sitting in the other chair gave him a start. He smoked quietly and wrote a note in the book beside him. La Touche paid no attention.

Dignified; undiminished. It came from generations of ease and assurance. From being used to universal respect. From being good at his job. Surely, too, from a sort of integrity. The man would never allow himself to commit or be in accord with a dishonest action. Large sums of public money were accounted for with minute exactitude. The detachment of the senior civil servant. One was perfectly aware of vast and shocking scandals, daily. Incompetence and mismanagement upon a vast scale. Equally, enormous corruption and public featherbedding. The gloriously bland silky hypocrisy of government where arms sales were concerned, or the misapplication of a gigantic sum for electoral purposes. The stranglehold of the middlemen —the ten, twenty, thirty bandits standing between the ridiculously low price to the producer and the outrageous sum demanded of the consumer. This man saw them all with detached distaste, and did nothing. That was rather like a policemen—wasn't it?

Long practice in the flexible and civilized manner —everything left unsaid—in which these senior officials reach compromises. An interesting lot. Much like the syndicate making up that English insurance group—Lloyd's wasn't it? Trust: word is bond: a signature on a scrap of paper a gold ingot.

They all knew each other. Many were related; all shared the same background. Frequently they had been in this world for two, three, or more generations. Gone to the same schools and training grounds. They were known personally to half the professors, quite a few of whom came to dine at the house. Birth, wealth, security, honor. A Rolls-Royce mind. Marriage, after graduation into an important department of government, to a suitable young woman. And wherever one went, everyone—from Ministers down—got up from behind their desk in acknowledgment of this effortless domination.

What was a man like this doing in a squalid interrogation room with a provincial cop? What could they possibly have in common? Was it the same blunting of moral sensibility, a sort of detached and even cynical indifference to human folly, greed, avarice? This man, too, was a policeman. On a grander scale. Yes, there was a lot in common. More, with an urbane and polished person like Commissaire Richard.

Castang felt a momentary sort of rage. This, surely, was all drawing-room comedy. The Procureur had come in person. Richard would be getting unspoken instructions. He himself had been left to conduct a preliminary homicide inquiry because it had no importance. He was regarded as a reasonably house-broken cop, able to go through the forms without making a mess of it. It wouldn't matter what he wrote provided he got it in the right language. The judge would pay no heed.

Shrinks would appear in number, making low-key remarks about pressure and the wife's instability, with parentheses regarding the daughter and too much intermarriage in old families.

A trial, respecting all forms. An advocate-general prosecuting who was somebody's cousin and would speak with studied moderation. A formal sentence suspended and replaced at discretion by voluntary treatment in a clinic. Retirement, not too premature. Memories of this tragic accident obliterated. Dear Gilbert had lost his wife and daughter in a ski disaster. Avalanche, yes; road accidents are vulgar.

"Once more," said La Touche a little diffidently, "I think I might guess what is passing through your mind. I shall hope that we come to know one another better."

The summer suit, and shirt, in good taste like the tie and the cufflinks and the inconspicuous English shoes. No crocodile there, any more than the wife would have dreamed of wearing panther. Such things were for the nouveaux riches, vulgar. Shit.

"I simply do my job," Castang said, hoping not to sound servile. "No efforts of understanding or any such things are required from me. Above all, no conclusions. I marshal events in a fairly lucid précis, and insure that the procedures are respected."

"I think you may be mistaken," urbane.

The door opened, and Richard came in, unfamiliar in his weekend sport shirt.

"This pistol is your property?" Castang said to La Touche. "And you kept it habitually in the drawer of the bedside table? As is the convention. Was it usually loaded? I mean the cartridges in the magazine? The magazine in place in the butt of the pistol? You are familiar with the mechanism? Did you leave the thing there with a vague idea of security, or did you sometimes take it out to clean? You practiced with it, from time to time?"

Richard quietly sat down, with a sign to pay no attention to him.

"This is Commissaire Richard," cross, and deliberately misunderstanding. "He is the head of the regional service. He will doubtless have things to ask you."

"Not for the moment." Despite the sport shirt, Richard looked smart: never windblown or ruffled. Tall, thin, handsome, quiet. Now slightly disconcerted, since La Touche got up at the introduction, held his hand out courteously, and said, "Delighted to know you, Commissaire, but I'm afraid I'm causing you trouble." For two pins, he would have said, "How was golf?" thought Castang sourly.

"There are worse things," laconically.

As frequently with remarks of Richard's, one was not certain whether this was a snub or not. La Touche took it to be one; two red spots showed for a moment on his cheekbones. With Richard's entry the temperature had dropped: the atmosphere of understanding and almost a certain friendliness had slipped away.

Castang studied his notes and lit another cigarette. "We have covered most of the facts," he said.

"There are so few," said La Touche. "Death of two women and a good man."

"You loved your wife and daughter?"

"I think I did. Badly, as is evident. Not enough, as is obvious."

"And they loved you?"

"I should have thought so. You may think I don't know the meaning of the word. You might very likely be right."

"You used the word 'good' in speaking of Davids. You admired him? He was a good painter?"

"He was a remarkable human being. One seldom meets a person of such quality. His talent—yes, that also: exceptional."

"Are you doing yourself justice in these answers?"

"I see no occasion to concern myself about that."

Richard was sitting immobile, without a flicker of the eye. His mouth had a sardonic turn, as though silently saying, "Theatrical performance." His face, ordinarily a healthy pink color, looked gray in the evening light, as if made of aluminum: the skin dull, polished here and there by much handling, by daily usage through many years. He has a very considerable experience, Castang was thinking; a great deal more than me. He is a good and unbureaucratic cop.

"Would it be fair to suggest that you felt envy for

this man? Perhaps on account of qualities inspiring affection?"

"Yes, it would. I did. And more—hatred, fury. Laughter—he was extremely funny. Sometimes I felt contempt. I qualify that. An unjustified contempt, because the man was astoundingly simple and open, like a child. I don't mean childish; I mean an unaffected naïveté. On the other hand, he was occasionally contemptible."

"I see. I don't think we need go any further at present. I'll give you this to read over and sign, if you will," Castang said, typing the final phrases of official formula concerning time, place, and circumstances. His eyes slid across to Richard, who shrugged very slightly.

"Thank you. We'll have more to talk about, but that will be in the morning, after certain verifications. I'm going to have to lock you up now. I should explain that you are as yet officially not charged with anything at all. You are held at disposal, as it is known, for twenty-four hours, after which the instructing judge decides whether to order your detainment."

"I understand. It is unnecessary. I admit openly all possible accusations."

"That may be so. We respect various safeguards the law insists upon."

"Are you always so punctilious?" murmured La Touche.

"Where crimes against the person are concerned, yes," rather more acidly than was needed. "Will you come with me?"

The jail was behind police headquarters, along a covered alleyway like a railroad tunnel, approximately whitewashed. Castang, who was used to it, felt an unexpected prick of shame at the air of dilapidated antiquity. La Touche seemed unconcerned. The warder had to fill in lengthy and tedious forms. La Touche glanced indifferently at drawings on the walls, did not even wrinkle his nose at a smell of stale cabbage soup, disinfectant, and ingrained dirt, which did little ordinarily for the detainee's self-respect. He was carrying no personal property at all, bar a handkerchief. Didn't smoke; no money or address book. Like royalty, who leave such matters to ladies-in-waiting. Castang went along with the incurious warder, thinking he'd better do something: La Touche had no idea. Richard would have made a face. What d'you want to do—tuck him in?

"Never been in prison before? Like during the war, say?"

"I have lived a sheltered life."

"I see. I have to have your tie. And the shoelaces. Are you wearing a belt, or braces?"

"I have no suicidal urges."

"It's the regulation. However, if you would like to tell me, I can find you some things at home. Tide you over the emergency."

"I need nothing."

"Nonsense."

"You are humane."

"I have to go back to the house anyway."

# 6. Czech Insistence on Being Contrary

"I'll be late for supper," said Castang on the telephone. "Got a homicide. Shouldn't be long, though—maybe an hour."

"Cold soup, anyway," said Vera's voice. "I'll expect you when I see you." That was that. He went to wash off sticky grime with kitchen soap and a police roller towel.

Even after sunset, it was still fearfully hot in the Rue des Écrivains. Smell of baked dust; the car smelt of ovens, baked enameled metal. Castang felt fatigue, an empty reverberation in the head sounding noisy and busy, though the street was now still and empty. Everyone had gone off to the supper table, switching on the television. Local news, before the national news: he wondered whether that cameraman had got his film ready in time.

The black-and-white marble of the hallway (there was something startling in the mixture of grandeur and simplicity here; the house was quite small, really, but all the rooms looked large, perhaps because they were so well proportioned) was deliciously cool and clean. The technicians had finished.

"No problem there," said Lucciani. "Waste of time, really. Clear as the Blue Lagoon. Here's the keys."

Simple as daylight, simple as champagne. All the simplicity bothered Castang.

Richard had said the same when Castang had got back from locking La Touche up. He was in his office smoking a cigar, tidying papers his secretary had left to be signed. He hadn't even looked up; the step of his subordinate was familiar.

"So simple it stinks. I've read your report. It's all right—hits quite a good note, in fact. Not that it matters very much. Without interest, all this."

"You think so? I thought him interesting."

"Naturally," dry. "He's anxious to be interesting. Been a bore all his life—now's his chance. He's throwing attitudes. He knows he's perfectly safe—how indeed could he be anything else?"

"Good, insanity plea—yes, of course—but is he insane?"

"What a silly question. Are you insane? They are and they aren't, as you very well know. At moments convenient to themselves they are. Kills the man. All right, that's insane—in an Inspector of Finance it is, anyhow. Killing a couple more puts him on the safe side. Make him that much more insane. Take off that wiseacre look; look at the facts. He could, or I'm much mistaken. He was sick of those two women: they'd been a horrible nuisance for some time. Admirable opportunity for getting rid of them. There'll be much sympathy, no doubt, for his point of view.

"Premeditation doesn't have to be something laboriously planned and thought out over weeks; it can take two seconds. This situation is much too complex, thinks a trained mind; he simplifies it."

"What happens now?" asked Castang stupidly, feeling fatigue in the bridge of his nose, stiffness in the back of the neck.

"Szymanowski will call for expert opinions. Nothing left to chance—if the first doesn't find the man is crazy, the second will. A bit of hemming and hawing over what constitutes crazy, but a formula gets hammered out that the Proc will accept. He'll make a show at the trial, but any good defense lawyer will find a bargain for the courtroom. Plea of diminished responsibility accepted—two quiet years in a clinic with woods around it and a tennis court, where the director gets called warden and has bars on his windows but wears a white coat and invites the inmates to play bridge. Yah. Just see to it that the papers are clean, though; Szymanowski likes to call attention to sloppy procedure."

"There's no technical hitch?"

"I've just phoned the house," said Richard simply. "The rich, my boy, are never interesting."

"I wouldn't know," said Castang. "I'm going over there to fetch the man his pajamas."

"Don't steal any little silver boxes."

Hitch? asked the technical squad—you're as bad as Richard. What hitch? Painter's been having a fine time, screwing these two bitches cross-eyed. Isn't it nice to be rich?

In the kitchen, he found a thin woman with glasses: Portuguese, voluble, distraught. Everyone was on holiday, she was the cook's cousin, the family had been in the country, she just came in to air the rooms —oh, what to do now, oh dear, such a quiet gentleman, so considerate, never gave trouble.

He went through the house again. Kitchen much modernized, pantry with china cupboards and stuff, a dining room, a dark study full of lawbooks. In the suite of drawing rooms on the first floor there were a lot of pictures hanging. In the bedrooms the technicians had done a thorough job. He found an overnight bag, male pajamas and slippers, added a couple of sets of underclothes and socks. If the man got a toothbrush belonging to his wife—well, she had no further use for it. A track suit, yes—sensible thing to wear in jail.

Tacking across the landing, he found two girl's bedrooms, one very disorderly. This presumably was the girl who had died, for the other looked as though it had been unoccupied for some time, although aired and dusted by the excellent servants. It was conventional, with little trace of individual personality. He wondered where the second daughter had gone. This painter Davids must have been a fine figure of a bull, but three together would impose a strain, surely. The things people got up to . . .

He went back downstairs. On one side of the drawing room was a library. He took a few books at random for La Touche. More pictures, including a very cleverly composed and intricately painted still life. In a classical Dutch sort of style—he wondered whether it was any good. Vera would know, but she wasn't here. It was only interesting to him because it was signed "Davids." Some of the things in the drawing room he didn't understand at all. One might, eventually, after a lot of time and study.

On the other side of the drawing room was a morning room, he supposed that was what it was called. A smell of fresh oil paint: the man had worked here. He really had been painting a picture!

The room was oddly conventional. A business room for an upper-class lady, the competent and well-trained mistress of an upper-class establishment. He looked at the bureau—letters, invitation cards, appointments book. Phone directories, address books, household accounts, menu cards, cookery books for planning parties. . . . The room was decorated with photographs of family relations and several horses.

And two large portraits, in crayon, of two little girls, about ten and eight, all most delightful and roguish, but they had traveled some distance farther since then.

The picture hung over the carved stone chimney piece, still unframed, perhaps unfinished. Hung to see how it would look, perhaps, or because the paint had been wet. He touched the surface gingerly: a scrap tacky. The man might have been working on it that day; how long did this stuff take to dry? Vera would know.

The painter's easel stood where it would get a good light. On the chair behind it hung his linen jacket, shapeless and bulging. He had been a big man. It could well have taken four bullets from that popgun to stop him. Castang wondered whether there could be a self-defense plea there, and shrugged: what did he care? He was interested, though, in this jacket— the technicians hadn't been fiddling at that. An uninterfered-with witness, so to speak. Lord, it was more full of junk than a peddler's basket.

This man at least had been real; a life lived intensely. Breast pocket: spectacles, and a handkerchief, silk but paint-stained. Side pocket: handkerchief, cotton, paint-stained. Crumpled packet of horrible menthol cigarettes. Bottle of pills. Other side: more handkerchiefs, of paper! Another bottle of pills! A little plastic bottle with a spray, for throat or sinus. And a handful of candies wrapped in silver paper. The inside pocket held a heavy worn wallet full of cards, papers, money, and assorted rubbish.

Trouble with his sinus and a liking for sweets. Castang was pleased. It was a life. The first homicide he had ever been on had been put together by Richard from the starting point of an uneaten meal. Richard had shown him how to construct an unknown man, identify him, and arrest him. From a liking for overdone meat, sugar in all the vegetables, and German mineral water.

So far, it had all been empty, staged, void of meaning. A brothel scene, lit with glaring, gaudy, but artificial lights. Depersonalized—there had been something, too, very irritating in the attitude of La Touche. One had to agree with Richard; it did look like comedy. Consider: man walking in, discovering this absurd great weltering sex scene. Calmly going to bedside table while the trio, presumably, stood about, fixed in consternation. Taking the pistol and loading it—a most important legal point, proving coordination and preparation, prerequisites for a homicide to be termed premeditated and the author an assassin.

And La Touche had behaved in a very stagy way afterward, also. Ringing up the P.J. like that (not just the cops from Police Secours) and saying "I admit everything" with a phony sort of flourish. He must have been aware, and well aware, that he was going— in three useful American monosyllables—to cop a plea. His answers, too, to questions were lucid and connected, but unsatisfactory.

One would have liked to ask the others questions. It was most annoying that they were all dead.

They'd been, though, human beings. Now carcasses, shapeless lumps of flesh. Might as well have been knocked to pieces by one of those huge bullets that tore the bones off your face so that it flew asunder like a smashed porcelain vase.

Castang looked at the occasional table. Laid with a coffee service. Three used cups. Nobody had bothered much about it. There was a little dish that had held chocolates. The dish was still there, but the technicians had eaten all the chocolates.

The painter had been a real man. A man who liked to have sweet things within reach to pop into his mouth from time to time: a candy, a girl, a biscuit. A humble small earthworm of doubt had come crawling into Castang's well-drilled subordinate's mind. He wasn't sure any more that Richard was automatically right, that this was no more than a formal exercise in legal technology. It must have been an unconscious revolt against everything being kept so smooth and pat and well-oiled, because Castang committed an illegal act. He unhooked the canvas on its stretcher from the wall and walked off with it. An illegal act because this, technically, was theft. Also because in a homicide case the disposal of all property is frozen, and nothing may be moved without the authority of the examining magistrate.

He locked up, made sure that the grille to the street entrance was closed and that there was a cop on patrol, and drove home. Two or three small knots of morbid sightseers were chattering and pointing, breaking off to stare at him. There wasn't much to see. A plainclothes cop with a flat object wrapped in old newspaper and an overnight bag. He left this at the wicket gate of the jail and went on home. Not really late. Ten past eight. In four hours, both a great deal and singularly little had happened.

Castang lived on the second floor of a house with no lift, in a quiet bourgeois street facing an old disused canal. Not an apartment block, but a smallish house: only four stories, and two flats on each floor. The street was inhabited by prosperous folk, and the rents were high—much too high, really, for an officer of police. Vera, his wife, who was crippled by an accident, found the getting up and down a slow hobbly business: she was not good on stairs. Finding an apartment on a ground floor, or in a building with a lift, had often been discussed, and as often turned down. She was too deeply attached to her poplar trees on the pavement opposite, to the grass-grown canal bank and the water that gave the view some distance and perspective. For nearly three years, she had been stuck in a wheelchair and this view had been all she'd had. She could take exercise now—laboriously. The half-kilometer of towing path, where other people walked their dogs, was a constantly renewed delight. The Castangs had no children, and no animals.

The summer evening, despite the early twilight of Central Europe, was torrid, windless, sultry. How was it in Memphis? People were lounging on balconies or at windowsills in sweaty undervests, scratching irritably. The canal water was not stagnant, but sluggish, and there were plenty of insects. The cafés were doing all their business on the pavements, and the streets smelt of ice cream—warmly, sickly.

The people paid no attention to Castang and his parcel. Even if it hadn't had the protecting fold of newspaper, they would not have looked: people are not trained to look at pictures. You could walk all the way down Fifth Avenue carrying a Rembrandt self-portrait without anybody noticing, except to wonder why you didn't take a cab.

Vera, sitting on her little balcony, had seen him arrive. Characteristically, nothing naked or sweaty there: she took a lot of warming-up at the best of times. She was addicted to cardigans and electric blankets when everybody else was puffing. This evening it was warm enough even for her, but she looked as cool as a freshly drawn beer, and as welcome, in a muumuu, a wide enveloping cotton shift of a bright primitive print, and she was far from naked underneath. She was both Czech and strictly brought up about cotton underclothes. Castang thought she looked good. Naked women are to most cops considerably devalued objects at any time: there were far too many of them around, even had he not just had two—and dead at that—on his plate.

Vera looked at the canvas he was carrying. Characteristically, she said nothing. Castang poured out the beer she had been keeping cold and had a draught to fortify him while undressing. Walked off into the shower, leaving clothes scattered. This annoyed Vera: men were incapable of being tidy. He came out rinsed, walked about still plastered and tousled, climbed into clean shirt and trousers, finished the beer, looked appreciatively at cold soup, bread, cos lettuce, and cheese, which was supper waiting, lit a cigarette, and was ready for a domestic chat.

Vera had the picture up on her working table. Herself a draftsman, an illustrator in India ink of some originality, she was looking at it with professional attention. This was the chief reason he had brought it home.

Vera looked at the picture; he looked at Vera. A bell of fair hair cut short; Slav features rather exaggerated, cheekbones pulling her eyes apart and squeezing them narrow. She was not in the least pretty. Beauty was something else altogether. He knew nothing whatever about pictures, but knew you had to look at them. He looked at his wife, and some-

44

times thought he understood art. She scooted her wheelchair across the room—this was still in daily use because she was expert at it and it was much quicker than getting up and sitting down again—took one of his cigarettes (it was characteristic, again, that she should do this instead of asking him to throw her one), and went back to the picture. She smoked in the awkward fashion of a woman who takes two or three a day just to be sociable, not eating it or drinking it.

"Where d'you get this?"

"Is it any good?"

"Have you bought it or something?"

"Would that be a mistake?" This question game was stopped by her turning around and looking forbidding. A picture was serious: she did not want to be teased.

"Not at all a mistake. But it's unfinished in several passages, and he was working on it this afternoon. Do you mean to say he let you take it like that?"

"He wasn't asked. He's dead. The thing is—or will be—an exhibit in a homicide. The subject is dead, too."

"Extraordinary." She didn't mean the homicide. Vera was used to homicides, having been married some years to a criminal-brigade cop. She had decided at the start to be detached about them, the way she was detached about danger, or his wearing a gun. (The gun was lying, on its belt, upon her sofa.) Even weird or horrible events do not bother artists. The subject of a picture, however gruesome—the "Raft of the Medusa," say, all about cannibalism—does not greatly interest them. It is the picture's being good— or bad—that has importance.

"You know who the painter is?"

"His name is Davids—mean anything to you?"

"Did he kill her?"

"The husband killed both of them."

"I'm not surprised. Let's have supper."

Typical. She would not talk about something serious without time and space. To think, but above all to stand back, to look again, to put herself at a distance. She had always been like this, even a a gymnast, before breaking her spine. It had slowed him down in a valuable way. Earlier, he had been too impetuous to make a good cop. Nowadays he knew how to look more, and think less. All cops of experience are stolid, and lack zeal. Only some are stupid. Looking stupid—being phlegmatic, and laconic—belongs to cops all over the world, and wasn't invented by Scotland Yard.

The soup had yogurt in it, and sorrel, and a clean bitter taste. Vera grew chives in a window box, as well as geraniums.

There was also a rule, much like the rule on small yachts: no drinking and no smoking before the washing-up is done. The flat was small, and like a boat in many ways. Vera even had a few ropes rigged at strategic points to help her round the deck in stormy weather.

"How's Richard?" polishing furiously with a dish-towel. She didn't mind being poor, but hated mustard glasses. A glass that one drank out of had to be crystal. Castang said that this was just Czech salesmanship.

"Being rather cynical about the fellow we've got. He's one of these obscure big wheels in the administration—Cour des Comptes or something. An Inspector of Finance no less, the fellow is, so naturally one thinks there'll be a careful beautiful legal whitewash."

"And will there?"

"It's early days yet. The instructing judge is Szymanowski. Polish, you know. Conscientious. Likes to give the dirty French a slap over the knuckles." There hadn't been much said during supper; a complaint about the bread. Vera sometimes baked her own, but only on weekends. "I've better things to do than worry about my belly" was one of her phrases. "All these amateur cooks with their endless chichi make me shit" was another. Sometimes she cooked well and sometimes badly. There were few dogmas. One was that he should make the salad dressing, because she tended to be too heavy-handed with the vinegar. *Right on.*

During the washing-up, she tacked off to write "scouring powder" on her shopping list. Finally she sat down and looked at the picture.

"Is it any good?" he asked. They were back again to square one.

"What do you think?"

"I thought it was. Balanced, stable. The fellow isn't sugary. Liked sweet things, though—would reach out and crunch a praline while working."

Vera laughed. "Of course it's good. You don't have to be so diffident."

"How should I know?"

"You mustn't pretend to be cretinous. For a start, the technique is tremendous. Hardly anybody knows how to do that nowadays, even if they find it valid. It will last. Extremely accomplished. Fellow knows his antique masters backwards. Painting is at a very high level of technical dexterity, but look, it's beautifully composed. Static, highly worked, and poised, but a fine movement and passion in it. What was his name?"

"Davids."

"It doesn't mean anything to me," said Vera, "but there's no reason why it should. I can easily enough find out more. Lovely painting. Good portrait. Is it in any way like her?"

"I've only seen her dead, with no clothes on."

The woman portrayed was alert and vivacious, with great charm and determination. The face was accustomed to getting its own way, and when it did, took on an expression of gaiety and delight. The portrait did not show what happened when she failed to get her way.

"I can understand shooting her," said Vera. "Shooting that good a painter is less forgivable."

"A candy-eating girl-tumbler."

"As though that mattered!" For Vera, he was welcome to crunch up all the girls he had a mind to. To get shot by some dim Calvinist lawyer was a great waste.

"So to you it's not a boring story," suggested Castang.

"Not in the least. The trial might be boring; they generally are. But not the instruction. Pity it's Szymanowski—Polish old maid," disrespectfully.

"You're just being Czech," said Castang with some truth.

# 7. God-Given Appearance
## of a Defense Attorney

Castang was a bit slow in getting out of bed; he lay there, in fact, five good minutes longer than he should have. For no particular reason, unless it was a private presentiment that it was going to be an extremely tiresome day and therefore to be put off as long as one could. He told himself he had a car, and would thus get to the office quicker than by bicycling, as he usually did. This was against all logic: he still got caught in the traffic jam. It was going to be another hot day. The streets were fresh from having been hosed down with water from the fire hydrants, but only in the gutters was there any moisture left: the roadways smelt already of dust. He arrived a good three minutes late, and was unsurprised to be told at once, "Richard's waiting for you. In none too good a mood. Seen the morning paper?"

"No." He hadn't had time to open it. The sense of foreboding had obviously been accurate.

Richard's office was large and bare, with a big desk over by the window and nothing else; it seemed a long way from the door, so that nervous trainees bowed three times on their way over to it, as though at the court of a Hapsburg emperor. He didn't look up when Castang came in, being busy reading the papers, which were strewn all about the desk.

"We'll have to start employing a clipping agency," said Castang.

Richard banged irritably at a page that crinkled in the middle instead of turning over properly. "A whole campaign already," he said in a lifeless tone.

Castang came round the table to read over his shoulder. "Where do they get all this? That lawyer? What's his name—Dieudonné?"

"God-given in more than name." Richard snorted. "Doesn't let the grass grow under his feet. Must have phoned the Paris papers after the television flash."

"I didn't see it. I got home too late."

"Nicely timed, to commit a triple homicide at four in the afternoon in August when there's no news. It was a dead evening and they fell upon it. God-given is the word. This is going to build."

The local paper was the usual gas-filled balloon, with a flaring headline saying, "DRAMA OF JEALOUSY," and featuring the bad pictures taken the evening before: Castang himself unrecognizable, he was glad to note, escorting La Touche—full-face, inscrutable, and dignified—to the car, and blow-ups of the courtyard and windows. Richard's face, so blank as to appear mentally deficient, and the text of his press release, plain and free from comment, but an excited footnote saying, "Turn to Page 7."

Dieudonné must have gone straight to the newspaper office, and they had given him space. Oh, nothing really prejudicial: on the contrary, full of prudent reservations about "when the judge is in full possession of the facts," but a lot of hairy innuendo about artists who destroyed domestic tranquillity, and the rights of respectable householders to do justice upon the thieves of their honor.

M. Szymanowski would be reading these effusions right now, and his lip would be lengthening.

So far, all this was banal, and no more than they were used to. But at the bottom was the source of Commissaire Richard's knitted brow: a subheading in small print saying, "Zionist Influence?"

A reliable source in the person of a close business associate of M. La Touche gave a hint last night which arouses speculation. "This painter Davids was, of course, Jewish," he told our reporter. "Frankly, I have been wondering whether Israeli Intelligence might not be involved." Questioned about this apparently enigmatic remark, he disclosed that La Touche has recently been acting as financial adviser to petrochemical interests in Near Eastern countries with very considerable funds to be invested in selected fields of European property and industrial markets.

"Just the kind of meaningless innuendo that does harm," said Richard, crossly for him.

The Paris papers had small paragraphs on the diverse-happenings page. These ranged from the sober "A Provincial Tragedy" in a serious paper to the sensational "Bloodbath After Orgy" of the gutter press. But they all had something. It was as though they had all been warned that this story had untold potential and could easily be "the-start-of-something-big" they all thirsted for.

The two policemen looked at each other, both wondering about the country's big evening paper. Coming on the street at lunchtime, it had missed a sensation timed for television. It might decide to make up for that by creating a splurge today. They were always hard up for an orgy, and this afternoon's edition might

51

well begin with a five-column headline like "PARISIAN SATYR WRECKS PROVINCIAL PEACE." They both shrugged. There is not a lot cops can do about the press. . . .

"Stuff about the painter, of unholy morals and dissolute existence, whose career has been abruptly terminated," said Richard, "is one thing. Anti-Semitic crap about Israeli Intelligence is another."

"He looked so Jewish," said Castang. "You know —big nose and curly lips—just like a cartoon in the *Volkische Beobachter*." It had been Dr. Goebbels's newspaper. "Misfortune for Jews that now and then they do look like Fagin."

"Virtually certain to be a canard," said Richard. "A dirty tactic but a normal one for a defense lawyer. La Touche behaved so level-headed and logical that the insanity plea, to the public, might look weak. So he throws up a smoke screen. We don't have to pay it any heed. I'll make a few phone calls." Richard was, being a sensible man, fairly friendly with the local political police, D.S.T., who, if one is to believe their carefully innocuous title, "survey the territory." This all sounded sensible. Castang knew that, however silly it was, it might do harm. There is always a small and crazy current of anti-Semitism. It is exacerbated by an equally small and crazy band of friends-of-Arabs. Governments, who are officially very tender toward oil-producing countries, and sensitive to their caprices, dislike being embarrassed by fantasies of this nature. And, one must admit, Israeli Intelligence exists. It has even been known to make a fool of governments. Homicides are bread-and-butter to the criminal brigade. Nobody, though, wants a homicide for a political motive.

Officially, to be sure, the Commissaire of the criminal brigade and his investigating officer couldn't care an ancient franc about the press. They had the author of the crime in a box, at the disposal of justice, fresh and dewy as a sheaf of gladioli. They had a full statement admitting responsibility, and no defense lawyers were going to set up a loud quack about extorted confessions, tortured suspects jumping out of windows, or such-like cheap ploys. Experience, too, gave them no exalted opinion of the press. Justice in this country is deliberate, and purposely so; one good reason is that the dust dies down. The press has a perfect horror of being a bore, and justice always is a bore. By the time—months later—an affair comes up for trial, the effervescence has ceased and the sediment has settled. The press itself is quite cynical about this, and feels free to contradict earlier wild fantasies, taking advantage of its own chatterbox superficiality.

The Great Public, whichever country it may belong to, forgets and forgives nearly anything, for deep down at the bottom of itself, where it keeps its conscience, there is an ashamed admission that the way down into the pit is steep and slippery.

Nearly any criminal, however base, can arouse sympathy. The most abject can arouse pity. When the appalling Christie—who killed women, raped the dead bodies, and in an effort to cover himself sent an innocent man to execution—came himself to be judged, it was noticed that the judge who pronounced sentence of death was in tears: for that handful of wretched women; for the man who had been hanged, an illiterate boy on the borderline of mental deficiency with a fondness for fine-sounding lies; for the police, the lawyers, and the judge who had killed this boy with

53

every respect for legal form; for this ghastly object who was still, somehow, a man; for mankind.

The public does not like its conscience to be awakened in this way. It is not grateful to be reminded for whom the bell tolls. The police, on an everyday level the repository of mankind's conscience, makes a damned fine whipping boy. The cop therefore is little better, in the eye of the public, than the common hangman. Worse; he is suspected of doing favors. Of pulling, stifling, blinding justice for favors.

The cop knows this. Not wiser, but perhaps humbler, he lives with it. He grows a protective skin, and, accused of cynicism as well as brutality, he becomes, with fatal ease, both brutal and cynical.

And the best of cops—Commissaire Richard was a very good one indeed—quails at the thought of a case covered by political protection, be it real or purely imagined. Once imagined, the public will persist in the delusion that it is real. The crooked cop is one of the favorite myths of mankind.

Mankind has always dodged its own responsibilities, and always will. The crooked cop is like the fornicating priest or the immoral artist. Does he not preach morality? Be sure, then, that he does not practice it.

Patient reader, forgive the rhetoric.

Not even Castang felt indifference—even knowing that whatever happened he would be covered by his boss. Commissaire Richard ran an efficient service because he was trusted by his subordinates. This, in turn, because he did not try to dodge responsibilities.

M. Dieudonné timed his appearance well. Castang had only just got to the foot of page 7 when Richard's secretary, Fausta, entered to announce his arrival. She was an enigma to the most experienced of detectives.

Richard himself pretended to an immense bland complacency at having so efficient, so pretty, and so heartless (it was supposed) a secretary. Quite as though he were Svengali and she Trilby. For no one else would she sing in tune. She had superb teeth, and brown hair she could sit on, though nobody had ever seen her doing so. Everyone *claimed* he had; he, only he.

A pushing man, this Dieudonné. Shameless as any cop. Just walked in, not waiting to be invited, a thing Richard detested. Fausta gave him a cold glassy look and no bonjour, for she detested it even more. At the best of times, she had a lack of sympathy for pettifogging attorneys.

"I asked you to be kind enough to wait," she said.

"Oh, come now, this is nonsense. We can dispense with formalities, surely."

"The Commissaire is engaged, and I do not tell lies."

"Yes, yes, my dear, you do your job; I realize," indulgently.

"I will let you know," said Fausta, cold as the circle of Dante, where attorneys among others are buried to the neck in ice.

Castang was repressing a grin like a sneeze, with a pain in the bridge of his nose. That Fausta had an infallible instinct. And to do Richard credit, little as he wished to cause offense to a lawyer, and especially this one, the principle of loyalty (and vanity . . . "My Fausta" . . . ) gained the upper hand.

"Give me five minutes, would you be so good?" Richard said with perfect urbanity.

Some people will never give up tugging. "My dear Commissaire—"

"I don't think you had an appointment, did you."

55

"One would think oneself at the dentist's." An offensive laugh. And Fausta with a beaming smile, showing her lovely teeth as much as to say, "We'll pull all yours out."

"Would you like to read the Paris paper?" A poisoned arrow, that. How did she know? She always did know, the cow.

Lawyers are never snubbed, or they would not be lawyers. Insubmersible, like a water-polo ball, he popped in again five minutes later as though for the first time.

"Well, well, Commissaire. Just thought I'd make my number. How naval that does sound. Battleships firing broadsides. Rather old-fashioned of them."

Round bustling man with an actor's face. Frivolous expression to mask the shrewdness. Fiftyish; sparse dark hair slicked back over a large round skull; much intelligence; merry twinkle in alert little eyes, amused indulgent folds round talkative, clever, tight little mouth; beautifully shaved.

"This is M. Castang, who is conducting the investigation."

"What investigation? As far as I know, there isn't any—am I wrong? No factual doubt, surely? You've got your author, and a pistol, and measurements and prints and chalk marks, all according to rule, all lovely. All nonsense, too, of course, but that's a different question. You've no worries surely, my dear man?"

"None whatever," said Castang politely.

"Have *you?*" asked Richard, interested.

"Me?" astonished. "I'm not a criminal lawyer. Abler hands than mine will pick up the reins. I am simply a man of affairs. I look after the family and financial interests of my clients. M. La Touche is in fact an old and valued friend. Nothing astonishing in that."

"Such dynamism," said Richard.

"Ah," in a deep bass voice, "my dear M. Richard . . . We're men of the world. We understand each other. You are aware—none better—that if one does happen by misfortune to get involved in a fight, a good rule, the best of rules . . . get in first. Avoid haste, avoid precipitation, avoid litigation—like the plague. Be mild-mannered, be circumspect. But if you have to hit somebody, hit him hard. And make sure—of course you'll agree—to get it in first." And all the wrinkles twinkled, together, in enjoyment.

"Good," said Richard. "So no shilly-shally; there's the defense, all mapped out. No hesitation at all. Regardless of what the preliminary inquiry may show, or the judge may conclude, or the instruction may bring to light. You've it all buttoned up! a campaign to blacken a dead man."

"Quite right. Dirty old lecher. Satyr. Lousy artist. I can't afford to hesitate, my dear man. There'll be a crew of worthy people clamoring, no doubt, that he was a hero of the Resistance and heaven knows what. An emotional smoke screen. Natural enough. Legitimate, too. Some of it even true, maybe?"

"Was he a Resistance hero, then?" asked Richard.

"Ribbon in his jacket lapel," said Castang.

"There you are—I'm simply anticipating the tactic. To be sure, M. Castang here, whose acquaintance I am delighted to make, will uncover further facts. Some may be seized upon. I won't say distorted, but perhaps exaggerated in a manner prejudicial to my client."

"Not by the police; heaven forbid," the lawyer said piously. "It can happen, though, can't it? I forestall," turning out the palms of his hands.

"You invite," said Richard. "Attack promotes counterattack."

"Possibly. But I will have been first. I play quite fair with you, you'll notice. I'll be seeing the examining magistrate this afternoon. I may or may not decide to call a press conference. He is bound to inculpate my client formally, as the admitted author of these acts, which are criminal within the meaning of the Code. No question of hearing him as a witness. From that moment, the defense has every right to protect our client. You can't quarrel with that attitude. No move of mine could be seen, by any stretch of the imagination, as a criticism of the police."

Richard's quiet voice contrasted with this volubility. "Very well. Nobody in this office is under any pressure to discredit a suspected or accused person. The facts are beyond dispute. There's a man in custody. He'll stay there until a judge decides otherwise. I don't myself call press conferences much—they generally call me."

"Quite so, my dear man, quite so."

"Nor do we know anything yet about this painter, until the judge calls for a supplement of information. Nor about his relationship with this oh-so-respectable bourgeois family."

"Oh, come, Commissaire—sarcasm . . ."

"M. Castang will look for facts to replace suppositions."

"Splendid," said Dieudonné happily.

"Thank you for calling, Maître."

"My privilege," beaming like an emblem of the Sun King.

"Overkill," said Richard after the door had finished closing. "What should he be so anxious for? We weren't going to do anything. But he's scared of something discreditable."

"He was just a little too God-given."

"You'll be going to Paris, my boy."

"Oh. What a godsend."

"We want to know a little more now, don't we? About artists, and also about these harridans of daughters."

"But the judge will send a commission. Paris can do the legwork."

"I think I'd like you to find out for yourself."

"Oh," groaned Castang. "It's much too hot."


## 8. Polish Intransigence of the Judge of Instruction

The telephone had rung neatly on its cue. This often happened for Richard. Some drivers are like that: as the auto goes down the avenue, all the green lights come on for them.

"You're to go over to the Palais," said Richard, "and see M. Szymanowski."

It generally presaged a tiresome moment for police officers. This judge had a reputation for being severe with the police and fussy about detail and for having a biting tongue; being in general a ghastly Pole from the barbarian north.

Castang was unalarmed, because to him, at least, the judge was oddly mild. He didn't explain this; it might be due to a number of things. Castang himself had a Slav look, wasn't quite "properly French," and had not, perhaps, an automatic assumption of superiority. And Vera—a Czech, who had been named for the national gymnastics team—her running away had created a small diplomatic nuisance; marrying Castang had put him—ever so slightly—on the shit list. And though M. Szymanowski had been French all his life, he would always be "that horrible Pole" to too many people.

And Szymanowski had come up from nowhere, through sheer determination and excelling in examinations. He hadn't married any Hélènes or important persons' cousins. It had made him an acid man, but not in the least neurotic. His wife was fat, plain, nice—and Belgian. Worse in some eyes than being Czech or even Polish. His house smelt of red cabbage rather. And his wife played Chopin badly but lovingly on the piano. And their daughter had unfortunately inherited her father's looks, being a bony, flat-chested young woman with no eyelashes. She was unmarried, lived at home, worked as a social assistant (was extremely good at this thankless job), and had, generally, a tendency to sanctity. They were very Catholic, and the house was full of Black Virgins.

How did Castang know all this? He had never been in the house, and couldn't possibly have known about the icons and the red cabbage. But Colette Delavigne, a friend of Vera's, the junior of the examining magistrates and the "children's judge," had been there on social occasions.

The man's looks were against him, too: he was thin and sharp-featured, with colorless, silky-thin fair hair, and gold-rimmed glasses that caught the light and reflected acrid glitters. And he spoke the hard French of the north, Béthune or Valenciennes, where he had grown up.

"Good morning, Castang; sit down. I wanted to see you before I look at this man. I know nothing about him at all. It could turn out a nasty mess."

Castang didn't have a yes or a no to that.

"The Procureur just goes pooh-pooh. He doesn't see anything in it but the habitual sensationalism and the inevitable publicity. Not really a public figure, he points out. No technical muddle—still, I'm a little less sanguine. A racial smell, and remember that appalling business up in Douai, a football match, bourgeois against the miners. I suppose you'll think I see Béthune everywhere."

"No; I think you might be right," said Castang.

"La Touche—what's that, Huguenot? And this wife, de la something du something else. Huguenot dukes, eh?"

"I'm not well up on dukes. But I'll find out."

"I'll handle the dukes," said M. Szymanowski. "But the fact is that France still hasn't got over the revocation of the Edict of Nantes, to this day. A lot of magistrates tend to be tiresomely allied to these old Protestant families: I'm being indiscreet but you see?" Castang did. "There'll be a lot of sympathy for this man. Since the woman's dead, they can black-sheep her quite safely. . . . What worries me more is this Jew."

A tiny trace of Polish anti-Semitism? Proper Poles don't know any Jews. One admits their existence, and they are part of Poland, and it wasn't Poles that staffed Treblinka—lot of filthy Latvian barbarians—but one somehow doesn't *know* any.

"You're thinking I see Poles under every bed, too," gloomily. "I can smell them a league off, it's true. This painter has a smell of backwoods villages in Galicia. I'm being frivolous, of course: I simply want you to find out." Down it went in the notebook.

"Dukes."

"Jews."

"The political slant is doubtless irresponsible invention."

"Richard is looking into it."

"Now, this daughter—well . . ." Her behavior had not been what the judge expected of daughters. "The Procureur has some acquaintance with this family and tells me the daughter was a tedious child, running away to Paris to be liberated. But there's another—he may have got them mixed up."

"Daughters."

"I've had Maître Dieudonné on the telephone, wanting access to his client, of course. Behaving very stiff—doesn't impress me, but he may know the answers to a lot of these things. You'd better try to get La Touche to fill in what he can before they build a hedge round him."

"Parlor," Castang wrote last, but that had to come first. The point of legal delay is a sore one. The Code says clearly that a suspect may be held by the police for no more than twenty-four hours before being seen by the examining magistrate, and a further twenty-four hours with the authorization of the Public Prosecutor. The police get accused of breaking this rule more often than most, and it is obeyed with an ostentatious strictness.

"The press is making a considerable fuss," said the judge, out of the blue.

"Yes, Monsieur le Juge."

"Well . . . I'll give them to understand that I'll be treating this affair with exactly the same severity that any Algerian immigrant would have to expect. No more, and no less. They'll find me quite intransigent on this point." And so would the cops.

"Quite so, Monsieur le Juge."

## 9. An Interview in the Convent Parlor

"Parlor" is the jargon term for the dingy little room in the house of arrest where detainees—for they may not be called prisoners before their trial—may talk to their lawyers, or the cops, without a guardian being present. It is remarkably like the "little parlor" in a convent. Not, of course, the real parlor, bewaxed and beflowered, where Reverend Mother receives monsignori, such as the Director-General of Penal Establishments, but an airless, badly lit, and horribly depressing small room with no decoration but an oleograph of the "little" Saint Teresa in a shower of roses, here replaced by a forbidding portrait of the General, with a rectangular mouth, telling the populace that liberty is within their grasp, which detainees find

63

an inept observation. In such a parlor, unimportant curates get given breakfast after an early Mass; poor relations are left there to stew while a nun is sought ("Dear Mother is just saying a prayer in the chapel"); and sometimes unwashed persons seeking charity get "stood," so that there is always a slight but unmistakable smell. There is in the parlor a bare table and four bentwood chairs, and that's it.

Nobody could look less like a detainee than La Touche.

He was spotless, with a shaved, brushed, showered look, wearing the carefully pressed track suit that Castang had left for him. This gave him the look of a distinguished middle-aged artist who has been engaged in strenuous physical activity: an orchestral conductor, let us say, just after rehearsal.

"Comfortable?" asked Castang, more or less without irony.

"Very," with no irony at all.

"Your Portuguese lady can leave parcels of laundry and stuff."

"Thank you."

"The food, of course, tends to be constipating. One can get fresh oranges from the canteen."

"Good."

"Nothing's a problem, really, when one has money."

"My dear Castang," smiling broadly, "you don't say!" It was no more than the buttering-up that is frequent when the cops wish to gain someone's confidence. There are several corny old gags, like "Would you want me to get the doctor to give you a sleeping pill?" "Inmates" have always the right to see the doctor, and distract themselves with the pleasures of hypochondria.

All this guff was not needed now. Castang was relieved, because he was only a hypocrite, really, when the job demanded it—though it happened frequently.

"You'll be seeing the judge this evening. All fixed up. Your lawyer's been in touch—dropped in to see us." La Touche made a polite gesture of refusal to the automatically proffered cigarette. The cops always offer their cigarettes. It is their way of saying, "No hard feelings, you know. Nothing personal."

"But you didn't come just to make these polite inquiries."

"No. But no interrogation. Background, on a pretty general scale. Things we need to get straight."

"I'll be happy to help in any way I can."

"Your wife's relatives, for instance . . ."

"You don't have to bother about them. They'll make a funereal fuss, but you can safely leave Dieudonné to cope. It's what he's for," with some aristocratic hauteur toward "attorneys."

"They'll doubtless be visiting you."

"They may feel that convention dictates a show of sympathy, if not solidarity. You think they may cause you trouble." At his game of good guesses again. "Don't be perturbed; they've no love for me—never have had. They're too frightened to budge, one way or the other. In any case, I've no wish for any visitors. You can forget, too, the idea of highly placed personages intervening on my behalf. When I see the judge, I've no doubt I'll be able to put the matter in its true light. They are essentially unimportant people, making an effort to persuade themselves that they may upon occasion have important roles to play."

So much for dukes. Castang decided to leave it at that, until somebody challenged him to a duel.

65

"I'd like to talk about your daughters."

"Yes, that's more complicated."

The impersonal tone caused a sudden intense irritation. "Yes, well, one of them, at least, won't be worrying you any further."

La Touche said nothing, slowly raised his eyes to the level of Castang's and lowered them again.

"Sorry," suddenly ashamed of a piece of police brutality that was a commonplace.

"You don't have to be. I deserve it. Nor will you be the last."

"No, but I didn't have to be the first."

"No more than I merit—but don't take that as a vulgar parade of remorse, designed to impress you. I feel little—too little. I tell myself she got what would in any case have been coming to her. She may have been beyond a better remedy. A nasty little thing. She was only a child, but she was old enough, too, to know better. She may have been badly brought up, but the debate would be futile. Her mother was not a bad woman. I was not a bad man, nor even a neglectful parent. They were brought up with some firmness, and plenty of affection. And showed themselves a pair of corrupt little cows." A crudity designed to prod Castang, and it did.

"What does that mean?" asked Castang, shrugging.

"Rubbing themselves against men, and if it succeeded, screaming," with a flat, cold clarity. "To giggle at male discomfiture and the abrupt subsidence of an uncomfortably erected penis gave pleasure. A vicious pleasure. And I did nothing about it. Inhibited, I suppose."

66

He wasn't mincing his words now. A little late in the day.

"I'll leave that to the experts," Castang said.

"I've handled these experts before now." Not contemptuously, but like a man under no illusions. Castang was taken aback. He had himself a vague respect for the "expert," but prisoners hang on to them as to life rafts. "Bombing the judge with my experts" is a favorite jail pastime and fantasy.

"Come, now, Castang; you're an officer of experience."

"Let's stick to daughters," Castang suggested.

"Yes," said La Touche. "One clings to bonds: blood, love, life shared. It's not to be written off like a bad debt. To cut is to cut into your own bone and sinew. I can't talk about it yet."

"You'll have time, with the judge. Still . . ." The wife was one thing, the daughter another. "I'm interested at present in your surviving daughter."

"Victoria?" as though speaking of an acquaintance one has not seen for some months. "She's a vagabond. She's an expert blackmailer, among other things. If she has not yet been arrested and indicted for numerous offenses, it is because so far she has known how to acquire a steady supply of money. It won't last. You're wrong to say she survives; she's on borrowed time."

"On dope?"

"Yes. She has been weaned a couple of times but it never lasts. Curiously, she was once rescued by Davids, who picked her up off the pavement in Paris. It was my first meeting with him. He persuaded me to take her back. Getting her to come back was perhaps harder."

"You said he was a good man."

"Right, and there's a proof. He did not—I should make this clear—worm himself into my house. I myself asked him to stay. I myself commissioned the portrait of Hélène. He made some drawings of Charlotte. It was stupid of me to throw her at his head like that."

"And Victoria?"

"Oh—she went off again. They find food, shelter, sympathy anywhere. There is a sort of grapevine across all frontiers. 'A sort of,' by the way, which is one of their favorite phrases, illustrates the confusion of their thought. They have a horror of anything precise. Now I," said La Touche a bit sarcastically, "am the contrary. Obsessive. Not on that account a maniac."

"So an anarchist group of sorts. Any political aims or definitions to your knowledge?"

"None whatever," said La Touche, plainly bored with the subject.


## 10. The Heat of the Day


To do any work in the month of August is ridiculous. This is a civilized notion, rooted in antiquity. The governor of a town being besieged by King Louis XIV, hearing that His Majesty was short of ice, promptly sent him some, with a courteous message: the thought of any gentleman going short of ice was a disturbing notion. How on earth did war manage to get declared in 1914? There was a cipher clerk left in the Foreign Office, eating three gigantic meals a day in the intervals of stupefying yawns, but anyone who was Anyone had gone to Scotland upon serious business. Grouse got shot in August: people didn't.

For the Law, and all to do with it, August is the Long Vacation. Dickens left a picture—vivid, as always—of London dead in a heat wave, of Mr. Snagsby, the law stationer, having a picnic in Cook Court, Cursitor Street, and the holy Mr. Chadband ingurgitating.

Somehow it is the emphasis that has changed, in our democratic times. Especially in France. Try to get a spare part. There may be a few factories open, and they may be—probably are—on strike, but no one pays any notice. It is, though, the People that are on holiday. The Establishment no longer withdraws to its country seat, there to fan itself in the shade while the merry merry peasantry gets the harvest in. Ministers and governments rush about, snatching the odd weekend, perhaps, but having to be brought back by helicopter because there is a crisis somewhere. As for the Law, it trots about, business as usual. It may be forgiven, perhaps, for taking roundabout ways on its errands, keeping to the shady side of the street.

It was hotter even than yesterday. Thirty-five: this is really hot. Castang took his time going back to the P.J. offices. Here the Law was at work. Languidly. So lucky that it was all so exceptionally straightforward.

Technical report on the pistol. Nothing wrong with it: it worked in a normal fashion; not rusty or anything. Short-barreled pistols were wildly inaccurate at anything beyond breathing distance, and a mixture of dust and congealed oil in the chamber made this one more inaccurate still, but that fact had played no part. The cartridges were old, but the thing still went off.

If you had wanted it to go off for some serious purpose—you were being fallen upon, let's say, by a rabid dog—it probably would have refused to fire at all. Notoriously chancy weapons, pistols.

Medical reports: no autopsies or pathological skill needed. These people had died of gunshot wounds that were in themselves mortal; that was enough, surely. The subjects appeared to be in rude health, apart from this unimportant detail.

Funerals had to be arranged. Contact had been made with relatives. No problem meanwhile in our progressive days: the Medico-Legal Institute possesses efficient refrigeration equipment. One no longer has to wait till the frosts of December to do a bit of pig-killing. Decomposition can be arrested, just like criminals.

Richard's man from D.S.T. hadn't been in the least excited by mention of the painter Davids. Briefly, he had said "Israeli Intelligence my foot." He knew nothing whatever about La Touche. Ask the economics squad. Nothing illegal as far as he knew about giving investment advice to people with a lot of money.

The economics squad asked irritably whether there was any suggestion of something fraudulent. Had any regulation concerning exchange control been contravened? No? Why were they being bothered, then? If the judge ordered an inquiry—well, they supposed that could be done. It would take a Very Long Time.

The Paris police was too busy changing its sweaty shirt and saluting tourists to be bothered with missing girls. Nobody had reported her missing. True enough, a year ago there had been a complaint. Information had been received—some café waiter, concluded Commissaire Richard—that the subject Victoria La

Touche, aged then eighteen, was being sheltered by a painter named Davids, who might thereby have been contributing to the delinquency of a minor. The complaint, however, had been withdrawn by the said minor's legal guardian. Affair classified: file would have gone to archives. If the judge really wanted . . . etcetera.

The painter Davids was a bona-fide person. No criminal record. Polish in origin, naturalized French many years ago. Had been deported, during the war that was now a dim and unimportant memory, to an extermination camp. Fellow was a Jew. Had somehow avoided extermination. He was a perfectly good citizen with various military and civilian decorations. Nothing known against him. No report that he was engaged in any subversive political activity.

All these people were keeping to the shady side of the street. And so was Castang. He went home to lunch.

Vera had made stuffed tomatoes, roasted them, let them get cold, and made a kind of aspic jelly with fresh tarragon leaves. So far, so good. But she, too, was keeping to the shady side of the street, and was in a tiresome frame of mind—what Castang called her talent for Invincible Ignorance. Saying things like "I fail to understand why women commit adultery." He wasn't going to argue. It was too hot. It was too hot today even for adultery. There were peaches for dessert, with a purée of fresh raspberries that were no longer fresh. The peaches had tough skins, so she had blanched and skinned them. And so pêche Melba got invented. With decidedly dragging footsteps, Castang went back to the office. This damned bore La Touche had to be brought up before the judge, formally inculpated with homicide, remanded into the custody of the House of Detention while the legal arguments got prepared, the experts called for, and the instruction generally set creaking upon its rails in a smell of hot softened asphalt. The thermometer in the concierge's office now marked thirty-*six!*

Richard wasn't even back before the telephone was ringing.

"Castang?" The judge. "There's some kind of demonstration afoot outside the Palais. I notify you because it looks as though, possibly, it might have something to do with our man. I've told headquarters to deal with it. Take a look, though, before you bring him over."

Central Commissaire Fabre, the head of the urban police, was on holiday. His replacement was another person with no ambition to fry eggs on pavements.

"I had a cop take a look. Nothing to it. A few hippies carrying banners—I don't know; something Zionist, or maybe anti-Zionist. Does it matter? Too hot for demonstrations. The judge is an old woman. What does he want me to do—turn a fire hose on them? They'd love that. Free window-wash. Could do with a rinse myself."

Richard, looking offensively cool, as though himself in aspic with fresh terragon leaves, arrived at this moment.

"What's the fuss?"

"Judge says there's a demo outside the Palais."

"Well, go and look."

The Palace of Justice is a building of unparalleled ugliness covered in statues of vaguely mythological nature. Nothing that he could see to do with justice. Orpheus in the Underworld or something. Some were

72

naked with beards; others swathed in flowing garments in which they had got caught out in the rain—in France called "draperie mouillée." The group outside looked as though it had strayed off the façade.

Anarchists, in the sense that they were mad dogs and Englishmen: they seemed to enjoy the heat. Not, though, serious anarchists, who would not be exposing themselves to identification in this way. The public has the right, of course, peaceably to assemble and to appeal for the redress of its grievances, and the police are careful to respect this. If they interfere, they are being provocative. Even if there is a disturbance of public tranquillity, the police does little, because there is little it can do, short of the riot squad and the water cannon.

The placards said, "Justice Has Already BEEN Done," "Liberate La Touche," and "One Zionist Spy Less." There were no more than forty-odd. He didn't think they were to be taken seriously. Certainly no call for the usual technique—the only one there is, short of fire hoses—of taking ringleaders down to the station "to have their identity verified." There was no need to do anything at all. They wanted to be noticed, so he wouldn't notice them.

They noticed him, though. In the forecourt of the Palais, a cop was strolling up and down, to whom they paid no attention, but at sight of himself a catcall went up. Damn that photograph in last night's paper.

"P.J. cop. Castang, Castang." And in chorus, "Rat Poison."

He went away again. A shuffle of the banners across the gateway told him what to expect. The Palais was only a hundred yards across and down the road from the back door of the jail. It was the practice to take prisoners on foot to see the judge, simply hand-cuffed to a cop. It saved trouble, and gave everyone a pleasant stroll. If they now let La Touche be seen, he would be recognized and there would be a scuffle. But if they put him in a police van, salad basket or Black Maria, there was a barrier to force. Drive slowly and you risked being blocked in a humiliating position. Drive fast and you risked some lunatic being knocked over, and then you were in real trouble.

He went back and reported things to Richard. Who simply said, "Use your judgment."

He took a plainclothes cop and an unmarked car, handcuffed La Touche to the first, and drove the second himself.

"They want to liberate you," he said to La Touche. "Make you a martyr."

"Really?"

"Maître Dieudonné will of course disclaim all responsibility."

"That is deplorable. I will accept it."

"You can't. You see, we are now responsible for you. Just leave it to me."

At the sight of the car there was a scuttle. A dozen assorted Tritons and Nereids sat down across the gateway. The uniformed cop on the steps came down them.

"Now—none of that. Out of it, I tell you."

"One moment," said Castang, getting out of the car. "You realize that by obstructing this gateway you are committing an infraction."

"Rat Poison."

He appeared to see the banners for the first time. He read them gravely. "Ah. I see. You wish M. La

74

Touche to be freed. Can't be done, as you know perfectly. Nor will it be done, by means like these."

"Hiding behind the judge." "Fuck the judge." "He's got the key—take it off him."

"Unfortunately, you're completely in error. M. La Touche has no wish whatever to be freed. What's more, he'll tell you so himself. Here." La Touche leaned forward, polite and controlled.

"Would you be kind enough to clear the way," he said. The fellow with the wreathed horn hung about, disconcerted.

"Do hurry up," said La Touche. "It's damned hot in this car."

"Look, don't you realize you're being framed?"

"So are you. And I'm in a position to know more about it than you do. Drive on, Castang."

"Get that stupid girl out of the way or she'll be doing herself an injury," said the plainclothes cop. "It's too hot, you know, for this sort of thing."

"Keep an eye on the car," said Castang to the cop as he unlocked the handcuffs, "and whatever you do, make no threats."

"One might add," said La Touche mildly, "never explain anything, and never argue. I'm sorry, Castang. I'm not at all pleased. I'll tell that ass Dieudonné as much."

"It was well planned," said Castang appreciatively.

"An effort to subvert the due process of law. That is not in the least what I want. Nice and cool it is, in here," he said as they entered the Palais.

"Has Maître Dieudonné arrived?" Castang asked the concierge, who was pretending not to have noticed anything, not being paid to defend the Palais with his life's blood: what did they think?

"Ten minutes ago. That's his auto—the green one. In the robing room, probably, having a smoke. I'll let him know you've come."

M. Szymanowski, who rather went in for the dignity of his office, had not been looking out the window. His clerk had, though, and so had the typists.

"Sit down, then, gentlemen," the judge said. "Ah, M. Dieudonné. We were waiting for you. Have you been here long?"

"No more than a few minutes," quite as brazen-faced as he had been that morning, in Richard's office.

"And you had no difficulty getting in?"

"Oh, you mean the demonstrators? Oh, I paid them no attention."

"And they paid no attention to you. I take note."

"I hope I do not understand the inference, Monsieur le Juge."

"I make no inference, Maître. Since the only inference possible is that a member of the bar should have been in collusion with persons attempting to interfere with justice, I take care not to draw it."

"That is quite unwarrantable and I protest. These people are manifesting their support of and encouragement for my client, as is their right, and having no interest in my humble self, they let me pass."

"I take note of your declaration, Maître," said the judge, lighting a cigarette.

"May I say a word, Monsieur le Juge?" asked La Touche.

"Do."

"Dieudonné."

"My dear Gilbert."

"Four words—five. Don't. Or I'll fire you."

Castang admired Dieudonné: he didn't turn a hair.

"Quite so, Gilbert. Would you like to recall, too,

76

that in matters regarding the law you would be well
advised to allow your counselor to use his own judgment, and that this would be the advice given by any
lawyer? Any one at all."

"Shall we get down to business?" asked the judge,
moving his ashtray a fraction closer.

## 11. The Cool of the Evening

It took some time, but it was no more than formality.
The judge, who had no choice in the matter, pronounced a formal inculpation for willful homicide.
Since, as he remarked, the legal responsibility appeared to turn upon a possible temporary unsoundness
of mind, he proposed to remand the detainee into the
custody of the House of Detention—provisional liberty being, of course, impossible—and to commit a
panel of psychiatric experts, who would formulate an
opinion and in the fullness of time make their find-
ings known to him.

Despite various suggestions put forward, he saw no
reason for accepting a political involvement, or need
to impound business papers. Doubtless—since Maître
Dieudonné here present was empowered to pursue
business matters—these papers would be at the disposal of justice if need arose. In the meantime, the
Police Judiciaire in the person of Inspector Castang
or such other officer as Commissaire Richard saw fit
to designate would be empowered to pursue the inquiry, and to endeavor to produce such witnesses as
might have germane information, such as this young
woman Victoria La Touche. A series of formal inter-

rogations would also be pursued upon the details surrounding this grave crime. That would be all for today, gentlemen; the greffier would now produce the record of this examination for agreement and signature.

It is all very ponderous and bureaucratic, and to the Anglo-Saxon eye ludicrously like the notice regulating the Behavior of the Public, as pinned up in pubs or buses. The Code Napoléon is like that.

However, the sniggering at pomposity tends to die away once a few myths have been punctured. Chief, and most persistent, of these myths is that under the Code a man is presumed guilty until he can prove himself innocent, or the exact contrary of Anglo-Saxon law. This notion is, of course, rubbish. The truth is that unless the judge is convinced, after exhaustive inquiries, that there is a strong case for the accused to answer, he will never go to trail at all.

There are two further very strong safeguards. One is that the defense lawyers are present at every interrogation, have access to every paper (and every word must be consigned to paper, for only the written word has weight), and can question every witness. The other is that the Judge of Instruction does not appear in the trial court, where he has no function, and no status. He merely forwards his recommendations. All pressure upon the accused person is thus removed.

The great disadvantage of this system is the immense amount of time it consumes, and the vast paperwork involved.

The great advantage is that shocking miscarriages of justice, such as have been far too frequent under the Anglo-Saxon system, are avoided. Nor are there any expensive and elaborate farces, like the trial of the Moor Murderers, where the question of their sanity was never raised.

Nor is there the squalid trickery, a commonplace in the United States, about the admissibility of evidence. Once the Judge of Instruction (or examining magistrate, as he is sometimes known) has raised the point—and he realizes, and raises them all, for he is a most painstaking person—all evidence is admissible to the trial court.

The system is, of course, open to abuse. First and foremost, the time involved. A perfectly innocent man, submitted to the sadly leisurely processes of instruction, can sit in jail for two years. And the caution—or hesitancy—of instructing judges has frequently meant that men and women have been kept imprisoned on relatively trivial charges for longer than the time of detention to which they would have been condemned by a court of trial for the offenses they have committed.

Inspector Castang knew all this. It wasn't any of his business. He went home. And was bored, because his wife started a tirade against "justice." She was far too sensible to do such things ordinarily. To get her dislodged from these barren complaints, he told her about the confrontation that afternoon.

"I don't understand these people—what do they hope to gain?" She was fiddling about with scrambled eggs, and watercress, and some leftover rice, and a couple more fragments, out of which she would produce one of her "potluck" salads that were strangely good.

"A crowd like that is like your cooking. Mostly bland enough. You can find people to demonstrate for nearly anything out of a hazy kind of do-goodery.

Being kind to poor downtrodden Arabs. Some are a bit more crunchy, and will seize on a pretext to embarrass authority. Much the same to them whether it's the cops or the rector of the university. Whatever seems authoritarian or paternalistic, they're against it. And you might find a couple who are pure hot peppers and real professional agitators. We've a file on them, and so has D.S.T. Fabre had a man down from Paris who gave a lecture on crowd control and had some of the best-known ones on film clips, but I was on duty and missed it."

"But did they really think they could prevent you taking the man in to the judge?"

"Of course not—come to that, one can get in the back way through the courtyard. One provokes them a wee bit to see what comes into the open. I mean finding out who's the cook. It's hardly likely that a lawyer like Dieudonné would go to such trouble on his own. He might have stirred it up, but he might have instructions from someone. But not, in any case, La Touche. Unless he's playing a pretty subtle game: lots of ostentatious collaboration with the law while quietly building up a big system of making it politically inexpedient to condemn him."

"Oh, it all revolts me," said Vera unhappily. "Bring it back to something I can understand."

"I wish I could," said Castang. "I wonder where that watercress comes from. If you ate wild cress nowadays, you'd quite likely catch typhoid."

"Better not ask," she said with a snap. "If you start looking too closely at things like that, you'd never eat anything."

"Good rule for a cop," said Castang with his mouth full.

The demonstrators had been gone when the group left the Palais. Because the heat had got the better of them? Or because they had made their point—or hadn't made it, since La Touche had refused to let himself be identified with these would-be saviors?

Nobody knew, and as Richard wasn't worried, or said he wasn't, there was nothing for Castang to be concerned about. He'd made his arrest and got his man booked for homicide, and from now on the police had no more than a subordinate role of interviewing a few witnesses and observing a few reactions.

Richard had been right enough about one thing. The judge had had no hesitation about sending him on errands.

"I've got to go to Paris tomorrow," Castang said to Vera. "No, don't worry: only for the day. I can take the plane; be back for supper."

"Why can't they do it there, whatever it is?"

"Because—you'll be pleased—the judge thinks the painter important. He wants me to interview the wife."

"What about the picture?" she said, looking across the room to where it stood.

"I mentioned it to La Touche. Not interested. Says he hasn't paid for it and isn't going to. So it's the widow's property. She can apply to the judge to have it back. It's not an exhibit or anything. We've photos of it."

"Did you see the evening paper?" asked Vera.

He had forgotten all about it, but came back to the office to find it lying on Richard's desk. There was nothing to worry about. Quite a lot of space had been given to the "DRAMA OF THE HÔTEL PARTICULIER," but as Richard said, they'd a lot of space to fill each day. The reporter had been lazy, or not very well

81

briefed, and hadn't made a big thing of the Arab connection or the Jewish artist. Color stuff. Photos of the pretty house in the Rue des Écrivains. Photos of the country house out in the foothills—the "château," as they called it. An interview with some viscount or other, the deceased lady's elder brother, who had been decidedly proper and tight-lipped. They hadn't gone to town on it. Their real offering of the day was "FAMILY SWEPT AWAY BY WAVE" in some Atlantic beach resort, and the fact that the rescue helicopter had been diverted at the crucial moment by a frivolous alarm for an overturned sailing dinghy.

Perhaps it had been an alert subeditor who had added what ginger there was. "Where Is Victoria?" ran the subheading, quite small.

La Touche has a second daughter, who has not been seen since the tragedy. She is, officially, a student in Paris. Less officially, an active figure in the forefront of various liberation movements. She was also, which makes her non-appearance the more surprising, a friend of the painter Davids. "She was with Lou for quite a time," a well-known personage in the art world told us. "One used to see them on the terrace at Lipp." When we asked whether this domestic setup had led to further acquaintance with a bourgeois family which on the surface at least seemed too prim to encourage such a relationship, our informant laughed. "Lou was always irrepressible. He must have wanted to make it a perfect score." We might conclude by remarking that if this was the case he was not well inspired. It would be the last "perfect score" Ludwig Davids was to make.

"The judge doesn't want to issue a warrant before he knows where he's going," Richard had said, tapping the paragraph with a fingernail. "I had him on the phone. He wants you to find out what you can, while you're on the spot, and perhaps see if you could have a word discreetly with the cops in the district. You know how it is when they're on dope; they don't react like ordinary people. She might just not be in the least interested. Davids had a wife, though—let's hear her first, eh?"

Vera cried a little quietly. "I find it miserable. Everyone so callous. A good painter. And the one idea everyone has is to make sure that this ghastly La Touche person isn't punished for it. Yes, yes, I know; don't tell me. But I'm just a private individual. I am allowed to find it lamentable."

"I'm not sure that I agree that he's a lamentable person or at all ghastly. And I think he might still surprise us."

"To me he seems quite unreal."

## 12. Life Class for the Investigating Officer

Castang took the morning express to Paris with a sense of novelty. There was precious little novelty about Paris, a city he had grown up in, but artists were new to him, despite Vera. It often happens, too, that men who are highly specialized, narrowly and even excessively sophisticated within their speciality, are not just ignorant but strangely innocent concerning phenomena outside their experience. To Castang, who had lost both his parents at quite an early age and had been brought up by an aunt—a pious

83

and narrow woman who kept a small shop selling paint and wallpaper near the Lachaise cemetery— artists still tended to be "Montmartre and all that jazz," and despite Vera he had never learned differently. Education at the classical lycée, reading law at the university, and many hours spent in the cemetery had given him plenty of information about the Romantic Movement. But his notions were still absurdly close to a stereotype, like those of most people. Artists were wearers of the broad-brimmed hat and the flowing beard, given to taking opium, writing sonnets, and catching syphilis from models. To be sure, Vera was not like this. But she was his wife and therefore quite different.

All these rubbishy notions were swept out of existence in a moment. To begin with, Davids had not lived in any picturesque squalor—in the Rue Mouffetard, say—but in a modern apartment block of primly genteel nature, well patronized by "middle management," in a street of no character whatever near the Val-de-Grace. Everything clean and well-lit, plastic tiles well-mopped, a lift that did not smell. Eighty square yards on the ninth floor, with ten more on a balcony outside the living room described by house agents as a patio. . . . And no smell of cabbage soup around here.

Mme. Davids opened the door to him, and again it wasn't what he had expected. The features could, he supposed, be called Jewish, but not strikingly so. A tallish statuesque woman of middle age, plainly and conventionally dressed in a cotton shirt and trousers. Pale auburn hair, opaque creamy skin, large fine eyes. Voice quiet, movements subdued, obvious misery under perfect control.

"Come in," she said. "Would you like some tea?"

She left him alone in the living room while she put the kettle on. Even for Paris it was conventional, and in Israel probably would be still more so. Light, simple furniture in pale varnished rattan, plain cream-colored linen curtains, and Tunisian rugs, off-white deep maroon flowers. Plenty of pictures but nothing excessive.

The room was cool, shaded by Venetian blinds. It was very tidy and peaceful; harmonious. There was nothing unusual in it but an old-fashioned parlor organ or harmonium in nineteenth-century walnut with a lot of sheet music on its top.

She brought the tea in a padded basket. China tea in thin handleless cups, good on a hot day, unsweetened. She sat quietly down opposite him and refused a cigarette.

"Just tell me anything you can," she said. "I know nothing." He did, disjointedly and, as it sounded to him, badly. Forthright, anyhow.

"I see," she said at last. "And you are puzzled. There is too much, as you remark, that you do not understand."

"Yes. If we knew more about Davids, we might get closer to grasping this other man's situation."

"There is not much to know about Davids. That you need, or wish, to be told." Her voice stayed even, and quiet. "An artist—it is a vocation for unhappiness. Very few things are important. Fewer still that the modern world holds important. This leads to much tension, and little content."

"Yes."

"The other thing is that people who have survived death camps . . ." She trailed off hesitantly. She was not sure that he could grasp. Decided then that she did not care. "Death has no longer much meaning. Nor have the affairs of this world. We believe, you see, in another world."

"Yes."

"That is important. But I have thought, sometimes, that to treat life here with contempt is an error. Even when it appears contemptible. It was given to us; to despise it is surely a fault of pride."

He sipped the scalding unsweetened tea.

"So why were we spared? If we were given a new lease on life—as I was when no more than a child, as Davids was when already a man—was it because we had something still to do?" She got up to bring him an ashtray.

She continued, "Artists try to heighten, and not to add to baseness." Now he was on more familiar ground. "Mammon is a glorification of greed. Vulgarity is a glorification of baseness, and what is baseness?" Yes; Vera, upon occasion . . .

"Everything, isn't it, that we fall into all day? You, as a policeman, should know something of that. Much —envy and vanity, callousness and cruelty, hypocrisy and crowd-pleasing. Petty meanness, timeserving, and shallow flattery. But the artist doesn't exist to combat that, as a policeman combats a crime. It is what he makes that counts. By his fruits you know him.

"Being what we are"—she spread her hands out and looked at them—"one can't get them clean. Always in the dirt."

"Some people are obsessive handwashers," he suggested, "always scrubbing away." She smiled.

"Good. I was afraid you might think me mentally deranged."

"Not by any means."

"He suffers, then, and he falls. He suffers, to be sure, the hatred of the base, the contempt of the vulgar, the envy of false artists. And his own baseness. He falls, often, into gross squalor. I have thought that this may be a search for relief."

"Perhaps."

She poured him some more tea. "Davids suffered much," she said simply. "Hunger, for a start. Have you suffered hunger?"

"No."

"Can you imagine it?"

"No."

"And very great misery. I am not, you know, trying to justify him. Nor anything that he has done."

"I realize."

"Do you, I wonder?" She fell into silence. Castang felt a kind of shame. A cop is an unimaginative animal, but sees much misery, and even, sometimes, hunger.

"Maybe I can give you an illustration," she said at last. "You know, we Jews are fond of little stories. Haggadah, we call them. Parables and little legends. Davids often told this story. It threw light, he said, upon artists."

"Good. Go on."

"In England there was a poet. A great poet. For some of the reasons I have touched on, he was often a great drunk, and surrounded by whores. He was friends with another poet, because of what they had in common. That one was an old lady, from an ancient family. Grand and aristocratic—and terrifying, too, from this age and grandeur. You follow? While this one was a rough, crude peasant boy. You follow?"

"Yes. Like Davids when he was young?"

"A little. Good. They were going to have dinner to-gether, and this one, who had been on a big bender, arrived very late, and much stained and disheveled, stinking of drink and whores, and feeling great shame. So he said, 'I am so sorry, I am very late and I smell revolting. You understand, it is the fault of the sea-side; I have been to the seaside.' And she answered, 'Yes, my dear boy, of course it is the seaside.'"

"And what happened to them?" asked Castang, who always wanted to know the end of stories.

"Oh, they died. He was only thirty-two."

"Yes," said Castang. "I should like to ask you how Davids came to meet this family." If he had really sheltered the girl Victoria for months, this woman must know. Or would she have more little stories?

"Ah, you find that important?" Her voice was so soft that it could not be called harsh. "He deserved to be exterminated, no? A gypsy, a dirty bohemian. Nobody can blame M. La Touche for exterminating such."

"M. La Touche will have ample opportunity for explaining himself. Davids no longer has."

She looked at him saying nothing. She leaned for-ward and took a cigarette from a box, studied him through the thin veil of smoke.

"Come," she said at last, stubbing it out quarter-smoked. "I will show you the studio."

It was upstairs one flight, the fire stairs quicker than taking the lift. In the European sense, a studio is only a one-roomed flat, a bed-sitter with a bathroom and a little kitchen. This one was a studio in both senses of the word. It was summarily furnished, with cur-tains but no carpet. There was a divan bed with a corduroy cover, a bare wooden table, a few kitchen chairs. Little else. Some canvases, and surprisingly few, were stacked against the walls. There was no mess. Castang had only been in one studio in his life: a sculptor's, an acquaintance of Vera's. He had a barn, in the country: a museum of old cigar butts and rusty razor blades, of broken furniture and old locks, and tools for everything from bricklaying to watch-repairing. He was certainly learning.

"You kept it clean?"

"Davids. I never set foot here unless invited."

"May I look around?"

"You are free."

The clothes cupboard held some lengths of furnishing fabrics neatly folded—for backgrounds, he supposed, or to alter lighting. Some old sweaters for the cold; shirts one could wipe a brush on, being no longer fit for society; an odd variety of hats. The kitchen shelves held some paints and mediums, and the sink had been used to clean brushes. There was a teapot, a coffeepot, and cups, but no food. Everything was wiped clean. The bathroom was spotless, too.

When he turned back, the woman had taken a canvas and set it on the easel, and was wiping dust off her hands with a paint rag. She turned the easel so that he got a good light.

It was a large canvas, placed horizontally. The subject was a naked girl, lying on a bed or sofa, her arms crossed behind her head. She was striking. She had a stylized pose, similar to that familiar from postcards —Manet's hieratic Oriental woman called "Olympia," or Goya's Duchess of Alba known as the "Maja Desnuda." Even Castang could see that she was very well painted. Having looked at the other picture—and been shown by Vera some of the things to look for—

helped. Sexy she was, disturbingly so, and wonderfully vivid: she was, too, enchantingly serene. Nothing there was jarring or violent, but the calm and harmony of a madonna. And this skin and flesh would not decay, these bones never become dusty. He was astonished to find himself so excited.

"And that's Victoria?"

"Yes. She lived here, in this room, for nearly six months."

"I've heard this story. So it's true? That he fed her, cared for her, got her off heroin?"

"He was good to her," simply.

"He slept with her, of course."

"Of course," said the woman with simplicity. To that one could only say "No further questions," like the District Attorney. There were too many, altogether. M. Szymanowski might choose to ask a few.

"Shall we go down again?"

"Is the picture for sale?"

"It is. Davids refused several buyers. I will be obliged to sell it."

"There seem few pictures."

"There were never many."

"They command a high price?"

"Yes. They are good, you see. I shall have to hope that his death puts the prices up," still simply, without bitterness. I'd buy her myself, he thought, and even wondered for a lunatic moment whether he could.

Back in the street, he had to remind himself that it was the real Victoria—but which was the real one?—that the cop had interest in. He went and had two Pernods in a café, which didn't bring him any closer to the answer.

Today, in Paris, it was not so hot; it was just a per-

90

fect summer day. The tourists everywhere were strolling, in a momentary perfection of content at owning Paris. A beautiful day, one they would always recall with bliss. The day they had laid aside all care and misery: the day they had felt that a sun-soaked Paris lay before them like la Maja desnuda. Crowding into the Louvre to see the Venuses and Dianas. Like most of the inhabitants, Castang had never set foot there.

The famous "empty Paris" of the month of August, with no traffic jams and no neuroses, has acquired its own folklore, but it has its points: the cops are for once not overworked. A lot of them are on holiday, too, and the ones that are left say they'll think about it tomorrow. Castang found a narcotics-squad cop he knew well enough to get invited out to lunch, in "a little place where the wine was still honest," up a flight of stairs and pleasantly like a nineteenth-century brothel.

Victoria was known, but not well.

"She got off the sauce for nearly a year. Prolonged her life."

"How'd she pay for it?"

"How do you think?"

She'd been lost sight of. Not altogether, but she had slipped outside the orbit.

"Got in with one of these political gangs. Anarchists. It's a mystery where they get their money. Some of our boys were interested because they had a notion that this bunch, sloppy as it seems, had done a few slickish post-office jobs, but it didn't hold up. I wouldn't know, really. Their security's tight enough; they wouldn't put up with Victoria—not, at least, unless she was pretty stabilized. Try D.S.T."

"They never tell anybody anything."

Correct: there the reception would be chillier. One had frequently the impression that they told one nothing because they didn't know themselves.

"At present, at least," the narcotics cop said, "they're doing well with arms. Plenty of market in Ireland. It doesn't amount to much, really, since they're cleverer at propaganda than they are at the real thing. They might perfectly well have SAM low-level missiles. Know better than to fire them off at anything, because they know perfectly well we'd have them inside five minutes."

Castang had met one or two D.S.T.s in days gone by, jovial types who got the giggles at things like anarchists. Perhaps things had changed. Perhaps it was just bad luck. These people always had a tendency toward airs and graces with plain stumblebum cops. They came neither under the Ministry of the Interior, like urban police forces, nor under Defense, like the gendarmerie, and quite certainly not under Justice, but were attached to the Prime Minister's Office, where the Intellectuals came from.

He was received in an office with a hush upon it, as though talk would interfere with the Extrasensory Perceptions. When the immobile man behind the desk condescended to speak at all, the voice was extremely slow and barely audible. He might have been put there to convince suspicious Americans that the French were neither noisy nor indiscreet. He was convinced that Castang was a very stupid person, and that this stupidity would lead to irresponsibility.

"I know nothing of this girl you describe."

"I am told she knocks around with the group in the Rue Delambre."

"What do you know of this group?"

92

"Nothing at all, which is why I come to you."

"Who is the source of your information?"

"A cop."

"I do not wish this group to be tampered with."

"I've no idea of any such thing," refusing to be insulted. "The girl has to be interviewed as a witness in a homicide."

"Show me your mandate. . . . It is most unlikely that a girl with the habits you ascribe should be affiliated with this group. Of which, it is plain, you know nothing."

"What I said. They may be using her for purposes of their own."

"If that were so, the more reason not to interfere. Until I know what these purposes are. I repeat. As a matter of policy, I wish for no meddling with this group, for however well-meant a purpose."

"Look," said Castang gently. "If there is no possibility, as you claim, that this girl is in their confidence, it can't compromise them or you if I ask her a few questions on a totally unrelated subject." If this worthy knew nothing about rumors that Davids had played some political role, Castang wasn't going to mention them.

"You fail to understand," bleakly. "If—and I say if —this girl has been used in some minor role, your appearance may be interpreted as a maneuver originating in this office."

"I feel sure you know how to avoid being compromised. I'm sure, too, that you prefer to avoid even the appearance of obstructing a matter of justice that is purely internal and domestic."

The man thought for a while. Then he opened his

desk drawer, took out a visiting card, turned it over, and wrote something with a green felt pen.

"If you meet"—staring at Castang—"anyone in the Rue Delambre who can give you any information regarding your inquiry, show him this. Since by so doing I am helping you, more than you may realize, I should be obliged if you will then bring it back to me, and make known any information you may gather. Is that understood?"

"I'll agree to that."

"One thing more. You wish to do well, in your career?"

With a wooden face, Castang took the card and left, thinking, Artists are not the same as ordinary people, Mme. Davids tells me. I'm learning a lot about art today.


## 13. The Unlucky Numbers of the Rue Delambre


A small sober flat in a building neither clean nor dirty. The flaked gray paint showed no affluence, or poverty. The door was of solid hardwood, the brass plate carefully engraved and recently polished. "Christian Bonnet," it read. "Expert in Questioned Documents." The doorbell was polished, too. The man who answered it was thirty, slim and light on his feet, with an open, friendly expression and a pleasant smile.

"M. Bonnet? Himself? I have a paper I'd like authenticated."

"Please come in." A room furnished simply as an office. "Do sit down. How can I serve you?"

"It is not in my interest to tell any lies, nor to pre-

94

varicate. Turn the recorder on if you wish. I'm not going to compromise you, or myself, or anybody else. I'm an inspector of police from the provinces. I'm looking for a witness in a criminal case, I'm told you may be acquainted with her; it's a very simple matter. I hope I'm not troubling you."

"By no means," politely. "But you spoke of a paper. Am I to understand that this was simply a pretext to gain entrance?"

"No, not at all. I have a written authorization from the Judge of Instruction concerned with this affair. No doubt you can tell at a glance that it's authentic."

"I'll be glad to oblige you. I must charge you, naturally, my professional fee."

"Sure," said Castang, perfectly serious. "Here, too, to save you trouble is my own identification. No fee on that, I think."

"Certainly not," laughing. "Thank you, M. Castang. Yes, these papers are certainly genuine. 'Victoria La Touche.' No, I know nobody of that name; however, there may have been some error. Is there anything further I can be of use in?"

"You haven't any trapdoors round here? You know, like Sweeney Todd? Push a button and I disappear through the floor."

"What a lovely idea," tickled. "Like Catherine de Médicis in the Louvre—zip, down the oubliette all the boring customers. But what on earth would one do with the bodies? Cat's-meat factory?"

"I thought Victoria might have gone down the oubliette: out of sight, out of mind. I really do want to see her—she used to know this man who got killed. Painter—you might have read about it in the paper. I've no curiosity about anything else; I'd hoped you might know where I could get in touch with her. Don't pay attention to the gutter press, by the way—this affair isn't sensational at all."

"Well, M. Castang, as to that, one would like a few guarantees. Nobody likes to get into the gutter press. Unwelcome publicity is harming to anybody in the professional way, of however humble a description."

"I think I can manage that. I've an introduction from a friend. Don't tear it up, though: he'd like to have it back."

"Good . . . That's certainly a serious recommendation. Now, this girl—to be businesslike—no, I don't know her, truly. The name is sufficiently unusual; I'd recall it."

"Perhaps an assumed name. One meets girls at parties. Here's a photo of her that her father gave me."

"Something vaguely familiar about the face. One can't be sure—these wretched girls change their hair and put on false eyelashes and you'd no longer recognize them."

"Try, though. I'd take it as a favor."

"Always glad to do a favor to one's friends. Tell you what, I'll try and find out. Make a phone call or two. Where could I get in touch—say, an hour from now?"

"How about my friend's office?"

"That'd be a notion. People bring the oddest girls to parties."

And with that he had to be content. He was so used to this childish rubbish that he took it as inevitable. These people were all moral imbeciles. On account of that, they were dangerous: they knew no standard but expediency. Nothing interested them but a gold bar, and even then they'd think it fake. Which was preferable, this group that pretended the girl didn't exist or those other idiots who were convinced she had never existed but had been invented to gain leverage somewhere? They thought him a sad simpleton. And he thought nothing about them at all. Any more than a gardener wonders why weeds grow quicker than flowers.

He went back to the secret-service crowd and found his man still sitting where he had left him, finger still on the pulse of the nation's safety.

"I haven't tampered with anyone," Castang said.

The man leaned back in a comfortable, well-padded leather chair. His desk was expensive, too. "Your people are holding this man La Touche?"

"That's what I've been told."

"Who started this rumor about Israeli Intelligence?"

"Somebody wanting to make himself interesting."

"There's nothing in it. Once more I say to you—don't meddle with what you don't understand. Now—what about this girl?"

"He's ringing me back at this number."

"Less bad," slightly mollified at finding Castang docile. "Tell me," in a more friendly voice, leaning forward again, "do you think she's worth finding?"

"In the evidential sense, she'd probably serve only to confuse a simple matter. She might have something to add which clarifies this action of La Touche. Which is fairly unaccountable. She was at one time on heroin. If she still is, she'll be useless, since they are interested in nothing but to satisfy their immediate needs. If you mean do I have a fancy notion that people got her laid alongside this painter Davids in order to keep tabs on his political activities—no, I don't believe a word of it. For a start, nobody on a drug would be the least reliable, or thought to be so by anyone remotely bright."

"I'm glad to hear you speaking sensibly."

"A girl of that sort, finding friends who seemed to satisfy her wilder aspirations, might get used as a tool at a very low level. Or for propaganda purposes, as leverage in an extreme case upon her family."

"What do you know about these activities of La Touche?"

"Very little. Frankly they don't interest me. They may you."

"Quite. If your judge has been reading spy stories and gets his imagination overheated, just be good enough to let me know. I'll handle it. There wouldn't be anything there for you. I make myself understood?"

"As long as it cuts both ways," said Castang. "I want to talk to this girl, about her father, and about this man Davids. On her personal relationships. Nothing more. If you don't like that, then there's nothing I can do about it. If obstacles are put in my way, then I will inform the judge. He can decide that for himself. The independence of magistrates is no part of my responsibilities."

"That's quite all right," said the man soothingly.

The telephone rang. The voice was the same, light, merry. "M. Castang? . . . That little favor you asked. I've been glad to do what I could, but I can't manage it for you. . . . No, you don't owe me a thing. It would have been a pleasure. . . . To tell the truth, I thought I could have fixed that. Just on the spur of the moment, when you mentioned it, I imagined it shouldn't be too difficult. But, to coin a phrase, the model's out of stock. . . . No, there's no act being put on; the person you really want to meet just isn't in Paris. Left the country, I'm told. You know how erratic these people are. . . . No motive at all that I can see, unless personal. You know—life is a bit of a bore, let's change the scene. Without being in the least rude, I'd hazard the guess that she thought meeting you would be complicated. To my mind, it's as simple as that. Fault of the press, I should imagine. Just couldn't bear to face the idea of a fuss being made. . . . I genuinely don't know. I'm told that England was mentioned, but I can't guarantee even that."

"Thanks just the same," said Castang. He put the phone down and said, "Well, that disposes of your worries. They decided she was an embarrassment and pushed her out. Probably sitting in the airport waiting room this minute. It wouldn't take her long to pack."

The man behind the desk risked his first, very faint smile. "My dear man, they know very well that if she left now I could have her if I wanted her. England, of all places, where there's a strict check at immigration."

"So you mean she's still here but they've deliberately lost her."

"No, I don't think that. They imagine I want her, and quite certainly they wouldn't want to irritate me for such a trivial motive, or if it were not trivial they would be tipping their hand, showing me that she had importance. No, it's probably true. She doesn't want to face the idea of being bothered by cops, and she just ducks it. That suits them. One thing they're really expert at is public relations and this is not a good terrain for them."

"I love that," said Castang, grinning. "Anarchists with a P.R. man."

"But of course." The man was unbending now, seeing that nobody was going to give him a troublesome moment. "What else is it, over 90 percent of the time? They plant a rumor, say, that they have a low-level SAM missile, and could fire it at one of these great lumbering things from anywhere round an airport perimeter. A thought well designed to make a good headline. Whereas, even if they had one . . ."

"Have they?" asked Castang, with some amusement: this man was proving that good public relations are never wasted.

"My dear fellow, who cares whether they have or not? They know that I could make their lives such a misery if I really thought they did."

Not you, thought Castang. You're only a pen-pusher.

"You mean you'd shove a few of them under subway trains."

"You ought to know better than that," prudishly.

"No," said Castang, "you shoot them up quite blatantly. Two useful results: in the public eye they're just gangsters, and they get persecuted by the criminal brigade—me, for instance."

"My dear fellow—we'll have to get you transferred to Paris." Shit on that, thought Castang.

## 14. Love Me Little, Love Me Long

He got a late-afternoon train, which would bring him home for a late but still reasonable supper. To this pack of poisonous phonies, a real woman like Vera was the only antidote. He had brought her a big bag

100

of greengages: next to cherries—that Czech fruit—her favorites. She wasn't able any more to climb the hillsides and go down on her knees to get close to the ground—for it is only when you are close to the earth that you find the wild strawberries.

On the train he read a spy story by a famous English writer, the specialist in moral imbeciles. It was of no interest. He scribbled in his notebook.

Monsieur le Juge,

1. I would be inclined to discount the whole political element, either as imaginary or as being an exercise in public relations by D.S.T.

2. The girl Victoria La Touche: inquiry among known associates met by time-wasting tactics and a sense of embarrassment. Likeliest conclusion: this group, politically sensitive, feels compromised by the noisy rumor of political scandal in the press. Information, probably reliable, is that she has crossed a frontier. Destination (unverifiable) England. Suggestion: warrant for interrogation via Interpol. D.S.T. unwilling and unlikely to act, their apparent policy being an agreed immobolism failing act of terrorism on national soil.

3. Davids: no ground whatever for supposing him an Israeli agent, unless the emphatic assurances of D.S.T. are taken to mean the opposite. From observation, such activities would be quite incompatible with character. Since the point is inconclusive, and in view of the strong obstructionism to be expected from other departments, my conclusion is that the entire political aspect should be excluded and treated as fictional, failing strong independent corroboration.

Respectfully,
H. Castang, O.P.P.

He threw it aside with a sigh. He was going home to clean himself. His habit of taking a shower directly

101

he got in was in a way symbolic. It wasn't just sweat that had to be scrubbed off.

The greengages, by a latter-day miracle, were not dry and juiceless from being picked unripe, but were full of blood, crisp even when bursting with ripeness, with a scent that filled the room, the bittersweet smell of her childhood: acid Slav scent of a little girl who could do with a wash, barefoot on a wooden ladder propped against the cherry tree. She sat eating them greedily, absorbed, immensely and simply happy. He sat opposite with his feet on another chair, propped on the bottom of his spine, where she had cracked hers, smoking a small Dutch cigar as a treat: rather heavy—they had mixed some dark Brazilian leaf in with the light Sumatra tobacco. More smokable, though, than the black things, skinny and knotted, that Richard affected and that knocked you down. He studied her: she was his balance wheel; without her, he thought, he would be nothing but a bum.

The Cattleya, the papers had called her. Such a stupid name; she was nothing like an orchid. But a play on her name, and because the strongly marked Slav features were exotic.

She hadn't changed much. The legs, of course: they were wasted and there was nothing anybody could do about that. But the face and the upper half hardly at all. The one a trifle thinner, the other a scrap heavier, but still in essence the same as when he had first seen her, at the Antibes competition where he was on security duty.

Antibes was not one of the top international meetings, but was regarded by the trainers as a good proving ground for the tougher work to come, for seeing who was in form, and especially for developing the younger, less known gymnasts. That year all three of the Russian stars were there. Roumanova, small and dark, the extraordinary jumper, amazing on the "horse" and in the ground movements. The very fair Liabouschinska, poetic and fragile, with beautiful arms and incomparable slow movements on the "balance beam." And the round-faced, doll-pretty Aronova, the reigning champion, not outstanding in any one exercise but unbeatable on average, so faultless and finished was her execution, her one handicap the slightly inexpressive features.

Castang, who had been a fair gymnast in the military team during his army days, watched with professional interest. Vera took his eye at once. She was far below the Russian girls, nowhere near accurate or inventive enough. Indeed, she was only substituting on the national team for a girl with a pulled muscle; but in this, the strongest rivalry she had faced, she surpassed herself, and in her best exercise, the parallel bars, she had come equal second with a Russian prima donna, and the crowd applauded madly. Castang had been a bit unprofessional about making her acquaintance. Still, nobody was more surprised than he when she ran away, suddenly, only three weeks later in Vienna. The press had been quite positive that this was a romantic attachment to a Czech ice-hockey star who had just done the same in Canada, and was disgusted when she married an obscure French policeman, neither photogenic nor likely to become so, and it promptly forgot her.

One day a year later, she again got a brief headline. She was training a class at the local club—slack-muscled French women. Ironically, it was on the parallel bars that a hand slipped, perhaps insufficiently resined, and the big somersaulted jump-off had pulled to one side, so that she fell awkwardly just off the protective mat and cracked pelvic vertebrae—or busted her arse, whichever you called it. Hadn't walked for nearly three years. Never would, in all likelihood, get much beyond the present hobble. He was the only person left who still retained, unmarked, the original cherry-eating Cattleya.

He had told her about Mme. Davids. She apprehended and understood it all so much quicker than he did. She was not intelligent in the conventional way, the way he was "a bright boy." In many things, she was painfully dense. And quite uneducated, never having paid attention at school, and shocking people by saying things like "Where is the Panama Canal?"

Now she was crying a little into the greengages, controlled as she always was. No noisy sobs and gulps or grimaces, only two white marks that came and went on the wings of her nose. Who was she crying for? It was not for the Cattleya, or for the wretched fate of the two young girls. She wiped it off her face with her forefinger.

"You saw the papers?" he asked. The campaign had gathered momentum in a nastily anti-Semitic outcry. Photographs of Davids, oddly clever at disguising the broad and noble features, all sensual mouth and greedy eyes. La Touche photographed well, with his distinguished, slightly pinched look of concavities below the high fine forehead.

"Dear sweet France, frightened again of offending the Arab pals and losing an arms contract. . . . Justice!" with bitterness.

"It's just a storm," he said. "It'll pass. And say this for Szymanowski, he has integrity. He'll have no truck

104

with this vulgar propaganda. Being a Pole, he hates Poles, but since he dislikes Jews, for a Polish Jew he'll bend over backward."

"But in face of a deliberate press campaign . . ."

"Pooh—yesterday's news wraps fish. He'll lie low for a while."

"That man," said Vera, "why does he kill his wife, his child?"

"Forget all this political crap. What are you left with? Passion, a genuine crime of passion? Only one thing we know about that—no journalism, no trial, no nothing can bring that out. Either you're clinical or you're sentimental. Best not try to understand."

"But I want to."

"Then go and see him. Talk to him. You might very well do better than me."

"How?"

"You've a prison visitor's permit. I daresay the judge will give you an authorization, if you ask him."

"Did he love them?"

"I don't know. Not at all, perhaps, and then too much. The shrinks will be busy with it. These very controlled, rational men . . . How does one know?"

Vera finished the last greengage and looked at him desolately. "Love me only a little," she said, "but love me a long time."

Castang laughed and crushed his cigar out. "Cattleya," he said teasingly; it always made her cross.

## 15. Tactics, and Tact

"Funeral this morning," said the judge, "and I want you to keep an eye on it, Castang, from a discreet distance. I've told that man—the viscount or whatever he is—there's to be no provocation. In the interests of justice, and in the name of decency and taste, I've laid down that it must be strictly private. He acted the horror-struck, and assures me that it will be a purely family affair, out in the village where they have their country house, far enough out to discourage the vulgar, so that I don't suppose there'll be any demonstrations. But that infernal Dieudonné is clever at orchestrating a show—black veils and sobs and photographers—so you'll keep an eye open, and see that nothing gets out of hand. There might, too, be a possibility of this girl Victoria turning up."

"Yes," said Castang.

"Quite so, I've read your report. The wretched press forces one's hand. They print all breathless that the girl is in hiding; she's only to pick up a paper to rush for cover. But there it is: I agree with you that she's a material witness and has got to be heard."

"I can't see her turning up at a bourgeois family occasion like a funeral."

"No . . . I've put the usual telegraphic notification through to Interpol. Finding her would put a spoke in Dieudonné's wheel, too; from what you tell me, it's clear that Davids protected and cared for her. Damned Pole, but I don't like this systematic blackening."

"The women egged him on. La Touche told me it had happened before."

"Damned imbecile," said the judge, meaning Poles. "Should have had the sense to leave young girls alone. If it had been the wife alone—La Touche was indifferent to her games, and makes no bones about admitting it. . . . Difficult subject, with that irritating lackluster manner. I'm not going to allow any blatant whitewashing: Maître Dieudonné has overplayed his hand. I've ordered two experts whose objectivity will be beyond question. Definitely not from Paris—one from Bordeaux and one from Lyon—and for heaven's sake see that neither of them is a Jew. . . ."

"Or an Arab."

"Just so, that's exactly the way the press twists one's arm. The swarthy complexion wouldn't do at all, and how does one go about asking for two psychiatrists, please, and see that one is Norwegian and the other Canadian—like these wretched United Nations soldiers who can't fight and who impress nobody. Very well, Castang, off you go. They're due to begin at eleven and it's twenty kilometers away."

Castang, climbing into a stuffy police car that smelt vile, winding down all four windows, was unaware that Vera was disembarking outside the Palace of Justice, making heavy weather of those broad flights of horrible sick-colored marble steps. She did not know M. Szymanowski at all. She was, though, quite close friends with the youngest of the panel of examining magistrates—Colette Delavigne, the children's judge —and through her had a prison visitor's card in her maiden name. One always encouraged prisoners with an interest in art. Those with literary aspirations less: there had been too many writing books about their experiences in prison. Vera made a good prison visitor because she did not pity herself and was curt with people who did.

In the country it was less hot. The city, in the broad river valley, was notoriously hot. Out here, it was still officially "the plain," but since leaving the town he had been climbing imperceptibly, and the land now rose in a ridge—or, more exactly, a whaleback—with a gentle approach from the city side, falling into an abrupt scarp on the other. The "château" stood at the very top, commanding a magnificent view over to the foothills. A real château, too; no gimcrack villa or false-classical pompery, but a simple, pretty country house in local stone with a slate roof.

The village was built up the whaleback, with cowsheds and farmyards up to the gate. Nothing but a slight widening of the unpaved street and two fine old lime trees marked the entrance: a wrought-iron grille and a graveled courtyard. There had been no room for the stables behind, where a paved terrace overhung the scarp, so they stood to the side behind a row of clipped acacias, and were now converted to cottages. Nice, too, thought Castang, as a grace-and-favor residence. Wouldn't mind the château, either, come to that: cost a bundle, though, to heat in winter. Serfs bringing in the yule log would be the thing, and alas, he was a serf, but wasn't getting sentimental about it.

The gate was open and a dozen cars were parked round the sundial. Castang had not been invited to drink sherry before the ceremony, or to lunch after, and went to explore. Good village: château and houses had grown up together, taking each other for granted, and would bury one of themselves in simplicity and solidarity. The church was nice, with the cemetery next door; box hedges and a lich gate. Lucky Hélène: no place here for urban louts or even earnest left-wing students cherishing their Arab brothers.

Everything smelt good; he wished Vera were with him to share it. Virtually everyone in France is countryman by instinct if not by birth, and he was no exception. Even Hélène. She would be remembered and loved here as a pretty young girl. The local people had groomed and shod her pony, washed her clothes, put cobwebs on her cuts, fished her out when she fell in the brook, and smacked her for disobedience. Charlotte, too, perhaps, with the more sophisticated urban upbringing, had come here to pick blackberries and mushrooms and been shouted at by village women for forgetting her sunbonnet.

Castang looked with appreciation at the "dependencies," all properly in their place: walled kitchen garden, orchard, vineyard, turreted pigeon cote. These people—how was it possible that they had not known how to be happy? Would one ever get tired of that terrace (sheltered from the vulgar gaze by trees, but cops are good peekers)? The sun setting on the far plateau? To come out after spending the winter months and the opera season in the equally delicious town house, and stay through the summer till after the vintage . . . this was the earthly paradise. And Hélène looked for it in witty-tongued charlatans, and Victoria in heroin, and the young Charlotte in brushing her behind along the arm of La Touche's stiff financial colleagues. Castang just didn't grasp it at all, and was glad not to be a psychiatrist.

The funeral procession had formed and was approaching. Quite a sprinkling of the older villagers had come to slip into the church, and about forty people were coming from the house; half of those would be relatives, with long black veils in the ancient style for the women; the curé, too, had dived into the past to dig the old "first-class" funeral trappings out of a musty cupboard—black and silver canopies and hangings. Castang lurked discreetly.

The chief personage was a stiff thin man of fifty, presumably the judge's viscount, in whom dignity had become the sort of carriage the French call "pètesec." Dry fart?—the translation makes no sense but the type is universal. The usual amazing number of faceless female cousins. There would be absentees among the family friends. Some of the neighborhood aristocracy were severely and militarily Catholic, and La Touche's colleagues had, of course, tactful prior engagements. But there was a fair sprinkling that lined up to shake hands at the end and murmur a bereaved word and depart with circumstantial expressions lasting till the car, and Castang looked at these, interested.

Among them, and striking enough to catch the eye in any company, was a tall man, with silver hair and an unusually bleached or blanched expression, whose black suit and black eyebrows made him look like Dracula. Entertainingly so at first: Castang had no other reason to single him out. During the service in the cemetery, he stood composed; one would say he was recollected but that his eyes, like Castang's, flicked about with more than idle curiosity or boredom, and when—as inevitably happened—their eyes caught, Castang realized that he got a longer, cooler stare than the others. He was being examined, in fact, with a cop's eye, except that this was no cop: too well dressed, and the long white hand wore a signet set

110

with diamonds. Nobody Castang knew, and certainly not D.S.T., had this subdued glitter, or the elegant nonchalance with which this man walked to his car and paused to light a cigarette with the kind of lighter no crooked cop would buy—he wouldn't even know where to find it. Nor would anybody paid by the government risk a Maserati, let alone such a plain and unobtrusive dark blue Maserati.

And yet the languid stroll was to let Castang catch up, and the performance with the lighter was to allow even a stranger to say a word in passing, such as two men might exchange when they belonged to the same club and needed no formal introduction. Castang didn't take up the offer, but he felt no doubt: they did belong to the same club.

The man got into his Maserati with the supple movement of a tennis player and backed it out unhurriedly. Castang slid into the little Renault, anonymous but for its persistent police smell inside, and did the same. At an interval of thirty yards, they pulled out of the traffic. They did not take the road to the town, but one leading farther into the country. Castang wondered where the hell they were going, but he was quite enjoying the idea of a tin-pot car tailing a Maserati—and an open tail, at that.

The man made no effort to lead him a dance; he stayed at an easy speed and signaled his turns in plenty of time, shepherding Castang along as a destroyer on convoy might a rusty old bitch of a freighter that at anything over fifteen knots would burst its boiler.

They took country roads, and it was nearly thirty kilometers before they slowed to enter a village whose name was vaguely familiar, but Castang had no idea why until the Maserati turned languidly to park in front of a long building whose terrace was a great splendid mass of ivy-leaved geraniums. To be sure. Les Armes de France was a restaurant with two *Michelin* stars and a red bird in a rocking chair.

There were plenty of cars in the lot and most of them expensive. The Maserati, as though by right, got a slot next to the front door. Castang had to take the Renault down to the end of the lot and plod humbly back. He found his man installed at a table for two on the terrace, and the service so rapid that the order for drinks had already been given. Two champagne flutes stood on the table, and as Castang walked diffidently up the steps the waiter came sailing up with a bucket. The silver-haired man smiled politely and patted the chair next him. Castang sat down.

## 16. Dialogue

"With your permission, I'm ordering lunch for the two of us."

"We won't get a table in this place, surely."

"Oh, we will, you know. I hope that this will be all right. After a funeral, do you think?" The waiter had brought a Belle Époque bottle of Perrier-Jouët and settled it in the bucket, giving it two neat turns—unnecessarily, for it was already cool.

"Cool," said Castang. "It, you, even me in a moment."

"Don't eat any of that rubbish on little trays; it'll only

112

spoil your appetite. Dr. Simon, Rainer Simon, at your service."

"Castang, Henri Castang, S.R.P.J., equally."

"Yes, I know. A bad photo, there in the paper, but recognizable to a man with any eye."

"Ear, nose, and throat?"

"No, law. 'Doctor' is a slightly Germanic way of putting it."

"What a lot of lawyers I keep meeting."

"There are far too many to practice as lawyers. I have commercial activities. These menus are large and time-wasting. Will you follow me or is that presumptuous?"

"You've already been presumptuous. Sensible, anyway—I don't know what all this means."

"Then I shall be guide in these labyrinths. And another of these, waiter, and tell the sommelier the Margaux in a magnum."

"I'll just phone my wife to tell her I'm lunching."

"I'd rather you didn't. She won't be anxious."

"It's a habit I have."

"To be perfectly honest, I'd rather there was no trace of our meeting. I did not accost you at the funeral; sensibly, you left me free. I had been prepared to eat alone, but I was much pleased at your joining me. I came down from Paris—no, not for the funeral, although Gilbert is an old friend. Nor to meet you. But, having met you—let's make a good lunch. I won't be mysterious, and strangely enough you can trust me. Equally, I will trust you. But I'd rather there were no phone calls."

"I'll be brushed with the angel's wing," said Castang, drinking his champagne and signing to the waiter that they preferred to take their own second helpings. "Discreet, this place," approvingly.

He had never before been in a restaurant this grand. Vera would be interested. It was a disappointment to both of them later that he had no idea whatever what he had eaten, except that it had been good. As for Margaux in a magnum, he couldn't remember ever having seen one before. Next time, he'd ask for a jeroboam. Insist upon it.

"Well," said Castang after they were at their table and his napkin had been unfolded for him and the second bottle of champagne had arrived with the soup. "Convey."

"Yesterday I made the acquaintance of Mme. Davids," said Simon.

"So did I."

"Yes, she told me. A good painter, you know."

"Did you see the big nude?"

"I bought it," said Simon simply.

"The subject interested you?"

"You mean the nude, or the girl? I'm a collector. I have no interest in the girl whatever."

"La Touche's daughter?"

"I know him, as I told you. I do not know his family. I went to the funeral, yes. For much the same reasons as yourself. I hope you like bone marrow." It was a beef consommé, with tiny medallions of delicate things that one must not allow to boil.

"What took you to see Mme. Davids?"

"Once more, the same reason as yourself. We are not parallel—we have converged, gradually." Red mullets in paper bags arrived, simplicity itself. The waiter spread the livers on morsels of toast and left them.

114

"I was curious," said Simon, "at this rumor of Gilbert dabbling in politics. It would be most unlike him. You see, not only do I know him well, but we are engaged in a similar business."

"Oh, you advise Arabs about their investments?"

Simon did not answer, but concentrated on boning his fish with care. "I know you to be intelligent," he said, finally. "There is no need for you to waste any time upon stupidities."

Castang was irritated. "Why not buy the judge lunch?"

"Ah. If I have not made myself plain, that is my fault." The delicate, beautiful skeletons of the mullets were removed. The wine waiter pulled the cork of the Margaux, laid it on a napkin after sniffing it with deep pleasure, looked at the light through the first half-glass, and said, "Solid as the bank. You prefer to help yourselves; just watch it toward the end."

"And bright as a new pin," said Simon. "Good."

"And there are few banks," said Castang, "that I trust my new pins to."

"I'm sure you'll agree that Davids was not any sort of agent. Neither Zionist nor even Mormon."

"It would surprise me very much."

"And it would equally and absurdly complicate your position if my poor friend Gilbert were engaging in politics."

"The judge wouldn't be happy."

"I should make it clear that Gilbert's activities in no sense overlap—lapped—mine, and that his domestic troubles cause me grief, but cause me no embarrassment."

"What business are you in?" Castang asked, looking at his plate and wondering what was on it. Looked like beef. Was beef.

"I sell aircraft."

"I see."

"Quite right. These idiot rumors gather headway. I'm open to you when I remark that Zionist agents are more apt to find themselves on my plate."

"But not today."

"No," Simon said, eating.

"Do you have an axe to grind?"

"No other axe to grind. If I can convince you, and I hope that I can, it will enable you to see through things more clearly, and if this rumor can be scotched—why, Gilbert is a friend of mine. It will also make life easier for me. I don't act directly as a government agent, but it's natural that the government is unhappy at these silly rumors. With any luck, they'll die—if they're given no further nourishment."

"Do you know Dieudonné?"

"Yes. He's quite an honest chap but he's a fool. I've told him so. I think he has the sense to stay told. That half-witted private army won't bother you any further."

"I'm grateful," said Castang. "And I'll do my best."

"Fine," said Dracula. "You like cheese? Or they do a thing here with prunes that's clever."

"Let's stay clever."

"I'm having both myself. There's a couple of glasses left in this bottle."

"Nothing wrong with your metabolism." That sounded like something the bishop said to the actress, thought Castang. He mustn't let this character put him in his pocket. Places like these did not make one drunk but they promoted euphoria. He had been

116

picked up cleverly, steered adroitly, had his brains picked thoroughly. Tipsily grinning and saying things like "Let's stay clever" with sticky vanity. . . . He'd better not get self-satisfied, because this man was not taking the trouble and spending the money unless he was getting value. He lit a cigarette, sent the waiter for coffee, and said so.

"I like that," said Simon. "I count myself lucky. You see, telling the truth has become an unfashionable pursuit. This makes it a powerful tool. Most people are so dishonest that they are flabbergasted by a scrap of truth. Of course you're right. I lured you here with the notion of sealing off a lot of clumsy police meddling that would perhaps handicap some business I have in mind. In certain circles, I am known both as a friend and a business associate of Gilbert La Touche. We have given one another introductions to people who are very rich. And people who are very rich—am I boring you?—who eat in these restaurants and who frequent people like me suffer from oversimplifications. One easily gets infected by that attitude. They are neurotically suspicious; everything becomes a plot, everything gets done with ulterior motives, and, being inordinately vain, they think always of a ploy to separate them from their pathetic little millions. I'm speaking naturally of Occidentals. Orientals are completely different; we won't go into that. Sorry—were you about to speak?"

"Just to say you're right about the prunes."

"Ah, I'm glad; I'm enjoying my own. You see, there's nothing a man like me dreads more than doing business with a man he can trust, and not realizing it. I'm perfectly satisfied—are you?"

"Yes," said Castang. "I made a proposal to the

judge that all this political stuff should be disregarded, and he wasn't happy. He'd be glad to have it confirmed."

"You tell him," seriously, "that you got a good opinion. From a good doctor."

"Less bad," said Castang.

## 17. Scuffle

Get back from lunch late—but businessmen are less concerned about this than policemen—and the rest of the day is gone in no time. Castang, going at a sober pace in the little Renault, took an hour getting back to the city.

Commissaire Richard, to whom an account had to be given of where he had been, listened to the story with an expression that could be called dampening, or sobering, or perhaps just deflating. Sympathetic, in a sense, because, being the divisional Commissaire, he held a certain position among the good bourgeois of his good city and, being the chief of the criminal brigade, it had also happened to him to be given a lavish lunch and lots of patter, though, as he had noticed—and now remarked—"The provincial bourgeois are mostly too mean to go beyond a one-star restaurant. Poor boys, they spoil the ship for a penny's worth of tar. Rather pathetic, but typical of that essential provincial pettiness, that they have never grasped the fact that a big bribe, a generous bribe, is more effective than a small mean grubby bribe. Have you drunk rather a lot?"

"If you mean did I fall asleep driving—no. My wife wouldn't like it. Assuming we worked neck and neck, which was roughly the case, I've had one bottle of champagne, rather fancy champagne, and one bottle of very fancy Bordeaux."

"Are you drunk now?"

"No. Tacking to and fro in those country laneways, I wouldn't have wanted to blow in any paper bags. But not now."

"That's as well," flipping his intercom switch and saying, "Fausta, dear, make some rather strong coffee. . . . I'll be seeing the judge this afternoon," he said to Castang. "I've a couple of jobs for you. Nothing very strenuous. You're to go and see the Israeli Consulate. He's been fixing up a funeral for Davids, being rather nice about it. Davids loathed the State of Israel and, being the tactless sort of fellow you'd expect, didn't mince his words about his opinion, and the rabbi took a distinctly dim view. From there you're to go—you've an appointment at six this evening—to see M. Jonas Meyer, who is a pillar of the local Jewish community and needs his ruffled feathers soothed because he's not in the least pleased with the situation. Watch him; he draws a lot of water. You should be sober by then. Don't tell him any Jewish jokes; he doesn't appreciate them. Rather you than me, in fact, but that's your horrible luck. . . . Thank you, Fausta, that's very nice. Does anybody invite you to restaurants with lots of stars?"

"Not unless they want to go to bed with me," said Fausta.

The Israeli Consul wasn't like any consul Castang had ever met, being exceptionally good-looking, bronzed, muscled, and in general looking about to take the helm of a twelve-meter racing yacht; dressed, too, in a silk shirt and sandals, with longish hair that shook back in one piece and would never be untidy or grubby. He wasn't wearing a gun, and was unimpressed by demonstrators, who had, he said, suddenly galloped off behind the mesa like Hollywood Indians, waving their spears and catcalling, giving the defenders of the beleaguered wagon encampment time to comb their hair and get their noses powdered. He didn't want to talk about politics; nothing could be duller. Davids he had never met, but, "having had the job of getting him buried," he had got interested.

"We buried him this morning—I just got back from Paris by the afternoon plane. I rather liked the widow."

"So did I."

"I would have liked him, too. We've plenty like that at home, but their energies are more easily channeled; they can always go out and irrigate an orange tree."

"Never did understand these Arabs," said Castang. "All they ever did was let the goats eat what vegetation there was, and sit scratching their own sores."

"Marvelous thing the press. Fellow pays a lot of money to print stories about dirty Davids screwing all these women. Wouldn't be at all difficult to print a lurid piece about bourgeois girls sold as white slaves in Beirut. Everybody's sick of being sorry for Jews, you see: they've done that for years. They'll be sick of being sorry for Arabs, too, quite soon."

"Tell me about Davids."

"Not at all an uncommon type. A deeply believing man, to whom his religion meant a great deal, but who simply hated what he thought of as lip service and excessive attachment to outward forms and letters. You know, curls and skullcaps and worries about eating lobster. The sight of what he called 'good Jews' simply maddened him. To an artist, you see, all that seems ridiculously trivial. Ever hear of Ernst Toller?"

"No."

The Consul leapt up, prowled along a wall full of books, whipped one out of the shelf, turned pages rapidly.

"Quote from autobiography. 'The words "I am proud to be a German" or "I am proud to be a Jew" sounded ineffably stupid to me. As well say, "I am proud to have brown eyes." Must I then join the ranks of the bigoted and glorify my Jewish blood now, not my German? Pride and love are not the same thing, and if I were asked where I belonged I should answer that a Jewish mother had borne me, that Germany had nourished me, Europe had formed me, my home is the earth, and the world my fatherland.' Now, Davids felt like that."

"Do you?"

A great shout of laughter. "Man, my wages are paid by the Foreign Office, like yours are by the Ministry of the Interior. What does it matter what you or I feel?"

"Few people understand policemen."

"The more reason why we should try to understand Davids."

"I've got to see a man called M. Jonas Meyer."

"Yes, well, you'll find him rather different."

You bet. Castang was received by the senior partner of Meyer & Sons in the senior partner's private office. The old gentleman was brusque, and had no high opinion of the Police Judiciaire.

"I ask you to get this rabble off the streets."

"We aren't encouraging them, you know."

"Yes, yes, yes, I know, I know," with great impatience. Just the sort of thing that put one's back up, not against Jews necessarily, but against businessmen. So very much the French industrialist, and dynamic as all hell into the bargain. We export for you, don't we? We pay bloody high taxes, don't we? It's upon us that you depend for your balance of payments, isn't it? Which gave them the right, the absolute unquestioned God-given right to put a 300 percent markup on their lousy shoddy products and grumble that the country was being run by plumbers' helpers. One could go anywhere in Europe or America and hear the same phrase. "Place is being run by niggers." This one had got so French that he exaggerated his Jewishness, just the way some black men compete to see who's the niggermost.

"I know nothing about this man La Touche and couldn't care less. That's a matter for the magistrates. If they choose to make a great fuss about the villainies of this Davids in screwing his wife and his daughter, that's all right, it concerns them. But to claim that this man was in any way whatever representative of the Jewish community in this city—that's overstepping it, that we won't have. I'm telling you this in private; that's correct procedure. You can tell your Commissaire that I'm not going behind his back, not trying to cut his throat. Get this clear, though. For the purposes of this meeting, which isn't designed as a basis for discussion, you can consider me as the spokesman of this community. You may or may not be aware yourself of the weight of what I'm saying. Your Commissaire may—or should. The Mayor does.

The Prefect does. The Public Prosecutor does. Paris does. I need only remind you that the aircraft industry is an extremely sensitive barometer to the prosperity of the country in the economic sense. And I'm not interested in who the aircraft get sold to, either, you follow?"

"Did you know Davids?"

Mr. Meyer lit a very mild, rather perfumed Egyptian cigarette from the good old Arab firm of Dunhill.

"I knew him," he said abruptly. "I bought a picture from him. I thought it good. Now I'm obliged to put it in the cellar, treat it as a dodgy investment. Might go up, might go down. That's not a Jew, that's a Yid. I've no use for Yids; they're a liability. The State of Israel, let me remind you, wouldn't exist long if it wasn't for the likes of me."

Castang, mindful of M. Richard's instructions, wasn't telling any Jewish jokes. The Consul had reminded him of the classic chestnut: when the tourists arrive in Jerusalem and ask to be shown the Wall of Lamentations, the natives bring them to the Ministry of Finance.

Ouf, the day had gone. Castang had wanted to see La Touche all peaceful and relaxed in his jail. He had wanted a few more things, too, like a nice siesta after lunch. And now he had to sit here and be this old schmuck's whipping boy.

He didn't get back to the office till after six, and it was already twilight when he left the office. His shoulders were sagging; he was very tired indeed. All Richard had promised him was a couple of days off "as soon as we've time to breathe."

It should never have happened, he thought afterward. Ordinarily I'd have been home a bit after six

—well, before seven, anyhow. It would still have been daylight. He'd have taken his bicycle, for ordinarily he kept his own car in the police garage, but he felt jaded tonight.

The pavement along the canal bank opposite his home was used by the inhabitants as a car park: it was wide, and there was room for everyone between the thick old poplars.

Castang dragged the keys out of the ignition lock; hauled himself out, yawning. And there was just this much luck on his side, that he was looking in the right direction. The fellow came sidling out from behind his tree, with a stocking over the face and the head. And a bicycle chain. In a corridor between cars, there was precious little room for maneuver. Room for precious little anything, bar instinct. The instinct was not to draw his gun.

He would have had time for the instinctive shot "offhand," as the combat instructor calls it, at under ten feet, squeezing one off from the leather; he knew the jargon. He could even do the trick, for he had been to shooting school. At this range, when a man is coming at you full tilt with an offensive weapon— very offensive—the thing is to have stopping power. Hence all the debates about the gun to carry: the instructor, who lives and breathes guns, goes boringly on about it. A .45 will stop anything but is such a vast clumsy thing that only the more loony gangsters still use them. There is also a thing called a .44 Magnum, quite useful against tanks, and a .357 Magnum, which will go through two Manhattan telephone directories and two innocent bystanders. Castang knew a couple of cops who had this kind of armory. One used a big Star, which is the Spanish version of the big Colt automatic; the other had been to America and come back with a Smith & Wesson heavy-duty, which is a .38 on a .44 frame. Castang disliked both men. A gun-shy cop is a danger to other cops, but a gun-happy cop is a danger to everybody. In these days, the old 7.65, which used to be carried by all European cops, is frowned upon. It probably won't hit anything and wouldn't stop more than a stray cat. Most professionals, including Castang, carry a 9 mm., like the Browning FN or the Walther; few are more fancy-pants than this. Lugers are still made by the Mauser factory, mostly for boys who like looking at themselves in full-length mirrors, and comb their hair before making with the pistol. These guns stop anything Castang had met, but it was an academic debate here, because he didn't try, and it wasn't from being gun-shy.

Be it a gun or a nail file, the thing is to be first; if you aren't, all the other rules are meaningless. Castang jumped toward the masked man. Seeing a blob instead of a face, he jabbed at it with his left hand. He had made himself small; the swung bicycle chain missed— thank God—his head. But it curls, it is flexible; some of it, at least, whipped through and fell upon his back and shoulder. He let out a short hoarse howl as it hit him, and gave the adversary, who was taller and thinner than he was, a short right-hand punch under the heart, which hurt as much as he could make it hurt, which was less than a bicycle chain. The masked man hit against a car, doubling up and falling off balance. As he sprawled, Castang hit him with a knee in the lower belly. Then, as he went down, Castang kicked him in the face. He was not a man who enjoyed giving pain, but his shoulder felt broken. The fellow made a noise, and got another kick to make him quiet.

"Now," said Castang with immense weariness, feeling the pain go down his arm and up into the top of his head, "we'll look at you."

He bent down and wrenched off the stocking mask and put it in his pocket. He decided not to bend down any more; it hurt too much. His vision was slightly clouded; he had a wish to be sick. He thought of grabbing this pretty boy by his long pretty hair, and took his gun out instead.

"Get up," he said. "Do what is told you and quietly. Or I'll kill you. Pick up the chain. Hand it to me. Now walk. Cross the road. We're going to have a tea party."

## 18. Tobacco Road

Holding the gun in his left hand while he used his right to twist a door key made the sweat run down inside his socks; he felt he was standing in a pool of blood. When he turned on the hallway light and caught sight of himself in the glass, he didn't like it: the eyes were bloodshot and the facial muscles twitching. He opened the kitchen door, said "Go on," pulled a wooden chair from behind the table, and said "Sit down." Vera appeared in the doorway, face white, eyes enormous, saying nothing.

"In the bottom bureau drawer is a pair of handcuffs, with the gun-cleaning material, probably under a lot of junk. Bring them to me, will you? And then get me a brandy and we've some codeine in the bathroom." Castang took a dishcloth, put it on the table, laid the bicycle chain on it.

"This, manny, is going to send you up. For three years. First, I'm going to re-educate you. . . . Put your hands behind you. Look, boy, I'll break your face with the gun barrel and think nothing of it. Make me a cup of tea, Vera, and then go knit socks, will you. I want nothing to eat."

"You'll eat," said Vera, "when I've called a cop and taken this off your hands. First I can see your back's hurt."

"It can wait."

"Possibly, but I won't. If you're going to make an interrogation, you'll do so as well with your shirt off. Can you lift the arm a tiny bit? I'll cut through it."

"No," said Castang, "it's a good shirt."

Facing him was a boy of about nineteen, fine-boned, the delicate features slightly marred by a nosebleed, where Castang had punched him, and a swelling bruise on the cheekbone, where he'd got a kick. From a soft moccasin, thought Castang; he's seen nothing yet. A pretty-boy Arab. A real little Yid. Racist I'm getting, but I've had a day full of Jewish Yids and all I needed was an Arab Yid.

"Yid," he said. "Pretty Yid." It was to be saying something while his shirt came off, because it hurt and he wasn't saying so.

Stung, the boy spoke for the first time. "I'm not a Yid."

"You think I can tell the difference between one Semite and another?"

Behind him, Vera gave a small liquid whistle and then a faint clucking noise.

"Is there a lot of blood?" he said. "It feels like it."

"No, that's all sweat. There's plenty of blood, but—what's the word?—subcutaneous mostly. There'll be one hell of a bruise. But is there anything broken underneath? Apart from that, it looks worse than it is. I want you to go and have an X-ray taken."

"No."

"Then I'm going to ring Rab. I've disinfected it, and I'm putting on a cold compress. . . . Now, let's just look at you," to the boy. "Keep your face still. A bit of cold water and you'll be as good as new."

"Don't get him too clean; I might want him dirty," reaching for a cigarette and wincing. Talk tough, he thought, knowing he wasn't going to hit this boy in front of Vera. She knew that. The boy didn't, though.

Castang had never yet hit a captive in cold blood . . . well, cooling. He'd seen it done several times. Twice he had seen a captive deliberately beaten up. Once after a cop had been shot; once when a man had hit a child—the child had lost an eye. The To-bacco Road type is now a rarity, not just because it is strictly forbidden, but because brutalized cops have got rarer, and the sadists have been diagnosed quicker. Castang wondered whether he would have slapped this boy's brain addled if he had him downtown. Here, in his own home, he wasn't going to do a thing. Vera knew this, too. Behind him came a thudding noise of ice cubes being turned out to make cold compresses.

He looked at the boy. There was no need to beat him. Being handcuffed to a kitchen chair behind your back is first numb, then painful. He had made them tight, and by now they'd be biting.

"Tea," he said as the ice-cold towel hit him, making him wince. The kettle whistled, answering him.

"I'm going to telephone," said Vera. "You still want a cop?"

"Yes," he said, "but no particular hurry."

128

He sipped the boiling tea, feeling it doing him good. The boy stared at him unwinking, determined to be a man. He'd seen movies, too. Vera changed the compress on Castang's back, and went out.

Brandy. Tea. Codeine. Towel wrung out in ice slosh. All four, he supposed. He had turned back into a cop. He just sat there, smoking, feeling the codeine slowly getting a grip on the pain, saying nothing at all. He felt like some more brandy, and had a cup of tea instead. He put his gun back in the holster, took the belt off, and went and hung it in the bedroom. He came back, poured himself a second cup of tea, sat down. The boy hadn't budged, but the face had got sharper. Bones were sticking through the skin. Castang went on saying nothing till the doorbell rang.

It was a uniformed cop off a patrol wagon. In no hurry: a cop on a night patrol never is. One has to get through those hours, and the less fuss the better. He looked at Castang's closed face in the hallway, said nothing, whistled slightly when he saw Castang's bare back, looked at the bicycle chain on the table, gave a long unwinking stare at the boy in the chair.

Castang went into the living room for another chair. Vera was knitting. Socks, for all he knew. He brought back a fresh packet of cigarettes.

"Tea?" he asked the cop. Together they sat and stared at the Arab boy. Two are better than one. The cop refused a cigarette. In training, he said. Castang didn't ask what for.

Rabinowics arrived five minutes later. He was a professor at the university hospital, not a "real doctor" at all, as he said himself. He had been Vera's orthopedic specialist after her crash, had become a friend. He had disclaimed all responsibility for her learning to walk again; said she'd done it by herself. He was rapid on his feet, always made an impression of displacing a lot of air in passage, and rode around in a Rolls-Royce to—or so he said—drive his neighbors into a frenzy. Castang's neighbors, who loathed having a cop in the building, were eaten up by envy and it served them right. Rab also teased cops, by parking the Rolls-Royce crooked, all over the place, and then pointing to the Aesculapius sticker with the twined snake on his windscreen, and blandly defying them to prove it hadn't been an emergency.

He entered into the spirit of things right away—he never needed anything spelt out. He looked at the bicycle chain, looked at the Arab boy, glanced at the handcuffs.

"Don't leave him too long like that."

"Good for the soul."

"But bad for the circulation." He nodded to the cop as though to an old friend, gave Vera an affectionate kiss, and took the compress off Castang's back.

"Ow," Castang said.

"Yes," said Rab, "the humor of it escapes me, too. Medieval sort of injury. Hence the invention of plate armor; less commodious than chain mail, but made for better insurance statistics."

"Ow."

"Lift. Lower. Lift. Lower. Tough little Gaulish skeleton. It's easier to make dints in a Frank. No displacement. Could be a hairline crack. You'd like an X-ray?"

"No."

"Want a few days off?"

"No."

"He wants to be tough," Rab said to Vera. "Very

well, dear fellow; the horse-liniment cure it shall be. It'll hurt for a while. Tickle for longer. What have you taken? Codeine; tut, it's illegal. Right, let's look at the boyfriend. Nothing wrong there. If he happens to fall off a truck at speed, don't come to me for a certificate. All right, girl, hop into the other room; I want to look at your leg."

Silence fell, and lay.

"He's screwing your wife in there," said the Arab boy.

Castang said nothing. The cop changed the compress for him, not too unskillfully. The ice had melted but the water was still cold. Rab could be heard taking his departure. Vera, sensibly, had gone to bed with a book.

"Take the cuffs off him, would you?" said Castang quietly. The boy sat and rubbed his wrists, and flexed his arms. Finally he made his mind up and said "Thank you," in a noncommittal but well-brought-up voice.

"Yes," said Castang. "It seems like nothing much at first, but it hurts after a while. Circulation . . . You're a student?"

No answer.

"I see your point," conversationally. "Try to see mine. A simple verification of your papers is all that is needed to know all about you. We're not going to hit you. I am sorry I hurt you; you understand that it was reflex action. We'll hold you." He nodded at the chain on the table. "There's no further proof needed, you see." Still no answer.

"I'm not going to threaten you with a heavier punishment. And I'm not going to tell you, either, that if you cooperate you might get off easier. You take the responsibility for what you did. No more, no less. No martyrdom, no press release, no nothing. Just a meaningless act. Nobody will be interested."

The boy was a little taken aback. He thought for a while and said, "It'll all come out at the trial."

"There won't be any trial. That's right. Sure, we could charge you with half the book. Unlawful everything: loitering, nocturnal aggression, possession, wounds and injuries, aggravated attack, assault upon police officer. And we don't need to charge you with anything at all. Except the possession. Your student permit will be canceled and the judge, in lieu of punishment, recommends your deportation within twenty-four hours. Everything wasted. Nothing to show for it. I'm asking you simply to think. There's no evidence at all. The doctor is a friend of mine. He'll say nothing. The man here found you in the street carrying a prohibited weapon. Recognized you as having taken part in an unauthorized manifestation yesterday in front of the Palace of Justice. Oh, yes, I saw you there. Were you paid?" asked Castang suddenly, in a contemptuous tone.

"No," angrily.

"Dieudonné organized you?" Indifferent.

"I had personal reasons," he answered, indignant at the mercenary suggestion.

"Really?" Incredulous. "Member of a political group?"

"Personal, I tell you."

"Who will believe that," without any interest.

"Charlotte La Touche was my friend, and I can prove it."

"Oh, was she?" Lackadaisical. "Why hit me? I didn't kill her."

"You're protecting those who did," pointing a heated finger like a public prosecutor.

"Oh," puzzled. "It was to protect La Touche, was it?"

"You know damned well. I knew Charlotte. She wouldn't have had anything to do with that Zionist spy."

"I'm afraid you still have a lot to learn about Charlotte," said Castang.

"Don't try to tell me lies."

"Ah. You didn't believe the press reports."

"Everybody knows the press here is run by Jews."

Castang raised his arms, and put them down quickly because the left one hurt him. "Well, my boy," he said slowly, "this is going to hurt you a lot more than beating you up would." One can't, thought Castang, really tell a lot from people's faces. It is an invention of fiction writers to talk about all the complicated things to be read in people's eyes. The eyes of most people are about as expressive as a bicycle lamp. This boy, though: lovely little lad with a bottom, no doubt, like a peach—dear, oh dear, the things that will be happening to you in the jug—is really the startled fawn. Apprehension, yes, that shows. The boy has been telling himself wonderful tales for the last three days. And is scared blind of evidence.

"Pass me the briefcase," he said to the cop. Not an artist, that police photographer. But a careful, sound, painstaking technician who left no margin for error. Everything done three times, using a reflex camera that blew up prints to cabinet size with no distortion at all. Charlotte's naked body, hardly bloodstained, was not pornography, since whatever it was it was not

133

titillating. It was hard, though, hard as granite. The boy didn't want to look and couldn't stop himself. The tears didn't mean anything to Castang. A lot of people cry, sooner or later, in the course of a police interrogation. It is themselves they cry for, generally. To be fair, there might have been tears for Charlotte, too.

The boy would not be able to stop himself talking now, either. He wouldn't even want to. Perhaps, thought Castang, it comes easier, too, here in the kitchen than it would in the office. He wrote it down in shorthand. Tomorrow morning one would get it typed. There wouldn't be any need even to have the boy deported. He'd run home by himself. He'd had enough of Europe.

It didn't add anything much to the central dossier. A calf love affair. It would serve, though. It would help demolish the so-called "political" angle. It helped demonstrate how a fact, any fact, could be made meaningless and even be disregarded altogether. And it threw light on Charlotte. An unattractive little girl, who had had a pet dog. She might have grown attached to it, but it was still a pet dog, and the fidelity of pet dogs to basically unfeeling persons is always a good illustration of the fallacies of sentimentality. In defense of Charlotte—she had been very immature. Would Victoria—two years older and, by account, brighter— be the same? She had lived with Davids for six months. And that picture he had seen in Paris—there was a great deal more to that than there was to these horrible photographs. A step further, thought Castang, and—feeling his shoulder—a price paid.

## 19. The Teddy Bears' Picnic

Even at eight in the morning there was no life in the air today. As long as the sky had stayed clear, it had been supportable; there had been a haze after dawn, but it had burned off quickly. Today it didn't burn off. The light was odd; the sky had a peculiar steely look. Castang had slept deeply but badly. He had hangover eyes. His back muscles were atrociously stiffened and painful. Vera did her best by massaging the back of his neck. She didn't want him to work.

"Rab told you. . . . It's a simple matter. . . . You don't need to have the X-ray if you don't want. . . . A certificate on demand just like that . . . Only for twenty-four hours . . . A day like this."

"There's going to be the father and mother of a thunderstorm."

"Why won't you listen to me?"

"Look, it may seem complicated to you but in fact it's simple. I don't want any official notice taken of that business last night. This affair is quite complicated enough."

"Oh . . . blow it," said Vera, who strongly disliked swearing, loathed any sort of blasphemy, and had been heard to explain "When I say fuck, I really mean it."

"Don't worry. It'll be an easy day. Nobody'll do anything on a day like this."

Since nobody would have dreamed of giving the police air-conditioning, he plugged a small fan in over a file cabinet, which swept through the ninety degrees and blew papers off his table, but for once nobody complained about the draft. The city sat under a smoggy pall. Fausta was in a bad mood. Even Richard, which was rare, was in a bad mood. Around him hung a peculiar chemical perfume, something like abrasive scouring powder. Castang sniffed when he came in, not ostentatiously, but he was detected at once.

"It's these aerosols that stop one sweating. My idiot of a wife . . . This one is supposed to smell of green limes. Try Fausta, she smells delicious."

"What is it you smell of, Fausta?"

"Bergamot," complacently. "But the real trouble is that Mme. Richard thinks people will notice he smells like me, and then they draw the wrong conclusions."

"So I smell like the kitchen sink," said Richard crossly.

"Don't make me laugh; it hurts my back."

"What's wrong with your back?"

He explained: Richard got back into a good mood.

"Sensible of you. The last thing we want is the press inventing terrorist gangs. You know, they even make the hotel-school apprentices buy these aerosols now."

"I'm very glad to hear it," said Fausta. "Who wants a waiter who smells of feet?"

"Yes, but even the cooks. This country isn't what it was. What have you charged this boy with?"

"Possession. Look: chain; stocking mask."

"Have it sent to the lab. Prints and stuff, to tie it to him firmly if need be."

"Yes, and my blood group," said Castang nastily. Plainly, no work was going to get done: sitting around waiting for the storm to break and talking about cooks' feet. But the smell of bergamot came suddenly floating back, carrying a telex carbon copy.

"You're going to enjoy this," said Fausta. Sandwiched into the jumble sale of prefixes and code letters and all the electronic and administrative jargon was a message in English, saying, "we have possible identification of victoria la touche but appearance altered and carrying valid lebanese passport. cannot hold without court order and u.k. magistrate would certainly refuse to grant same without more positive identification. can maintain light surveillance but instruct rapidest and if possible send officer prepared to affirm. sorry but u.k. law exceedingly fussy about habeas-corpus 1066 and all that. please contact sergeant metcalfe message ends."

"Blub-glub," said Castang.

Richard turned a stony eye and said, "You'll get on splendidly with Sergeant Metcalfe, so sharpen up your blub-glub. But what's 1066 and all that?"

"Some regulation or other. Deporting undesirable aliens, or words to that effect."

"No, no," said Fausta, who had a degree in history. "It's the Norman Conquest. They used to own Aquitaine and have never forgiven us for wanting it back. Queen Aliénor they call Eleanor."

"And she probably perfumed herself with bergamot—they didn't bother about little things like washing."

"But not today, for God's sake," said Castang.

"No, no, stop fussing. Find some photographs and stuff for identity, and I'll see the judge for a strong court order. No point in your going unless you can bring her back. Fausta, you get a telex off to this Metcalfe and leave out about Aquitaine, and book

137

him plane tickets for the direct flight tomorrow morning. You can have the rest of the day free, Castang, but you'd better go down to the clinic and get some physiotherapy, deep heat or whatever, because you look a perfect wreck."

There was a slow distant rumble of thunder.

"Here it comes," they all said, looking out the window. The sky had gone yellow and was darkening.

"Put the light on, Fausta." Richard was lighting one of his thin cigars as a preliminary to business. "Keep your pad; I'll dictate that message in a moment. I want to finish with Castang first. Can Lasalle read your shorthand? No, well, if he can't Fausta can. We have to hold on to this boy, but of course the judge will agree that he doesn't want the La Touche affair messed up by any more Jews or Arabs. Never mind, leave that to me. When he sees that chain and the mask, the Procureur will agree perhaps to deporting the boy with no further ado. Undesirable in every sense of the word." There was another, closer rumble of thunder. The lights went out and the fan stopped. The lights flickered and went on again.

"I'll have Lasalle charge this boy—no, no, better still, you had him picked up by a uniformed cop; we'll get it done by Fabre, and the P.J. is out of it altogether. Found carrying a concealed prohibited weapon."

There was a really huge clap of thunder. The lights went out again and the telephone rang.

"Yes, Richard. What? . . . What? . . . This thing's going blub-glub, can you hear me? . . . No, sir, I'll be over as soon as I can. I've some matters to discuss with you. The Metropolitan Police in London—damn this thing—no, I said London. . . . Yes, Victoria La

138

Touche, but this line's hopeless. . . . No, I have to come over anyway for your signature. . . .

"Go get some infrared or something," he said to Castang, "and make yourself extremely unwound, because there are dramas right and left. Must be the storm has made everyone silly, or it's full moon. That La Touche has short-circuited: he's fired his lawyer, is entering a plea of guilty, and the judge isn't happy at all. He's freezing the whole thing until the psychiatric reports are ready, and he wants a new set of reports from us."

Hailstones were bouncing off the sills. From everywhere in the building could be heard the sound of windows slamming shut.

"That'll strip a few vines," said Richard, magnetized toward the window despite himself.

"If you go down in the woods today, you're sure of a big surprise."

"I'm not going outside in that," said Richard.


## 20. Francophile Behavior of Metropolitan Policemen


The knife, fork, and spoon, from a cheap doll's tea service, were plastic. The plane, inside if not out, was plastic. If one went by appearances, so were the passengers. The stewardess had a strong resemblance to a rubber dolly bought from a sex shop. The food, naturally, was all by-products of the petroleum industry. Castang did not give any of these things attention or thought. If, as was always being threatened, there were suddenly no more oil, he supposed he would traverse Europe by bicycle and like it. As long as the airplane existed, he would take it, and disliking it, was whimsical. He did dislike it, because it was a great waste of time: nine-tenths of these journeys were totally unnecessary and the people concerned would have done much better to write a letter. But if one gave way to this sort of thought one would do better being a municipal gardener, bedding out the calceolarias. "I wish I were," said Castang, disciplined himself firmly, and thought, I'll only talk English for the rest of the trip.

"I like—I want"—no—"May I have a box of matches, please?"

"What bus—which bus—goes to Aldwych?"

Which witch goes to Ipswich?

"Can I see Sergeant Metcalfe, please? He expects me." It would get better as he went along.

"No, Miss, thank you not a drink, but have you got some Evian water?"

"I don't know; I'll look." Well, she'd understood, anyway, even if, to judge by exteriors—and what else did a cop have to judge by?—her mind was furnished with moisture cream and roll-on deodorant. His back hurt, but less than yesterday. He'd had needle sprays of electricity and water—they had more or less the same feeling—to break down the adhesions or whatever; the physiotherapist had been rather technical about it and he hadn't listened properly. In fact, he'd successfully fallen asleep for twenty minutes at a stretch and dreamed with slight indecency that Fausta was tickling his shoulder blades with her hair.

"Sorry, ladies and gentlemen; slight panic in Heathrow. We're liable to be stacked for a while we

140

hope will be short." Windsor Castle, Slough railway station, what might have been Virginia Water and was more likely the Hanwell Water Filtration and Pumping Plant.

Rattle-te-tat on concrete full of puddles, and airlines belonging to countries where one would never want to go, and couldn't imagine anyone who would, and stewardesses with bared teeth and blue faces and their hats held on by scarves, and the huge dangling plastic sleeve leading to the grain elevator, which, instead of disgorging floods of rice to all the starving peoples, devoured Henri Castang and sent him on the long march to immigration. Identity card scrutinized with the utmost attention, and his face stared at with a cop's blank unwinking gaze, and the "Thank you" that sounded so much ruder than silence, and flow on, and change some money—Molière's face swapped for the amazingly bland features of the Defender of the Realm—and then trundle trundle past innumerable factories making chewing gum and the thousand little gardens all identical, and then at last the plunge into the Inner Circle Tube smelling of synthetically perfumed toffee papers, and Victoria Station with the sirocco blowing and posters inviting him to be whipped and massaged with "Wank" written on them by fourth-form City gentlemen, and the smell everywhere of sweets, which the English call "confectionery." So misleading to the European eye, to which confection means ready-made clothes, but not to the nose.

"Sergeant Metcalfe? Are you sure? What I mean is, did they say to ask for him? You see, I don't know really whether he's . . . Oh, I see. . . . Oh, well, I'll phone. . . . Metcalfe? I've a French gentleman here; do you . . . Oh, you do: . . . . Well, that's all right, then.

I mean, does he have to fill in a form? Oh . . . yes, I'll tell him. He says he'll be right down. If you like to sit down, you'll find some magazines and things."

But Sergeant Metcalfe was "right down" before he'd had time to work out who Mr. Punch was.

"Hallo. Delighted to see you. Now I wonder whether we should go upstairs, and you might like some coffee or something. . . . No, no," deciding this wouldn't do at all, "that's all absolute nonsense; we'll go and have a drink. I've left my phone on automatic record; you've had a beastly journey, the pub will be nice and quiet."

"I'm very obliged—no, *much* obliged."

"Certainly not, you're not even just obliged; we are. Now this is quite a nice pub; would you like some wine? It might not be very `nice; would you rather a whisky?"

"Yes, please, with no water if I may."

"Nor ice? Oh, do stop being so polite. And a gin-and-tonic. And cheers. And now," in very good French, "let's talk about lunch; that's very important."

"You don't want to talk about business?"

"No, no; lunch is much more urgent."

Sergeant Metcalfe was all a policeman should be. He was very large, "second row in the scrum," with a large smooth shaved face that shouted "cop" a mile off, but not in the least bovine. He handled his big body very neatly. He was extravagantly dressed, thought Castang at first—changing his mind quite soon—in a sports jacket of Prince-of-Wales check; poor old Edward has at least sartorial immortality. A silky white roll-neck pullover. Nice trousers of Bedford cord, which Castang, who was addicted to them, envied. Big well-shaped hands, oddly white and very clean. Complicated but comfortable-looking cowboy boots, with chains and buckles and everything but spurs. These English . . . Castang felt very small, meager, and froggish in his Havana-brown linen suit that had seemed so suitable at home and looked so pompously formal here. He had left his gun at home because of the hullabaloo it would cause on the airplane and because the English didn't wear any.

"I should be talking English," relaxing rapidly.

"No, no, man, hospitality. We talk French here, and when I come to see you, then you can talk English; that's the way things go. You're looking miles happier already; do have another." The gin-and-tonic got drained in one massive gulp.

"I thought you weren't supposed to drink on duty." It was tactless but he couldn't stop himself.

"So we aren't. But shush. The Assistant Commander turns a blind eye, because he's read those awful Maigret books, and is quite convinced that French policemen become exceptionally sharp after about four Pernods. And they ride everywhere in that lovely old Citroën. All those English actors in képis—their heads are the wrong shape for képis. Quite pathetic. And now we're going to go chez Solange and eat blanquette of veal—oh, don't worry, it won't be all that nasty."

Castang felt much happier.

"So by that logic, when you come to us I should find you one of those places where you can take away your curry."

Sergeant Metcalfe gave a great happy laugh. "We're trying very hard. You know, this year there was the pistol-shooting competition and you only just beat us. We're really working."

Castang couldn't help it: this absolute refusal to

143

talk about what he had come for was very sympathetic.

"I felt awful. The suit and the shoes—all wrong."

"No, no, perfect; I could drive you straight out to the Teddington studios; they'd snap you up. You have, you see, that intellectual look. By definition, the English policeman is bound to appear imbecile."

"Don't go thinking you've the monopoly," said Castang. "It might be all right for us to look bright, but God help us if we act it. What made us choose this lousy job, anyway?"

"They had a good rugby team," said Sergeant Metcalfe.

"Right. I was fair at gymnastics."

"Oh, yes—eleven boys balanced on one motorbike."

"When they aren't wearing big white gauntlets, riding very slow and solemn in front of a politician in an open car."

"Not worried at all about a hand grenade, but living in mortal terror of a well-greased banana skin. It's very good, really—the first lesson we have to learn is to accept the monumental stupidity. The only lesson, I sometimes think," gazing sadly into his gin. "You're lucky; over your side there's much more sense of reality."

"But less humor. Is it true anyway, about the reality?"

"Oh, Lord, yes. We're so hemmed in by myth. I'll give you just one example—the business about being unarmed. Supposed to be no guns in England—you know; every bloody air gun licensed by magistrates—whereas every little gas-meter bandit has got one. And we're expected to go for him, presumably filled with courage by the vision of our widows getting given a medal by the Palace. Here, come on, you must be absolutely starving; let's go and eat."

"I feel absolutely at home," said Castang, unfolding his napkin, "except that the wine's far better than anything we ever get. Crafty old England."

"You wouldn't say that if I took you to the police canteen and you were pressing down the spaghetti on toast. I think in fact you're right, though. There isn't any difference between us. The fear of foreigners, and particularly a dislike of the French, is a ridiculous and ignoble piece of balderdash, assiduously fostered by politicians frightened of losing power."

"Good phrase," said Castang admiringly.

"And we," said Metcalfe, with his big deadpan face, "know that only the French can make a good phrase. There's a good one, by the way, about justice being meaningless. Pascal, I think, or maybe Montaigne."

"Of course," said Castang. "Learned it first week in law school. 'Comic justice whose frontier is a brook; truth this side of the Pyrenees is heresy on the other.' Pascal."

"What did I tell you? 'The bastards have a phrase for everything and worse still the bastards are always right'—Raymond Chandler."

Feeling delightfully euphoric, Castang drank a big glass of wine.

"Seriously, though," said Metcalfe, "I've been saving this up till we were a bit mellowed—I've bad news for you. I haven't got Victoria."

"Ah," said Castang, turning back into cop. "She slipped off, did she?"

"I hope you're not going to be angry. I blame myself, but it's no good saying I'd have done better if I'd been there myself instead of being stuck doing paper-work; I don't think I would. We're short on manpower, of course—don't think I'm making excuses. One man seemed adequate. I wanted it to be unobtrusive. That's a mistake, I know: two or even three are much less obtrusive than one, because he has to stay too close. I just didn't have another man. You see," said Metcalfe sorrowfully, "I wanted to keep this a criminal-police matter. The moment it's political, and Special Branch get into the act, the whole thing gets out of propor-tion."

"I've had the exact same problem," said Castang. "Look, don't give it another thought. Our judge at home will be cross, of course, because my coming back without her is a black eye, and this evasiveness leaves a big question mark because the inference is that she knows more than she should and is unwilling to talk about it, and why? Probably she knows noth-ing, of course; it's this irritating trick they have of drawing attention to themselves, making themselves important."

"Oh, yes," said Metcalfe, "it's familiar: slipping off to Spain hoping to get an evening-paper headline about the 'Missing Witness' and maybe the *News of the World* will make a bid for the memoirs. But I'm afraid . . ."

"No notion where she's gone? Sweden, I daresay. I don't care: the judge won't bother following it up. It's just, you see, that she was daughter and sister to two of my victims, and ex-mistress of the third. And the assassin's surviving daughter—it isn't without in-terest, from the evidential point of view. It's all cut and dried: the whole thing's going to revolve round his state of mind."

"Look," said Metcalfe heavily. "I'm misleading you. She's not in Sweden. She's in the morgue. The Serious Crimes people have her. And they aren't optimistic."

"Merde," said Castang.

"Yes. Merde and remerde. Doubled, in spades."

## 21. Breakdown in International Cooperation

"Fuck it," said Metcalfe angrily. "I'm only a pissing sergeant."

They were back in the office. A gray cell in the big modern building. Lots of gray plastic, one wall nearly all window. Plenty of modern machinery that wasn't helping either of them. The cell was holding a high concentration of gray matter, but this wasn't helping them either. Metcalfe had played the tapes of his telephone calls back, and the result was a lemon.

"No, come," said Castang. "I'm an officer, good, and what does it mean? You have plenty of C.I.D. sergeants doing more important jobs on their own than I'd ever get a sniff of."

"You don't understand," said Metcalfe bitterly. "Sure there are, you're right; there are sergeants who know their jobs better than most chief superintendents. But there are two factors you leave entirely out of your reckoning. First, that you—I really envy this—all have a far stronger theoretical formation. One sees it in everything; doctors, engineers, pharmacists— you've all got degrees, you've all had that really thor-

147

ough intellectual training. We have this pragmatic empirical formation; it's fine, I have no criticism, absolutely typical: take a Marshal of the Royal Air Force to train the cops, teach them to be self-reliant when the engine fails—good old Trenchard, keep the lip straight even when your parachute doesn't open, devotion is the thing. Christ," furiously, "the bloody inspector guarding the Princess, nobody gave a fart that he was so badly trained his gun didn't work because the stupid clown had always left the magazine in and the mainspring had got fatally weakened. And I mean fatally—Christ, a Walther nine millimeter, beautiful well-made German gun, marvelous craftsmanship, and in the pinch it lets him down because he didn't know how to maintain it. Fellow just barely squeaks through with his life, and what does he get? A kiss from the Queen and a sodding medal—how incompetent can you get? And second, this miserable stinking hierarchy: you're an officer if you talk nice; otherwise you stay a sergeant. I ask you, Castang, how are you going to run a cop force on this mincing crapping difference between a grammar school where they've gray matter and Stowe where they've architecture. So I have a fellow whose arse I have to wipe," furiously, "and he's an inspector and I'm a sodding sergeant." Castang was discomposed. He was saved from agony by the door opening.

"Jesus, Metcalfe, what a stink in here—those filthy French cigarettes."

"This is Inspector Treadwell of the Serious Crimes," said Metcalfe in a majestic rolling tone. "And this is Inspector Castang of the Police Judiciaire." A curt nod.

148

"Do you speak English?"

"It'll do."

"Well, what d'you know about this woman?"

"Nothing," said Castang.

"Won't say, eh? Well, hereabouts we do our justice in public. Here's a woman dead of an overdose and you say 'Nothing.' Since I'm led to believe there's a warrant out for her and that an accident can be ruled out, I'm bound to investigate. I'd be inclined to see it as suicide if it weren't that some of these people she was frequenting might be more than small pushers to support a habit. May be a distribution network there. I look for you," to the air somewhere between the two men, "and you're out to lunch, while I'm left to sweep up the broken china. So now what about it?"

"If my English gets not good enough," said Castang quietly, "then I ask Sergeant Metcalfe to translate—all right? I say nothing because I know nothing. When you find out a thing, and when you tell me, perhaps I can make . . . link—yes, thanks—and then I tell you. This woman was a witness to background, to character. Perhaps important—maybe, I don't know. But nothing suspected, nothing accused. I come here to try to talk to her, hoping for no drama, hoping no need for court order, to ask magistrate for extradition. About the drugs, we know she had a small habit. Bit of pushing to support that habit, as you say—yes, likely. No evidence for anything else, as I am assured by our narcotics squad. If now you find differently, that is your inquiry. I don't interfere, I don't complain, I accept what your inquiry finds. Any cooperation I can give, I give, and I don't accept any contrary suggestion—all right?"

Inspector Treadwell had listened with no sign of

impatience, unless it was brushing at his mustache with the nail of his forefinger, which might have been a tic.

"Very well. You give me that assurance, naturally I'm bound to accept it. I don't know how long you're staying, but I'll certainly see to it that a copy of my conclusions—when I reach them—is communicated to you. Since you tell me you know nothing about this woman's associates, or perhaps you mean that you simply aren't interested, then I see no point in your being associated with the inquiry—if I decide, that is, to pursue it. I'm not convinced either way. I'll ask you to excuse me now, since I'm busy. I'd like a word with you, please, Metcalfe. Nice to have met you, Mr. Estang."

Metcalfe looked anxiously to see if Castang was vexed, showed relief in a large wink—Treadwell was already in the passage—and got up leisurely.

"Forgive me a moment, Castang," he said loudly. "That's to say, not longer than a small quarter of an hour, and I mean that. It'll be the quickest way out, for you. Here's some pornography to read; we've so much we're blowing our noses on it."

He was as good as his word.

"Un vrai con," he said as he came back, grinning.

"What's that in English?"

"Oh," very blandly, "I think we'd say 'a perfect prick.' I got all we want; frightened him by hinting it could go to a higher level. Embassy makes a protest, question in the House of Commons. Is the Minister aware that there is reason to suppose a grave dereliction of duty on such a date, arising out of . . . He's picking his nose now. I'm sorry he was so rude. Nasty smell, indeed. He's one of these people who do press-ups and admire General Montgomery: they think rudeness will excuse, if not disguise, their invincible ignorance. However, he's competent, I will say that for him. He didn't like the overdose at all; that's why he was vexed. What do you think?"

"I don't think it matters either way. I'm just feeling a bit sorry, because the likelihood is I killed her. Nothing to do with my homicide, probably, though not provable. She had no interest in her parents, and the painter was an episode which she'd quite likely half forgotten. But mixed with these anarchists, who are fond of Arabs because there's lots of money available there, and money is always nice . . . She could have killed herself, and she could have been killed for a dozen reasons. She didn't have to know anything; she had just become an embarrassment or a liability, probably by the mere fact that the cops were after her. No, I'm mistaken; I didn't kill her, though I was the instrument. The press killed her, simply by irresponsible suggestions that her father had a political motivation. We've been trying to deflate all that—you understand; that's why I had no enthusiasm for Special Branch."

"Right. The drug-distribution stuff is bullshit, by the way. Treadwell sees a headline in it for himself. Our active and ever-alert officer has again smashed a network. Bucking for a promotion. Bollocks to him. But still, is there anything at all I can do?"

"Turn into a plane and I'll fly you home," sadly. "I just wanted to talk to her. Poor little bitch. And La Touche, now . . . he's certainly made a clean sweep, all around him."

"We'll go somewhere nice and have tea," said Metcalfe, determinedly cheerful. "I don't want that Treadwell to see me; I'm a living reproach."

"Yes, it was embarrassing. I was going to open my mouth and tell you that you're talking nonsense, when bingo, the door opens and in walks this fellow who's been to Lancing or whatnot."

"And he knows about as much law as a street sweeper," said Metcalfe happily.

"Why is it that the English have tea, when everyone else drinks it?"

"Now, isn't that odd?" Metcalfe said. "I'd never noticed. In Jane Austen, we all drank tea. I've no idea. But have you noticed, too—in England we 'have' sex? It's exceptionally depressing. In France you say 'enjoy.'"

"From time to time," said Castang cautiously.

## 22. The Scruples of the Prison Visitor

"I'd like him to have a visitor," said M. Szymanowski, the Judge of Instruction. "It would do him good. He's far too closed in upon himself. The psychiatrists won't pronounce, of course, until they have finished, but without exception they tell me in confidence that they're unhappy. I tell *you* in confidence, Madame," shaking a finger.

"Monsieur le Juge," said Vera, timid but obstinate. "You know I wouldn't repeat your confidences. And I wouldn't repeat his, assuming he gave me any."

"It's a case of conscience for both of us, Madame, and it worries me. In the old days, a man on a murder charge was on the secret list. No access. Nowadays we take a less rigid view. What worries me is that if the defense were to find out you were the wife of a serving police officer—and, what is more, the very man who was charged with the preliminary inquiry—they would shriek improper tampering at the top of their voice, which is loud."

"There isn't any preliminary inquiry," said Vera.

"Very true. And I would very badly like someone to break this last piece of unhappy news, which is that the surviving daughter has met a violent death in England—we probably never will know how or why. Brought by myself, I fear, this news would only push him further into apathy. In short . . . well, you've done this job before; you know the dangers. . . . I'll overcome my reservations. Permission granted. If you infringe, be it ever so little, the private capacity —you do see that I'd be obliged to come down more than usually heavily. . . . All right, my girl. As long as you realize that I grant this request for strictly professional motives."

"I accept that, Monsieur le Juge, knowing it not to be altogether true."

"Off with you," said the judge, shaking his paper knife at her.


She was extremely nervous, and it had little to do with the intimidating surroundings, for she had been here before, and things like having her handbag rummaged through by the guards or having a guard present (not really listening, but inevitably a wet blanket), did not worry her. She was frightened of La Touche, of whom she knew too much and not enough. Her fingers were trembling; she was glad to have a cigarette.

"How's the legs?" asked the guard in a friendly way. He knew her, but did not know she was a cop's wife.

"All right," said Vera, "but not very reliable. I find myself sitting down when I least expect to." They had a laugh over that.

"I'll get your man," said the guard.

La Touche, in his nicely pressed track suit, was very polite and formal. Strangely enough, that stiff courtesy made it easier for her.

"This is Mme. Spaniera," said the guard. "You'll get on well with her; everyone does."

"Delighted," said La Touche, kissing her hand. The light cool voice was as Castang had described it. "What are you an expert in?"

"I'm not sure," she said, not trembling at all any more. "I think perhaps my dustpan and brush."

"Ah. I've got pretty sharp with it myself. But do you mean to say you've no doctorate in sociology? Or anthropology?"

"Nothing at all."

"Then to what do I owe this pleasure?"

"Not even vulgar curiosity. I thought someone who wasn't anything at all might be a good idea, and slightly to my surprise the judge said yes."

"He's a good honest fellow," said La Touche. He might have been praising a conscientious subordinate, but Vera had been prepared for this.

"Well," he went on, "that's nice: I'm not anything either. You were quite right, M. Morel; Madame is a light-bringer."

"No, don't put me at a disadvantage," said Vera. "I'm nervous enough as it is."

"I'm nervous, too, and it makes me rude. I beg

your pardon. I'm afraid I'm not yet clever at
my new identity. Committing a violent crime c.
one a good deal."

"It doesn't change you for me at all."

"I'm a corporal work of mercy? Has it a religious connotation?"

"Heaven, no, that would be horrid. If you mean am I Catholic and are you my brother, I'd have to say yes, but please, no self-conscious virtues. Going to cheer up poor old Charles because he's in the hospital and it must be depressing for him isn't my idea at all. I don't know who I am. The secretary, maybe—not very efficient but willing. A bridge to the outside world. Change your library books. Inform myself about anything you're interested in. Run errands. Fix any buttons the laundry tears off your shirts. Gossip. Conversation. I'm afraid my intellectual level's not very high, but I'm interested in most things—as long as they aren't too abstract. Things like—oh, you know, the foreign policy of the Chinese—I'm sadly uninformed about, I'm afraid."

La Touche actually laughed. It was sufficiently unusual for M. Morel, peacefully engaged upon *Reader's Digest*, to look up for a moment with a glance of astonishment.

"My dear girl, you're heaven-sent. I'm sorry, I would like now to be very informal. We can do better than the secretary. May I say Vera? My name is Gilbert. It would make the hospital bed softer, and be a kindness. It's true that I've always been an artificial person, evolving in artificial milieus, and here I'm more so than ever. This is a torrent of oxygen. May I ask you personal questions?"

"Please do."

"Who are you? Will you tell me something about yourself?"

"Oh, yes, though it's brief and boring. I'm Czech; it's written on my face rather, and I'm married to a functionary in the administration and I'm twenty-seven and I've no children, I'm afraid, which rather saddens me. I've not much use for being liberated, which seems to me selfish and superficial and fundamentally self-defeating, and I had a baddish accident, which left me hampered, as you see, which is a bore, and I draw a bit, illustrations to various things, some children's books, and really I think that's about all; now you."

"Ah. Well, to adopt your style, I come from a rich and narrow-minded family in the high bourgeoisie— What was your father, by the way?"

"He made barrels."

"Exactly. A craftsman, and useful. Mine was just the opposite, but I thought him admirable."

"Then he probably was."

"Something to be said for that. Kind, anyway, and less rigid than I am. I am, or was, a servant of the state, which is a family tradition. I was trained to examine and verify state accounts. I am rich. I married money. To say that money doesn't mean much to me is no compliment: it's easy when one has always had it and is trained to use it. Poor Hélène—my wife—came from the ancient noblesse, rather God and Fatherland. She worried about her investments and, of course, they kept losing value, having been badly made. I've never been much good at enjoying life: I'm a dried stick. And dear, oh dear, where do we go from there?"

"I'd say there were plenty of places to go. One starts again."

"Like you. I disagree, but we won't go into that."

"I only meant that one feels completely shattered. Without boasting, I was a gymnast—quite a good one. I mean for years it was the center of my existence, and when I broke my spine I thought it was the end. But I was just too young and stupid to realize. There are so many other centers."

"Oh, look," pleaded La Touche, "I'm enjoying you such a lot; don't be like those tedious psychiatrists."

"I'm so sorry, I didn't mean to. But isn't there something to be said for them?"

"Probably there is and I don't want to sound irritatingly haughty. But they search, you see, for things they can measure. Mental health is a fact like another; well, I agree, and it's reasonable that they should look for the causes of an accident, a breakdown in myself quite similar to the neurophysiological trauma you had. But to me, you see, this is quite irrelevant. I think that the breakdown was a moral one, and that the dried-out stick once snapped cannot be repaired."

"I don't like metaphors," she said. "A human being isn't a stick."

"I beg your pardon," said La Touche. "It is unforgivable to be talking about oneself all the while. Prison makes one sadly egoist. By the way, there are a few books I should like from my library. Do you think the judge would allow you to go to my house?"

"Yes, of course; just give me a list. I can come twice a week, like the butcher's van."

La Touche looked at her, as one looks at something beautiful that is going to disappear. Venice, perhaps.

"You are good."

"Mmm," said Vera. "You'll change your mind. I

157

want now to say something I've been dreading. I'm afraid Victoria is dead."

He appeared to shrink in upon himself that bit more. His face did not change much. He sighed a little.

"Very well. Tell me."

"Not much is known. The judge heard today. He thought you'd prefer to learn it in private. It was in England. A cop"—she had come dangerously close to saying "my husband"—"had gone over to talk to her. She was on dope, as you know. Apparently somehow she got an overdose," gabbling it.

"Yes . . . I suppose one can't be surprised at that," he muttered. The eyes had gone absent; he wasn't looking at her.

"I'll go now, if you'd prefer," said Vera timidly. She hadn't known what it would be like to bring a man news of his child's death. And when he himself had killed his other child . . . She put that resolutely out of her mind. It was irrelevant. She wasn't a psychiatrist, thank heaven. "If there's anything at all—no matter what—I can do, please please don't hesitate."

She had not very much experience as a prison visitor, enough to know that "feeling sorry" was a trap to be avoided at all costs. But there must be some sympathy, in its literal sense of suffering-with. There must be some solidarity. She was married to a cop, and was trained to avoid sentimentality. A prison is damn well not like a hospital. In her notions of justice she was very theological: very Czech, said Castang, laughing, very baroque Jesuit.

"I'm grateful," said La Touche. "That's a sign. There's nothing now to hold one." The remark was not addressed to her and she decided to pay no attention. She waited patiently for him to come back, which he did at once.

"I said you were good. I repeat it. Now let's talk about you. Have you done this long?"

"Not very. It's not much. Three hours twice a week. There's a Yugoslav man—he learns Czech from me and I learn Yugoslav from him, by talking together. That's good, you see. I mean he's a poor man and uneducated and he's teaching me. And there's a man I teach drawing. He can't draw, and I rather hate it because he's getting an illusion that he can, but he enjoys it a lot and that must do good. And the director would like to give gymnastics lessons to the girls, but we've no equipment, and no money to buy any."

"And what can I contribute? Not much. Hmm. I'm rich. I'll talk to my imbecile lawyer. I think the judge would allow me to spend money on gymnastic equipment."

"That would be nice, but don't do anything for the wrong motives."

"Whose idea was it to come and see me? The judge? One of those damned psychologists? Tell the truth."

"I will. Mine. But if I tell the truth it sounds so—so patronizing."

"Nevertheless."

"I don't think things out much. I just thought it was awful for you—all right, I'll say it straight out—to have made such a hole in your family and perhaps it would be good if a woman came to see you. This was a very crude idea, you understand, so I asked the judge. What ideas he may have, of course, are no business of mine."

"Well," said La Touche, "I think that very good.

159

We won't talk about lessons. There's sadly little I could teach anyone. I'm a wretchedly sterile person. I've never done anything. Even elementary bookkeeping or Latin would be beyond me. And it's too late for me to learn much. I haven't such a great deal of time."

"Yes, you'll be out of here before much longer. Sometimes those instructions do take such ages, but I mean yours should be quite straightforward."

"That's not quite what I meant, but no matter. I'd be content simply to see you come back."

"Of course. Now the book list. Can I give the pencil and paper, M. Morel?"

"Sure," said the guard comfortably.

Vera was home in time to cook supper for Castang, who was cross, tired, and frustrated by his English experiences, but interested in hers.

"So the judge allowed it—never would have thought it. I was joking when I suggested it, and there she goes, trotting off solemnly to beard the lion in his den."

"He wasn't a lion at all. All these judges are reasonable when you handle them right. He's very rigid, poor old Szymanowski, but he wasn't troublesome at all."

"You're to cross-check on the psychiatric opinions."

"You know better than that. What do I know or care about psychiatric opinions?"

"They'll play a big role in this case. No law involved at all, hardly. This and no more—how far was he over?"

"He certainly isn't now. A difficult person, yes. Withdrawn, badly closed in upon himself, deeply embittered, a strong sense of inadequacy and, I'm afraid, a lot of bad melancholy—but not despair."

"But was he off the rails at that moment? That's the thing."

"Oh, yes, of course he was. Anybody is. But I'm perfectly aware that to claim so isn't law and isn't sense and isn't justice, and I have no interest in all that; to me it's perfectly irrelevant."

"That's right. I'll be a witness. Won't budge off the facts. Luckily they're quite unshakable. Everything depends on how the Proc is going to pitch his case. It's certain he'll go easy, because otherwise the court is on the hook. If this is sanity, the whole definition of an assassination plotted in cold blood is present. Opens the door most uncomfortably. But if the shrinks pick up a lot of stuff showing that this personality can become quite disabled by an appalling vision—I mean, fair enough, catching your wife and daughter together in bed with the same man is an appalling vision—then his actions are dictated and the cool and collected manner is just one indication more. Did it like a sleepwalker."

"I haven't any doubt but that this is so," said Vera. "He's under terrible strain all the time."

"Then nobody has any worries. Not even me, as long as we keep this political stuff from getting out of control. Feel fairly safe about that now. You see, to admit a political element would now be an embarrassment to the English government as well. This chap Metcalfe is a very sensible fellow. He'll see to it that they remain quite happy with the notion of accounts settled in some drug gang. She was making off with the supplies or something, creating a private black market, so they dealt out punishment. Perfectly plausible, too.

Or simply chopped her because of the extradition demand—attracting the attention of the cops, she's a liability: out. It would all be quite consequent."

"This is horribly cynical."

"Why? It doesn't affect La Touche. Look, what does it all boil down to? I'll try and demonstrate. Forget this stuff about Israeli Intelligence; it's crap. This painter happened to be Jewish, and was serious about it. I mean his Jewishness was essential to him. But as a painter: funny games in the State of Israel don't interest him. I feel sure of that, after talking to the wife.

"Now La Touche. He's an expert on finance, above all on financial management, on what's well run and what isn't. Pretty good choice for an investment consultant. Above all, knows everyone. Excellent contacts in all banks and insurance houses, hand in glove with all government spending and purchasing agencies, been at school with half the senior civil servants. Money, money, money—all this revolves around money. Semi-officially, some people are quietly asking him for advice about sponging up a bit of this vast pool of petro-dollars we hear about. Unofficially, he is used as a sounding board about governmental intentions. Some stuff pretty close to the bone there, like aircraft and arms sales. But he isn't acting dishonestly, he isn't taking bribes—at least I don't think he is. Legitimate commissions on various things that aren't contrary to the 'national interest' or disguised consultancy fees: it doesn't matter.

"Here I fall into guesswork. He liked this painter. Maybe he has secret Israeli sympathies. I know nothing and why should I ask? Maybe he saw a man in the painter that was a good man as well as a good painter. Better than himself, creative, uncorrupted—

call it what you will. He's not worried about his wife; he's cynical about her. If the painter screws her, jolly good; keep her from doing sillier things. But about the daughters he has terrific guilt feelings, and I leave all that aside—it's for the shrinks. Finding the wife and the daughter together is just too much to swallow. He goes mataglap, takes the pistol, executes the lot, and then, being a very serious person and determined not to embarrass the government or the job or the family, he rings me up and says 'I've killed; take me in.' And that's really all there is to it. I've no doubt I'm over-simplifying."

"And Victoria?"

"Ah, that's more coincidental than anything else, perhaps. Victoria is in total opposition. Nothing to do, maybe, with Jews or Arabs, but she's on dope, she is irresponsible, she gets the weird ideas they do get when on dope, and she's an active girl. Instead of just going off to be dim-witted and go 'Hare, Krishna' in a dirty yellow nightie, she joins an anarchist group. Trouble with them is they're dodgier than her simple little mind can comprehend. Some of these anarchists are genuinely dangerous. They link up with the I.R.A., with those mutton-fat fedayeen, with Tupamaros and fanatic armies of every sort. There's a parallel in that wretched child of the newspaper magnate—Hearst, was it? Very troublesome, and all the political police sweat blood over them.

"These people benefit from a quite large degree of toleration, as a consequence; too troublesome and expensive to do anything else. In return they try to avoid being too flagrant, knowing as they do that it's nice to have three regular large meals a day and a comfortable bed: they don't want to take to no maquis."

He stopped: this was all useless, and a mistake into the bargain. Vera had the look of extreme imbecility she wore when she wasn't listening and didn't want to listen. It meant she couldn't cope, and didn't intend to try.

How, anyway, to explain the unexplainable? How to say that a cop—if he is to hold on to some sensitivity, retain an awareness of integrity—goes white with black spots in order to avoid going gray all over? There were areas in which he "didn't want to know." There were one or two where he would say "Find somebody else." Where a superior officer with any sense would not force him to obey orders, because that would be the quickest way of losing a good cop.

A bit of folklore concerning Basque separatists was one thing. Rounding up a fellow and saying to him, "You're making too much noise here in Bayonne; the government would like you to go and live in Lille for a while" was fine. But mixing too much with the complete moral anesthesia of the hard core, the ones who would smash anything, kill anybody—a classroom full of small children, say—led to becoming morally retarded yourself.

There were cops who were all black, all the way through. One or two in every department. Castang knew two. He shook hands with them in a corridor, murmured a meaningless cordiality—"How goes it, vieux?"—found himself having a drink with them once or twice a year.

These were the ones used. To whom a senior commissaire, a Richard, would say now and then, in as

164

few words as possible, "See to that." They would knock you off any way that was handy: a gun, a knife, or a leaky gas main, with no hard feelings. Much worse: with no feelings at all. If people were terrorists—real terrorists, not just chatterboxes—you used terrorists against them. These people were like the executioner and his assistants. You didn't see them very often, but they could always be found when needed.

This total moral insanity is one of the proofs of the existence of evil.

The ones who were really all black would not live very long. They would return to the master who sent them.

What kind of husband and father does a bad cop make? The ones that were just dingy gray all the way through?

Castang switched the television on, and he and Vera watched a cowboy film, with an all-white hero, and a villain who was pretty black but died bravely.


## 23. Psychiatric Opinions


Commissaire Richard, running over a list, prepared for him by the admirable Fausta, of engagements for the coming month ranging from the unavoidable to the purely protocolaire, got past "Prefect's reception and wine-of-honor for Mr. George MacDermott," opposite which Fausta had penciled "An Assistant U.S. Attorney, s.s.o. [some sort of] fact-finding mission: heads of departments requested to attend." American double-talk, like Treasury meaning narcotics. F.B.I. or something. This was always complicated and tiresome: one had to look back to see how often one had skipped, in recent months, infernally boring functions of this sort, and how many one could skip in the near future without its being commented upon. One had to keep a few discards in hand: there would be people even more grindingly protocolaire than Mr. George MacDermott.

"Date set Assize Court, trial Gilbert La Touche." He picked up the internal telephone.

Castang was deep in bread-and-butter police work; that is to say, nothing gaudy like homicides. Things pinched. With effracton—robbery. Without effraction —larceny. Complaints. The tide of complaints was swelling to the point where somebody—originating with Commissaire Fabre of the urban police force— would have to think about taking measures, because there'd been too much mugging, and too many editorials in the local newspaper about "Why Are Our Streets No Longer Safe?" What were all these people doing wandering about lonely streets at two in the morning, carrying, invariably, thick wallets stuffed with banknotes? Why were they so stupid? Been running after whores, nine times out of ten. No patience with them. And they were always the ones who complained the loudest and most persistently, and always said they had brothers, highly placed, in the Prime Minister's Office in Paris.

If only one could put a stop to the torrential sewer of hypocrisy. If only, just once, one could put a notice in the paper: "Communiqué to the Public from the Police Judiciaire," saying, "Listen, grow up and have some elementary sense."

His phone rang. Richard. A concrete person. Vaguely phrased pep talks were a rarity. If Richard wanted to give you the sack, he invited you out to lunch.

"Castang? Come in here."

Cigar going. Where did he get them from? Said to be Brazilian, but perhaps he grew them in his greenhouse between the orchids. Black tarry chewy things, knotty, as though made of vanilla. One always expected sputterings of saltpeter and then a blue flare, like the flares carried by clippers in the eighteeneighties, when collision at night appeared imminent. Economical, anyhow: nobody in their senses would take one when offered.

"La Touche is coming up for trial. The instruction's finished; I forgot to tell you. You'll be wanted as witness. I'd like you to see what you can of this trial; you'll be called early, so the observation part is easy. I won't be there at all, thank heaven. I've a lot of time-wasting rubbish anyway," looking crossly at Fausta's list, which was worse than usual, and his own diary beside it.

Castang was surprised. "It's a snip, surely."

"It's not that much of a snip. I don't mean there's anything wrong with your showing in the inquiry; that's all solid. You'll get the usual barrage from the defense. He refused a Paris lawyer. Defended by a junior off the legal-aid list."

"Good God."

"That's by no means all. Fellow said, I quote: 'I wish we had English law: I'd plead guilty; avoid all this nonsense.' Charming. Can you see the panic?"

"What would it mean?"

"I'm not quite sure—not a mandatory death sentence, I think, because the English have their hangman in abeyance still, I believe. Hanging by a thread." Richard was quite good at gallows humor. "Or did they reintroduce it for cop-killing? It's of no consequence, because of course the folklore won't do here, and they're hunting for a very severe Assize Court President who'll stand no nonsense. Braunschwig would do nicely but this isn't the Paris jurisdiction, alas. But there's worse than that. Szymanowski's much aghast; he's got all the psychiatric reports."

"You don't mean—?"

"Oh, yes, I do. Perfectly sane in all respects and at all times. And La Touche said quite openly, 'Thank heaven for some psychiatrists with a little common sense.'"

"What's this fellow preparing in the way of a nasty surprise?"

"Quite: that's the question everyone is asking. Before closing his dossier and declaring the instruction completed, the judge wants to give himself a loophole."

"Supplement of information?"

"If need be."

"What the hell does he think further police work could dig up at this time of day?"

"None, I think. But when he starts like that—and I'm reduced to basing my own working time on 'I-think-he-thinks-that-someone-else-may-be-thinking'—So stay here for a moment—I'll tell you why in just a while—and I'll try and get light shed. Fausta," into his phone, "get me a line to M. Szymanowski at the Palais. . . . Now about these muggings: Fabre's being tiresome. You remember the other day there was a party for that old imbecile Roupeyrolles." This was a worthy but wooden-headed old inspector who had finally retired, much to Richard's relief, after forty years of devotedly mediocre police work. There had been an official "apéritif," with a presentation of a medal and a chiming clock. Castang had congratulated himself upon finding a foolproof pretext for absence from these rollicking solemnities.

"The sous-chef appeared." The big shot from Paris, M. Marty, known as "Eminenza" inevitably, since there was a cardinal of that name, but the cardinal was a more amusing person than the sous-directeur of the whole P.J. apparatus. Castang knew vaguely that the occasion had been taken for a vast pep talk involving "Working in Harness Together."

"Well, he was very tiresome indeed." The phone rang and "Judge for you," said Fausta.

"Good morning, sir. To come straight to the point, I see that a provisional date has been set for the La Touche trial. . . . Ah. . . . I see . . . yes . . . yes. . . . Castang's with me at present. . . . Quite. . . . This afternoon already: one moment till I look. . . . Very well. . . . Yes, sir, I'll tell him. . . . Yes, I do realize. . . . Very good, I'll arrange accordingly. . . . It's understood, sir. . . ." Richard put the phone down, and said blandly, "Do you know, in the course of Hitler's war the Italians produced a phrase book to assist municipal functionaries in their dealings with the occupying power—to wit, American sergeants. Among other masterpieces was the useful phrase 'Permit me to present to you the Count'—can't get anywhere without counts. So there it was all nicely printed. 'Posso presentare il conte,' and the English translation opposite. 'Meet the Cunt.' "

"Ah, Sergeant Metcalfe would like that."

"You might bear it in mind, too. There's going to be a conference this afternoon in the judge's office. Fabre, myself, the brigade chief of S.T.; likewise of Renseignements Généraux." R.G., survival from the old Sûreté Nationale, another branch of parallel police. It is like M.I. 5, and the Special Branch; all these people have an invented sound.

"Another pep talk," said Castang with disgust. "The judge, this time, instead of Marty."

"And you instead of old Roupeyrolles."

"What have I to do with it?"

"Your wife."

"What's she done now?" genuinely startled. There had been the moment when Vera had "chosen freedom" and been a slight embarrassment, but what . . .

"Do I have to spell it all out?" asked Richard irritably. "Your wife has got to know La Touche quite well in these last few weeks, but that stays unofficial; the judge doesn't want it misinterpreted. Since nobody grasps exactly what the man is up to, you will please possess yourself over lunch of any lights your dear girl can shed."

"She won't tell me."

"Be a bit serious, Castang. The judge wants a consensus of opinion before he decides to close the dossier of the instruction. What's La Touche playing at? Working up for a show trial? Thinking with this precious lawyer of his of a grand denunciation of government policies in the Middle East? The judge—and small blame to him—doesn't care for the thought."

"What would she know? They chat about Mme. de Sévigné and her daughter."

"You might just verify that."

"It's ridiculous," said Vera. "Call for a psychi. opinion on Richard, and that Polish bastard."

"Spare me all that," said Castang curtly. "Be serious, because this is. Three shrinks declare La Touche sane, so he goes forward to trial. He's not calling any experts in rebuttal. His lawyer is obliged to convey some notion of the defense, but before closing the instruction the judge would like to know what's coming."

"Oh, why can they never understand?" said Vera angrily. "I can say it all in about three words. If I'm visiting a detainee, as he's so prudishly described, I don't talk politics. I'm not that soppy; I'd have been dismissed my first week. Nor do I encourage them to pour out grievances. La Touche is a highly intelligent and sensitive person who is most careful not to embarrass or bore me. He has lovely manners and it's a delight to see him. He's also a simple person. He trusts me, I think and hope. We talk about all sorts of things. Books mostly, which I haven't read and he has. It helps him, I believe, and I'm even damn well convinced. I'm not telling anything, because it's all in confidence, his confidence, and I'm not doing any espionage for that Polish bastard. He's got to learn," said Vera with Czech peasant wisdom, "that if you try and hold a fart back it explodes the louder."

"About three words," said Castang mildly, "and don't think I'm going to relay confidences; I won't. As you ought to know. Just one thing. Is La Touche planning some sort of political demonstration—to your knowledge? It's just that it could kick back. Richard will stand up for me, but bad police work will simply send us both to Madagascar to lecture on the Penal Code to natives. Mad dogs and Englishmen. Just try

171

## 24. The Bounce of the Ball

We're a funny lot, thought Castang. As the junior in this distinguished gathering—a mere inspector—he was keeping his mouth shut.

The rest were socializing. They were not friends in any sense of the word, and colleagues only in the most superficial. They had no particular liking for one another, and the professional cordialities they exchanged when they met were the thinnest of shiny chrome, peeling rapidly before corrosion, exposing the base metal below. Good enough metal, in that these were all men of some quality. Good products of the system: intelligent, sensitive, quite cultured, of strong character, widely read, much traveled, deeply impregnated by all sorts of civilized values. But how little it all added up to. These metals were made brittle, as cast iron is brittle, by the almost pathological suspiciousness they suffered from. This went a good deal further than interdepartmental rivalry.

Having all met recently—at the apéritif for the retiring cop, where they had been summoned to hear the P.J. sous-chef deliver his famous lecture on "Working in Harness"—they had at that time exhausted the joviality that obtains among men of this type who do not see one another more than once a month: the jokes and the exchange of good stories. They had done their duty then, they all felt, on an occasion they could none of them well dodge. Now they were all bored, because this was a waste of time.

Each of them felt that he was not concerned by this small matter, and nobody among them wanted to become concerned, because nothing could come of it save "emmerdements," that useful word which in French conveys the abstract notion of being covered-in-a-shower-of-shit.

M. Szymanowski, the present "chairman," did not know any of them well. Richard he knew best. Richard, a quiet and exceptionally secret person—nobody present had ever met his wife or his two sons—was an unknown quantity to everyone. He had not much small talk, and was talking about golf. Since golf in Europe is a considerably more exclusive, expensive, and snobbish leisure pursuit than it is in Anglo-Saxon countries, and the tax inspector regards it like ownership of a yacht or a racehorse, the others were all thinking, Typical vice-squad performance. Typically P.J. Typically Richard. Since they all knew that Richard did not take bribes, this made them cross. How does he do it on his salary? M. Szymanowski, to whom a golf club was a dangerous blunt instrument likely to cause grave injuries to the bystander, preferred to change the subject.

Commissaire Fabre of the urban police—the "Centrale" of all the municipal police brigades, criminal, moral, traffic, public order, and so on (he was what he had to be: a skillful reconciler of warring factions, soother of municipal councilors, good administrator, diplomat with mayors, prefects, and chambers of commerce)—was a burly man, with heavy muscles now running to an overweight look, and large black-framed glasses. He campaigned assiduously to keep his weight trim, and was quite a sharp tennis player in doubles. He also liked music, and went whenever he

174

could to all the concerts and operas given rather grudgingly by the city to its public. When alone in his office, he was notorious for a robust "tum tum," half humming and half singing, recognizable to the initiate as barrel-organ Verdi. So jammy, so firmly constructed, so beautiful, so good. This trait was thoroughly attractive. But Fabre had an abrasive side. He was extraordinarily mean about small expenses, a perfect terror about postage stamps and turning down the central heating, and had made everyone at his drafty gloomy headquarters replace their hundred-watt bulbs with forties.

M. Frédéric-Alexandre Marre, brigade chief of Surveillance du Territoire, was nearly as small as Castang, but broader and thicker. He cultivated a casual look, and was always seen in a Harris Tweed jacket, a flannel shirt with small checks, and mysteriously a bow tie. He had abdominal muscles like Charles Atlas —power springs from the pit of the stomach where the nervous centers are—decorated by an expensive belt in crocodile leather that did much more for him than holding his trousers up: he never wore a pullover. He had a furry teddy-bear voice and tiny shoe-button teddy-bear eyes, and the falsest smile Castang had ever seen. He had a slight resemblance to the secretary-general of the big Communist trade union. He enjoyed and cultivated this resemblance. He was an enthusiastic theatregoer.

Cardillac, Ambroise Édmond, was a complete contrast. He was best known to everybody for having been, a few years back, for thirteen whole weeks the champion of a complicated and esoteric television game involving the identification of the names of movies—nine or ten of the damn things every week—from the meager clues of the director, the supporting actors, and the scriptwriter. The contestants were each week given a theme of a star once famous but for the last thirty years forgotten save by people like M. Cardillac, who possessed all the back numbers of *Cahiers du Cinéma*. Perhaps it was part of Renseignements Généraux, translatable vaguely as "Spying on Everybody," of which he was the local linchpin.

His morphological type was that described by the cliché "cadaverous." He was not very tall, not particularly thin, not even very bald, but his forehead was bumpy, his jaws concave, his neck strangely bony. His ears rather stuck out, and black fuzz grew out of them. He had extremely intelligent bright and mobile eyes. These for the television cameras had been masked by dark glasses. Even now, his lenses were tinted a rather horrible cold bluish color, giving people in the same room fear that a laser beam might come suddenly popping out to castrate them, or something equally nasty.

It is notoriously hard to say what it is that R.G. actually does. Surveying of the Territory is a fairly transparent euphemism for counterespionage, but what does General Information mean? Like "Normal School," it means more than it seems but has a vaguely old-fashioned ring, connected with peculating financiers like M. Stavisky, and Presidents of the Third Republic who got heart attacks while in bed with somebody's wife. This combination of vagueness and legend is a puzzle to foreign journalists who are studying the institutions of the Republic. Suffice it that R.G. is minatory, muddled, and supposedly makes of the Minister of the Interior a mighty man, since he has access to all the dossiers involving dirty stories. Aha, Mr. President-Director-General (of some boring textile factory in Roubaix), we know all about your filthy doings with tiny girls under age: always known, nobody knows why, as "ballets roses," with all the implications of elderly and vicious but impotent voyeurism.

I'm the low man, the smallest and least fiercely grimacing figure, on this totem pole, thought Castang.

Isn't it strange? Supposedly, the company here present ought to have a dossier on every man, woman, and child in, say—put it in small, manageable figures—a hundred by a hundred; that's ten thousand square kilometers, which is a lot. How is it that they miss so many notaries who whip off with the trust funds, wine merchants who have craftily mixed up the green tickets (controlled original appellation) and white tickets (limited superior quality—meaning largely undrinkable), or, to change scenery a bit, confirmed alcoholics who habitually torture their children?

How is it that the P.J. hasn't got the remotest notion who composes the gang that twice now has done such an extremely smooth job on major post offices and got away with the equivalent of a hundred and fifty million dollars?

How is that R.G. has never found out that Millennium, that admirable and practically universal tranquilizer and happy-pill, is sold for three francs a dose and costs one third of a centime to produce? The difference, familiar to policemen, is between knowing a thing and being aware of it.

They had told—or had not told—the German government quite a long time ago that the Chancellor's personal aide was a listening post. If they had told, it might have appeared peculiar that nobody had paid the slightest notice. More likely they hadn't told, being well aware that nobody would want to know.

In La Touche as a person . . . well, all policemen have the defect of never seeing the people they deal with as persons. We all of us, thought Castang, probably know something about him, but add us all together and it won't amount to anything recognizably human. In all likelihood, the only person who would be the faintest use around here is Vera, and she has her trap firmly shut.

"Good," said Szymanowski in a hurried indistinct voice, "you are aware of my concern over this seemingly unimportant and stupid case. The facts are unsatisfactory and everything so far adduced leaves an atmosphere of confusion. Perfectly good system of defense and the man seems bent on ignoring it. Why? Between us, and in confidence, there might be scraps of knowledge we can collate into some coherent whole. I ask you in turn to contribute what you can, and to examine the results informally. M. Fabre?"

Fabre took his glasses off and closed his eyes.

"There was a brief flurry, at the beginning, of loud talk and slogan-writing, which to my mind had no significance. It could have been in the interests of a variety of people to make us believe that this man was either being unfairly attacked—or improperly protected. Depending on which side you stand of opinion. Opinion is always polarized and some people seize every pretext for polarizing it further. Accuse the Communists of Fascist activities. Conversely, use the same fact to claim that crypto-Fascists are seeking to split the unity of the workers. Classic, and anyway 'post hoc, propter hoc.' Aside from this, and for the rest, my services haven't been involved. I'm aware that an attack was made on Castang here, which could have made propaganda. It was the subject of a confidential report by myself to the magistrate. The young man in question was deported for carrying a concealed weapon. Since no charges were preferred, there was no prosecution. Further, nothing."

"Castang acted sensibly, and with my approval," said Richard. "That Lebanese boy was inflamed by the girl Charlotte. Since she's dead, we can't interrogate her. But it's clear—calf love, and she hung about with a group of Arab students. Tunisian, Moroccan —a type the girl found physically attractive. I had a couple interrogated by Lasalle, in his well-known baby-sitting manner"—nobody grinned—"and there was nothing else to it. That man Dieudonné saw an opportunity for a little publicity, which he might have thought would distract us from more sensitive aspects, if there are any. M. Marre, as I then gathered, was of the opinion there weren't."

"And still is," Marre said.

"One second just to say that while I wasn't concerned with the inquiry at its beginnings I am totally satisfied that Castang's handling of it was scrupulous in the extreme," Fabre added.

"Nobody has queried that," said the magistrate mildly.

"Just for the record, Monsieur le Juge," said Fabre. "I won't be a witness at the trial—or not if I can help it."

"M. Marre?"

The teddy bear had put a big long cigarette between his front teeth. Red-and-gold packet. So like them to smoke Dunhills. He spoke with his index

179

fingers together on the point of his nose (his elbows on the table) and the second fingers on the dimple in his neatly shaved chin, forming a diamond through which his mouth spoke with the cigarette sticking straight out between. Witch doctor, thought Castang, putting on grotesque mask to frighten natives. Me rain god; you ignorant niggers. No listen Tarzan; he white man's friend.

"And still is. Nothing that has happened here concerns me, since there isn't any threat to state security and never has been. I have received a report from a colleague in Paris, which I bring to your attention within the framework of confidentiality mentioned by Monsieur le Juge. The girl Victoria had some contact with an anarchist group. On, as I understand, a very casual basis. In other words, she was seeking to make herself interesting. This lot aren't handling drugs . . . because doubtless . . . they'd be arrested by the police if they did. . . . As a known user of drugs, it's of course obvious that she would not be used as any sort of go-between—far too unreliable. She was not a source of information to our office; I make the point in order to dispel it."

"Any idea why she was killed?" asked Richard. Castang knew he'd asked the same question in private. He'd said "Alex" then.

"That, I should imagine, was the concern of the English. She may have compromised people in ways we know nothing of."

"Which would seem to imply that she did have some knowledge it was thought worth suppressing."

"Not necessarily. I make no criticism of M. Castang here: he was doing his job. Somebody may have seen English cops standing around. Even if only an affair of illegal entry or a faked passport—the English are sensitive to such. People draw hasty conclusions. These groups are apt to meddle in what doesn't concern them, just to make money. They're vulnerable that way."

"I can't make out what you're talking about," Richard said.

"I'm not talking about anything I don't know about," said Marre. "If the Channel ports are full of stateless Pakistanis, that doesn't interest me in the slightest."

A perfect smoke screen of confusion and innuendo, thought Castang. If she had a phony passport, and if somebody was making a lot of money selling them, and if there was a likelihood of her being interrogated, then quite adroitly M. Marre was suggesting that Victoria's being assassinated was all the fault of the English immigration officials.

Nobody wanted to pursue this, which was presumably what Marre intended.

"M. Cardillac?"

"I'd better begin by saying that I will not entertain any suggestion whatever that the parties in this case, which I see as a clause in the Penal Code and nothing else, were manipulated for information purposes. A report of a certain conversation taking place between Castang here and a certain Dr. Simon was brought to my attention. I know Dr. Simon. I had a chat with him. As a selling agent for heavy industry—with, I may add, the perfect knowledge and approval of the authorities—he was interested in the contacts M. La Touche possessed. I summarize these as people with money to invest in foreign securities; the connection is obvious. I am not aware that any serious suggestion has been made that La Touche used knowledge he may have possessed in an improper manner. In view of his access to confidential information in the fiscal area, he had been subject from time to time to security checking. I go into no details: they are irrelevant."

"Were the checks negative?" asked Marre amicably, dropping ash into his cupped hand and tipping it neatly into the ashtray.

"They were, my dear Alex. I repudiate totally any suggestion that this painter was an Israeli Intelligence agent: it's preposterous. They don't work that way, outside of bad fiction. Anybody with a grain of sense can see that in matters of finance Israel is not short of intelligence. I conclude: La Touche was of no interest to my services. It follows that nobody in his entourage was, either."

"This meeting, at least, serves its purpose," said the judge. "Any red herrings raised by the defense can be forestalled. Castang, I come to you last, for reasons you divine. Perhaps you'd like to sum them up yourself?"

"With respect, sir, I draw two conclusions. That since interrogating La Touche I have come to know a bit more about him, and because of that I can make a shot at adding this up."

"Yes."

"And that on your instructions I pursued the investigation on a more personal level?"

"Very good."

"Can I say that we'd all agree after listening that all these relationships were personal and no more?"

"That all these elements are fortuitous, and not causally connected? I think you could. You gentlemen agree? Go on."

"That these different people have died—it may mean something to La Touche: it doesn't mean anything to me. I'm no wiser than when I began. On the purely personal level, pursuant to—"

"Yes, yes," irritably, "we understand."

"I've talked to the people, the prison officials and so on, who've been in contact with him. It overlaps the psychiatric reports, I believe. He's perfectly friendly and flexible, not unnaturally withdrawn or rigid, will talk about anything, but not on any grounds concerning his family life or relationships. End of story."

"Really?" said the judge. "I'd been quite counting on that woman who's been visiting."

"Yes, I got her to realize that. She was reticent, naturally."

"It is to her credit. But you got her to see that it is genuinely in this man's interest—?"

"Yes, Monsieur le Juge. Her opinion is that, quite simply, the man doesn't care a damn about his interests."

"The man's abnormal," said the judge crossly. "He can't possibly not realize the gravity of the situation."

"She hasn't any opinion to offer on that point," said Castang.

M. Marre took the dead cigarette butt out of his mouth and laid it tenderly in the ashtray. M. Cardillac fidgeted as though his bladder were giving him trouble. Richard just sat and looked unemotional. Fabre still had his eyes shut.

"I don't know what the Advocate-General is going to make of this," said Szymanowski, letting the file close with a snap.

## 25. Upheavals of the Prison Visitor

La Touche had had his hair cut. Nobody expects prison haircuts to be dainty, but it startled Vera to find him crew-cut: grayer, harsher, the face seeming a lot thinner.

"Are you well?"

"In rude health, thank you," smiling.

"It suits the shape of your head, but they've been a bit radical. I do my—" She bit it back; she wasn't here to talk about her husband.

"I told them to be radical: I'll be entering the ring quite soon and I'm in training, so to speak."

"So. What's the news, then?"

"They're beginning to talk about a trial. The judge is rather mournful. Such a thin dossier. Good bureaucrats like it rich and complicated, like Christmas pudding—something that takes a lot of digesting."

Vera knew this, having been given a law lesson by Castang. "Instruction's finished," he had said. "Yes, 'What, already?' That's what everyone's been saying."

"I never quite grasp why it all takes so long, as a rule."

"Ho. Justice is inquisitorial, as opposed to the English system, which is accusatorial," Castang had said. "No—not an inquisition: an inquiry. The whole principle is to judge the person, not the fact; the criminal, not the crime. The examining magistrate is not a trial judge—total separation of functions. His role is to shed light upon the personality more than the mechanics, and to dig into all the background."

"Building up the case against the unfortunate."

"No, that's a common mistake. That is the prosecutor's role. An instruction is strictly neutral: 'à charge et à décharge' is the golden rule. Inclines actually toward the defense. Before every interrogation, the defense counsel gets copies of all the papers—the day before—and a list of all the questions put. That's one reason why it all takes so long—assembling and organizing the defense. Szymanowski's in despair because there isn't any defense."

"Keep still." Vera, who at that moment had been cutting Castang's hair, snipped carefully behind his ear. Castang was fussy about hair; it must be long but not untidy.

"And what happens then?" she asked La Touche now.

"Oh," he said, "it's all very formal. Papers go to the Chamber of Accusation, which is a sort of judicial committee, and it examines the dossier to insure that the instruction has been correctly made and the legalities have been respected, and if everything is absolutely fit and proper, then they send you to trial. You are no longer a Presumed; you're an Accused."

"Incredibly laborious."

"My dear lady," in a parody of his old stiff manner, "you underestimate our passionate attachment to hair-splittingly precise formulas. What d'you want, then— a people's court and barrelhead justice? Every hair on my head would prickle, if I had any. I'm not in the least impatient, having a long and profound experience of lawyers, though only on the civil side so

185

far, I'm bound to admit. This is my first acquaintance with the criminal courts, but the judges are the same. Naturally I've been trying to hurry them up, chiefly by not giving them vast amounts of paper to play with. By the way, they might not let me see you any more once I'm committed for trial."

"Oh dear." Second shock. "I'm quite uncertain; I'll ask the judge."

"Are you disappointed?"

"I'm upset."

"That touches me very much. I've become very attached to your visits. In fact, if I may be allowed to use simple language, and you give me the only opportunity I have, I've grown extremely fond of you."

Vera, angry with herself, blushed.

"Yes, it's bad, in a man who killed his wife and daughter in atrocious circumstances. I'm sorry; we'll speak no more of it. Can you—I'm alas obliged to fill out a shopping list in a hurry in case they remove you from contamination—get me, do you think, a Book of Hours?"

"You mean the psalms and things monks have?"

"Those prescribed for recital at given times, that's right. 'Lord thou knowest my down-sitting and mine uprising'—subject of scatological humor to schoolchildren."

"I feel sure I can."

"The chaplain will be puzzled but pleased at these upwellings of religious fervor in times of trial."

"Is that what they are?"

"I've no idea. I'm simplifying, that's all. Continuing to simplify—my own existence, and, if possible, other people's."

"I've no earthly right to say it—but does the outcome of the thing—the trial—does it not worry you at all?"

"It would worry me a great deal if I thought it could go wrong."

"I'm sure it won't, you know," with some fervor. Vera indeed believed utterly—and had said so to Castang—that no murder could be committed by an amateur unless he was laboring under temporary insanity, and she was sure no reasonable person (Assize Court judges were surely reasonable persons) would disagree.

"What's your definition of a professional, then?" Castang had asked her.

"Well, committing a crime for interest: money, in the long run."

"And when there's no evidence as to state of mind? Then there's technical guilt."

"Oh, technical. The judge is a technician. That's what he's there for. They simply don't pass those ferocious sentences any more."

"Hmm." Castang felt a little bothered sometimes about Vera's belief in persons of responsibility being essentially right-minded. It reminded him of Neville Chamberlain's belief that Herr Hitler would certainly be responsive to a handshake from his right-minded self.

La Touche now was wearing the sort of expression described as whimsical. "The English, you know, have a quaint medieval custom. A clerk gets up and says, 'How say you, prisoner, are you guilty or not guilty?' I wonder whether anybody has ever said, 'Oh, all right, guilty, since you ask.' Court quite relieved—get home early for lunch. They'd never allow that here; it wouldn't do at all. Incidentally, Madame, I've never known your first name. Do you think our acquaintance has sufficiently progressed?"

"Vera. I do, rather."

"You embolden me. I'd like to ask you something intensely personal, on a basis of strict impersonality. Not as paradoxical as it sounds. Assuming you were not a married woman—or, shall I say rather, assuming that you had no family or emotional ties. As you see, that's very impersonal."

"Not as much as all that. It's the way you describe your own situation, and I understand your viewpoint. At least I think I do, sometimes."

"Then impersonal is the wrong word, but I'm looking for a technique. American lawyers use one called the hypothetical question. We hypothesize a situation in which both of us are in the situation as described. Would it be possible for the female person described to form an attachment to the male person described?"

Vera applied herself to this with the concentration she gave to every question seriously put, an anxious care that amused Castang, and for which he had much respect.

"The hypothesis, I take it, allows of a free man?"

"It would have to, I think," said La Touche, with a laugh, glancing at the stolid figure of M. Morel, who was solemnly eating candy Vera had brought him.

"Then this relationship you describe would grow into a sexual relationship, don't you think?"

"I don't know. I suppose that's possible. Might it be platonic?"

"I've no experience of platonic relationships. I've no great faith in them."

"Then accept the condition."

188

"I think in that case your hypothesis seems reasonable, but I don't like it; it's divorced from reality."

"It is, I'm sorry to say."

"You're talking about you and me, aren't you?"

"I am."

"It's a mistake you know, to talk about myself. It's against my rule."

"You're quite right. But will you take the risk?"

"Yes, I might," she said after thinking. "It might be good. But the consequences less good. All right. You see, I am a married woman of a basic sort. With complicated notions of honor, and conscience—all rather Spanish. I wouldn't—I mean I couldn't—start things I didn't know how to finish. And I have a real feeling for you. I refuse to let it get sentimentalized. Pretending that M. Morel wouldn't look and then imagining sleeping together is just mawkish."

"I completely agree."

"Oh dear . . . You see, I can't say I would, because I might, and I couldn't." Losing all command of French, or Czech, or any other language. "If I could—oh, damn. Then . . ."

"Don't cry," said La Touche softly.

"No, of course I won't. But you see, having said that, I can't come back any more. That is the consequence."

"I understand."

"I have to tell you something else. I've said to you that my husband was a civil servant. That wasn't quite true. He didn't know I came to see you. He does at present. He doesn't ask any questions. He wouldn't try to make—gain—anything from it. I don't betray anything you say, and I haven't, and I won't. You see, he's the cop who arrested you. My name is

Castang." She stood up and said, "M. Morel, let me out, would you."

"Thank you for coming," said La Touche. "It gives me much happiness."

"Me, too," she said. "I'll look after the book."

M. Morel brought the book next day. She had written on the flyleaf, "Coriolanus says 'There is a world elsewhere' and this surely is not just quixotic." He studied this for a time: the handwriting interested him. One had lots of time in jail, as well as very little. It was quiet. The chief guard, sympathetic to his polite manners and to his never giving any trouble, as well as impressed by an "intellectual," had given him a good table and chair, and was amiably lax over writing materials. For the greater part of the day, it was not even noisy. For dinner, there were lentils stewed with bits of bacon. The canteen provided virtually everything he needed, and he had lots of money: a great deal—far too much. He was, though, more grateful for far-too-much than he had ever been. In jail, money has more value than anywhere else. By "canteening" cigarettes, and a little extra fruit and soap, he got devoted service and friendship from the penniless and a chess partner whenever he wanted one.

Prognosis about his case was widespread: in a house of detention there are people serving short terms—a month or so "confined to barracks"—but the aristocracy are those who, having committed felonies, or even crimes, are being "instructed" and enjoy prolonging the instructions as long as possible. "It all helps to pass the time" and will be subtracted from the eventual sentence. But they look forward, too, to their trials. A trial is interesting, exciting, there will be publicity. And once the prisoner is sentenced, there is the move to a long-term prison, a "centrale."

"Properly organized, you are then. Not like this pissy dump. Get a little camp stove, you can, and make a cup of coffee." An earthly paradise . . .

"Psychiatric institute, that'll be you. Soft. Do a little gardening for the guards, grow some fresh vegetables for them; they'll eat out of your hand."

This trial was a bore. One would have to go through with it. He'd got that wretched Dieudonné to give him a list of his investments and goods, both fixed and portable, that could be realized. It was an agreeable surprise how much there was. That would do something, he hoped, for the poor, the ones who could not "canteen." In France, with money, you can do anything.

La Touche went back to a book he had been reading, one of those Vera had brought from his library, solid literature much respected by the guards and all the prisoners in for "intellectual" crimes like fraud. This one was a rediscovery, forgotten since student days. A gem: Rudyard Kipling is a writer who has always been highly esteemed in France, and who translates well. A volume of short stories. One he was especially fond of, a fable—and he enjoyed fables—called the "Children of the Zodiac." After looking at the Book of Hours, passing his hand over the binding the way a man who loves paper does, studying the little message Vera had written him, he went back to this story looking for a particular passage. When he found it, he underlined it in pencil; he had been discovering the pleasures of annotation. If things go wrong, he told himself, I can make a "commonplace book."

The passage read: "After Leo's death there sprang up a breed of little mean men, whimpering and flinching and howling because the Houses killed them and theirs, who wished to live forever without pain. They did not increase their lives, but they increased their own torments miserably."

## 26. Diplomatic Illness
## of the Ministère Public

Judicial mills turned, even when they had little to grind. M. Szymanowski's instruction dossier went to the Chambre d'Accusation, a particular type of tribunal which does not sit in public, which verifies that the instruction has been properly carried out, that all the defense rights have been correctly respected, and that there are no legal flaws in the case to be presented against Mr. Thing. It works quite quickly, and after the occasionally interminable tergiversations of instruction the rhythm accelerates noticeably. The Procureur—or, as he is known in legal jargon, the Ministère Public—gets the dossier first, and within a strict time schedule is obliged to present his conclusions to the tribunal. There was precious little need here for time: the conclusions were simple and succinct.

"A triple homicide in circumstances allowing of no doubt, confusion, or mistaken identity.

"A Police Judiciaire inquiry carried out strictly according to rule and with every respect for defense rights. Medical opinion both immediately and subsequently confirms clear-headed and rational behavior of the presumed. Experts of scrupulous independence and integrity agree upon total lucidity. A unanimous opinion that personality problems are minor in nature and adequately compensated.

"Exhaustive inquiries reveal no political motivation or shading. No element herein could conceivably be held to compromise or embarrass any national interest. The sensitive and responsible position held by the presumed as a State Functionary can in no sense be held relevant to the actions alleged against him.

"The use of the word 'allegations,' while obligatory pending the decision of the Chamber to lay this information at the door of the Assize Court, must be considered a legal fiction. At no moment during the preliminary inquiry by the P.J., or the instruction subsequently set afoot, has the presumed departed from full and free admission of his entire responsibility. The rarity of this circumstance can in no terms be accepted as an indication of mental instability.

"In view of the detached, dispassionate, and disillusioned attitude of the presumed toward his wife and daughter, the Ministère Public sees no alternative to a prosecution based upon culpable, deliberate, and willful homicide."

The Chambre d'Accusation, to nobody's surprise, marked the dossier with the republican equivalent of "Le roy le veult." It is only the third stage in the six different phases of a condemnation for a major crime, and the most impersonally formal. It is roughly equivalent to, say, a Grand Jury of the Commonwealth of Massachusetts bringing in a true bill against Thing. We the People consider that Thing must be brought to

193

answer for his disturbances of the public tranquillity.

Behind these sedate affixings of seals to parchment there was a sense of scurry. An Assize Court sits every three months, except—as in Paris—where there is too much crime to cope with at this leisurely interval. It is a serious affair. There are three judges, who must all be Counselors to the Appeal Court. The Advocate-General, presenting the prosecution case on behalf of the Ministère Public, is likewise a person of much weight and substance. As counterbalance, in major criminal trials there is traditionally a formidable array of defense talent. Half a dozen names, of advocates whose reputation in criminal pleading is worldwide, crop up over and over again. Unless one or more of these names is present, the authorities are uneasy. Without them, it is felt, the jury may feel itself browbeaten by the thunders of the Procureur and the authoritative, sometimes haughty airs of certain Presidents—and the President of an Assize Court has very wide discretionary powers.

It happens occasionally that a relatively young and unknown defense counsel, by his skill, brilliance and determination, can make himself a mighty reputation and enter the ranks of the great operatic tenors. (All pleaders are actors, but not all overact.) But without a good strong cast, the public, and the press, may make nasty remarks about justice being seen to be done. Here La Touche, tiresome in many ways, had been unusually tiresome.

In a way (said the Procureur in private), that imbecile Dieudonné was at the bottom of it. One didn't understand how a sound lawyer, albeit no pleader and with no experience whatever of courts, could lose his head to this extent. Ten thousand advocates never go near a courtroom, and are the harder-headed for it.

Was Dieudonné perhaps in secret a sympathizer with the extreme right wing—that vague appellation containing a multitude of oddities? Certain it was that he had approached a Paris advocate of notoriously extreme views.

It could be something more personal and more deeply buried, a hankering for theatrical behavior in a man who had never done anything in his entire existence but write legal safeguards into contracts. However, said the Procureur, we aren't trying Dieudonné.

Directly he had heard the name of the Paris lawyer proposed, La Touche had flatly refused even to see him. Various people at this point had taken Dieudonné aside for a word in his ear. Trying to give a political complexion to an affair of this sort is a perversion of justice. A sound trial lawyer would see that it wouldn't wash. La Touche at this time had appeared to oscillate between apathy and cynicism, going as far as to say to the judge that he "washed his hands of the whole business" at a moment when he was much annoyed at the appearance of the psychiatrists. Since he had nobody but Dieudonné to represent him at the sessions of instruction, the judge had asked crossly for somebody, for heaven's sake, from a big criminal practice with experience of trial procedure. And when, after all this trouble, a really big gun had been persuaded that it wouldn't be a wasps' nest, and came down in person to see his client, accompanied by his bright young man who would do the donkey work during instruction sessions, La Touche had been extremely vexed. Suddenly coming out of his mantle of mute disinterest, he had said politely that sorry, but he didn't want this simple affair dramatized by a Parisian pleader whose presence alone in a courtroom would be a honey pot to journalists. Even more vexed at a session of asking reasonable questions and getting obstructive answers, the judge suspended the instruction and sent for Commissaire Richard.

"It doesn't matter what we call it—say, a supplement of information. I want to find out what lies behind all this."

Richard said nothing and went away wondering what he was supposed to do.

"Castang, look," Richard said, "they're so tangled up in lawyers that Szymanowski's becoming highly fractious. Nothing to do with us, but he doesn't want to use coercion, so a negotiator is needed and that's you; you've always got on well with him." And, dragging his feet, Castang had gone to the "parlor." The P.J. can interview a detainee with nobody else present.

"At least you've got no axe to grind," said La Touche. "One can't talk to lawyers, who are incapable of understanding anything."

"I'm a passive instrument. My work is done and I've no further role to play. If I can do anything unofficially to help you, I will."

"Help," said La Touche. "I hadn't thought, in my arrogance, I would need help. But I've been wondering how to extricate myself from an impossible situation. The judge fusses about defense: I can't make him grasp that I neither want nor need any." And I'm not going to be a witness to your insanity pleas, thought Castang.

"I can't do anything with lawyers," he said tactfully. "All these judges and procs are my hierarchical superiors."

"I realize that. . . . I'll trust to your discretion," suddenly. "Between us, then, in all simplicity."

"Your experience ought to tell you that they're only trying to respect form."

"Having respected form all my life, which is too long, I wish to get this back into a human context. I'm resolved on that. I'm stubborn on this point."

"You can, I think, go along with them without hypocrisy. What were you intending—to stand mute?"

"More or less."

"It doesn't work—they go over your head and behave as though you weren't there, and the position is falser than ever. The judge commits a lawyer off the legal-aid list, and he is regarded as your mouthpiece. That he hasn't the remotest clue about your thinking doesn't worry them: the forms are obeyed; you are defended. You simply make a farce of the entire proceeding—it seems unlike you to approve of waste and stupidity. It makes no difference to me. I'm a witness, but neither for nor against you, a witness on procedure and not on the heart. I think I'm genuinely unprejudiced, and that you can trust me if you want to. If you don't want to, all right. The passive instrument will go back and tell the judge to forget it. But I remark that there is no lawyer or guard present here. You can speak, and freely."

La Touche looked at him queerly. "Logically, my whole position lies in being illogical. You won't be offended if I say that to put trust in a policeman sounds illogical."

"But you must put trust in somebody. Not lawyers. Not cops because they've a secret tiny tape recorder and will play it all back to the judge. Who, then?"

"Very well, tell me."

"In this affair, I've only met one," said Castang seriously. "The painter's wife. She impressed me. I suppose she's Jewish—she doesn't have a funny nose or wear a wig or anything. Jews have that intransigence that forces one's respect."

"Ah," interested. "This is the party to which I should like to belong. Los intransigentes. The extreme republicans. Nothing political about that—do you understand? Nothing left-wing."

"Sure," said Castang. "My wife is, too."

"Tell me about the painter's wife."

"He was intransigent, too. As I understand. About art, I mean."

"Yes, indeed. In fact, that is at the root of this affair."

"I see . . . At least, very dimly I think I glimpse. All right. She refused to make any complaint against you. No court action, no appeal for damages, nothing either civil or criminal. She was too young to have been in a camp, but I've met this attitude in a woman who'd lived through Ravensbrück."

"Yes. I hadn't made the bridge. I know nothing of camps. I have not, you see, lived at all. I simply want to end as a man."

Strange, thought Castang, how these lawyers—for this is just another lawyer—adopt weirdly sentimental attitudes. A few weeks in jail, and he starts throwing heroics.

"Reduced to essentials," Castang said, "she doesn't bother about forgiveness, or justice, or any of that nonsense. Nothing to forgive. What justice? Belongs to God, huh?"

"We won't indulge in theology," said La Touche dryly. "Stick to this world."

"By all means. Compromise with it. Go with the

punch. Since they want you to have a lawyer, take one. Tell him what you please. As long as he can talk, at the trial . . . You have to go through with the trial, you know. As long as the shrink doesn't pronounce you unfit to plead." As dryly as La Touche.

"Over my dead body."

"Good, then, I've done my best. Given you, I hope, good advice. Do something with it."

La Touche was polite to the judge at his next session, and Richard was pleased with Castang.

"That's fixed up," Richard told him. "Fellow off the legal-aid panel. Bright, too. Delighted with this. His name's Weber. They were a bit fussed lest it sound Jewish. He looks a bit swarthy, too. We're getting like Heinrich Himmler around here, worrying about the physiognomies."

"All that's needed now," said Castang, "is to make sure that none of the jurors are called Abdul."

"The Procureur," said Richard, swinging his swivel chair and stretching his long legs out, "is going to have a sudden attack of a virus infection. Oh, no worries— nothing to put him in the hospital. It won't last above a week or so. But an acute laryngitis, depriving him of vocal cords."

"Has he Arab blood?" asked Castang with an innocent look.

"You may well ask. He can disqualify himself on grounds of personal friendship with a Counselor to the Accounts Tribunal, meaning they've both got money invested in the same concerns. Odd, by the way—did you know that if you're a civil servant in the Accounts Tribunal you're exempt from jury service?"

"La Touche says continually that he's lived his entire life divorced from reality. On the other hand, so is a cop exempt from jury service."

"I should bloody well hope so," said Richard. "How did you find him, by the way? Without going into any details."

"The shrinks say he's sane and who am I to contradict? A bit spiritually illuminated—one often finds that in intellectuals serving a spell in the jug. The monastery syndrome."

"Ah, yes, devote ourselves henceforward to prayer and good works: it's all that peace and quiet."

"Opting out."

"Shave your head. Wear sandals. The 'Hare, Krishna' performance."

"They're selling stuff on the street called Spiritual Sky Incense," said Castang. "Smells awful. Jasmine and all."

"Sounds like that stuff Lasalle puts on his hair," said Richard. An unusual piece of disloyalty, from him, but they both disliked the oleaginous Commissaire who was officially Richard's second, but who preferred his office to the street. "All right—just thought I'd let you know. Now we've work to do; where's Fausta?"

"Is this Weber German or what?"

"Oh, Alsatian or something. Safe, anyhow."

"Who's going to be President? Not that old anti-Semite Mirecourt?"

"I don't know, but rest assured, if it is he'll be striken with laryngitis, too, at the crucial moment."

"It'll be even more of a farce than at present seems likely unless they've someone good."

"Where have you been, then?" asked Richard as the door opened.

"Changing the typewriter ribbon. One has, you know, to wash one's hands," said Fausta blandly.

## 27. The Witnesses

The life of an officer in the Police Judiciaire has lengthy stretches of monotony and wearisome bureaucratic routine. He forgets the paradox of his vocation, which is its ambivalence. When engaged upon an inquiry, he is an officer of the law, part—and supposedly the sharp point—of the judicial apparatus, armed with great powers as well as a technical bag of tricks and a gun, restrained by powerful safeguards from becoming a petty Hitler through the arbitrary exercise of these powers. In the different stages of his inquiry, he is directly responsible to the Procureur of the Republic, the Judge of Instruction (who possesses such strong legal instruments that Napoleon remarked that he was the most powerful man in France), or the President of the Tribunal. It would seem thus logical that the P.J., executor in penal matters of this legal grip, should depend from the Ministry of Justice. In fact, in nearly all countries he belongs to the Ministry of the Interior. One is reminded of the comic interchange in the English farce, between the Home Office and the Foreign Office.

"They're aliens. Consequently in your department."

"No, no, my boy. These are undesirable aliens. Consequently in your department."

For about nine months of the year, the average P.J. officer uses his gun to stir cups of tea with. His life is that of any civil servant, translating reams of statistics into more statistics, to feed the voracious appetite of other civil servants for nice, neat, manageable figures that look well on the page. And, like every government functionary in the world, he is always a year or two behindhand. Talleyrand, it is now universally agreed, was a very great man, and never more than in his notorious, abominable, appallingly intelligent instruction to his civil servants. "Not too much zeal."

In France there is a long and amiable tradition of exciting, sometimes brilliant cinema, the French equivalent of the Western, concerning the conflict between a bandit, mostly heroic, and a cop who is a cynical bastard and a badman. The badman has to win, a type of masochism much enjoyed by audiences, who are put on the rack and love it. In this tale, Commissaire Richard would be a cynical Mephisto, manipulating everything because he's a raging psychopath; Castang would be shot—he might show some gallant futile courage—and . . . But the reality is, as Vera is rather relieved to find out, a little less catatonic. Most of the time, Castang is unzealous, and comes home promptly for meals. A typewriter basher, he forgets all about being an officer of the law, and consigns people like La Touche (administrative equivalent of the rough end of a pineapple upon the digestive tract) to oblivion. Vera—concerned if unzealous about soot on windowsills, the health of the trees opposite, the ridiculous price (doubled in twelve months) of a small tin of tomato concassée, and the nagging need for doing-something-about-that-ghastly-bathroom—does the same. When La Touche actually came up for trial, it was a shock.

Vera wasn't a witness to anything. She had gone

back to the judge after her last interview with La Touche.

"You gave me a hard task, and I'm not really up to it. I don't think I can reconcile my conscience to any more." M. Szymanowski had been nice about it.

"I wish a few more people would act according to the dictates of their conscience. Very well, I won't ask you. I take note that the man has become more co-operative, and there are small but healthy signs—he's more in touch with reality, less catastrophically apathetic. I don't know how much you have contributed to that, but certainly your influence has been a good one."

To Castang she said only that she found La Touche "too complex: I didn't feel firm ground under the feet. I'd do better to stick to fraudulent managers. Assassins are like eating giraffe; it might taste good but one feels so bloody guilty." Castang just said, "It's for you to decide—did you remember to buy black-currant juice?"

Castang was a witness. He sought an interview with Commissaire Richard, who said he didn't know but Fausta would; she always did. Fausta had it all written down; her memory was exceptional, but, like a Judge of Instruction, only the written word was valid.

Fausta said, "I had a long girlish chat on the phone with the Procureur's secretary—you know? She has red hair and smells rather peculiar, but she's perfectly human with women. I know you'll say she's a bit lesbian, but it's not true at all: I can tell, believe me. The one Lasalle fancies, but he never got anywhere. Good." After this brief but telling sketch: "The President will be M. Ziegler."

"God, another Alsatian."

"Next best thing to M. Braunschwig."

"Good; next."

"The assessors are M. Tatin."

"Oh, God, Demoiselle." Poor man, he suffered from his name. There is a sort of French dessert, an upside-down affair of apples and caramelized sugar, most delicious when properly done, called "tarte Tatin." Who the Demoiselles Tatin were is a piece of information long lost in the mists of gastronomic myth, but alack, Judge Tatin had an old-maidish way with him.

"And—this is very good news—Mme. Marie-Laure Rampollion."

"Hurrah." Marie-Laure was a perfect sweetie, and by far the prettiest judge in France, and at forty-seven her figure aroused the fierce jealousy of Colette Delavigne, the children's judge, who was twenty-eight.

"Those lovely gentle eyes," said the men, sentimentally.

"That great huge sexy mouth," said the men, even more so.

"Sensitive," said Fausta. "And I know about her throat, so please . . ."

"Next."

"The Procureur is going on leave."

"Aha."

"Not—I quote textually—on holiday. Nor is he ill. But on medical advice, at a good time of year, he is taking the thermal cure at Contrexéville, for nervous overtension."

"Oh, that's absolutely brilliant."

"Occupying, consequently, the seat of the Ministère Public will be the senior substitute, M. Mars."

"I don't know him," said Castang.

"I do," said Richard. "Blond hair in waves as though lacquered. A piss-vinegar expression. Very quiet and controlled. And extremely, frighteningly bright."

"Oh dear."

"In this instance, an unknown quantity."

"Oh dear, pity the poor policeman. I have nervous overtension."

"You can go to Contrex for the cure when the Proc is back. Can't risk meeting him there, wrapped in his little towel with his navel sticking out."

"Can't I go to the Pyrenees?"

"No, no," said Fausta, "that's only for women with gynecological troubles."

"But that's me," said Castang despairingly.

"Keep your eyes firmly fixed on Marie-Laure."

"Yes, that's something. But what will the jury be?"

"Artisans, housewives, respectable craftsmen. And no Jews or Arabs."

The intercom phone rang.

"Castang, a lady would like to see you."

"Does the lady give a name?"

"A Mme. Davids."

"Tell the lady I'll be right down." He found her more than handsome, in gay and pretty clothes, and asked her out for a cup of coffee.

"I'm not wearing mourning or anything," catching the approving eye. "I've got to be a witness, and since you're the only person I know I ask for a bit of guidance in this labyrinth, which is frightening." She sounded joyous, and he felt some embarrassment.

"I'm afraid that the defense may try to blacken your husband."

"No," calmly. "I'm a defense witness."

"Oh . . ."

"Maître Weber wrote me a very nice letter. He's going to plead insanity."

205

"Naturally. He may have a hard row to hoe; the experts seem against him. He could have asked for a further check before the instruction closed—too late now. I imagine he thought it unlikely to find any more favorable conclusions. It's his only way out, of course."

"Psychiatrists don't know everything. Yes, thank you, I think I will have some cake. The man's spring is broken. He has let himself die. It is a phenomenon similar to what was seen in the camps a lot. The musselmen they were called. They refused everything progressively, and simply died of inanition. But I think he can be brought back, and I want to do my best. I'm sure it's irregular, and improper, and everything else, but I want to appeal to you. If you can reconcile it with your conscience—not to be too severe. I must add," hastily, "I'm not an emissary from the lawyer, and I'm not trying to interfere with you."

"The lawyer wouldn't have tried," said Castang, smiling. "I'm a piece of colorless glass; the light goes straight through. I'm only a technical witness. I haven't any real opinion about his state of mind—and if I had it would be inadmissible. I'll certainly not be hostile, but I'm only allowed to testify on procedure. You, on the other hand, will be much more valuable. You could have asked for civil damages, and you haven't."

"M. La Touche's civil lawyer offered me a large sum. I have refused. To do him justice, he wasn't trying to buy me."

"But the suggestion might have been made."

"Yes," turning her candid eyes upon him. "And I would have refuted it."

"I suppose yes, it is improper. I'm a bit on your

side, but I can't show it. A word, if I may, of completely private advice—don't pitch it too strong. The court might think, Oh, emotional appeals, and react against you."

"Yes, I understand. And thank you very much. You give me the courage I needed."

"You won't quote me to the lawyer? I'd be obliged as well, you see, to react against him."

"I won't. And he's a sensitive man. Which is perhaps better than clever. He's clever, too—I think he'd see that it wouldn't do."

He reported the meeting to Vera, who listened with her face held carefully reserved.

"I've changed my mind," she said afterward. "I think after all I'd like to come to this trial. Do you think there'll be a great crowd?"

"Yes and no. The political stuff has been so carefully and elaborately defused that there isn't any whipped-up manifestation. Inevitably there'll be the morbid—hoping for sexy details."

"Revolting."

"Justice is public, girl. They can't put too severe a filter on who gets in—defeat their own ends. There'll be a lot of reporters—it's undoubtedly going to be more interesting than seemed likely. No trouble where you're concerned—the police have a few methods of polite bribery. I can get the doorkeeper to hold you a place, and keep it quite anonymous."

"I won't arise theatrically in denunciation."

"I should sincerely hope not. Anyway, Ziegler has the reputation for standing no nonsense from anyone."

"I don't agree in the least that La Touche is a musselman. It's interesting, though, that she should take that attitude."

## 28. The President of the Court of Assize

"Gentlemen, the court," said the doorkeeper in one of his moments of glory, unnecessarily loud. Everyone stood up, Vera hoisting herself.

She had never seen La Touche in ordinary clothes. In a gray business suit with an unexpectedly bright tie he was impressive. The prison pallor did not show up; the prison haircut suited the austere face. The haggard look she had last seen had been replaced by composure, serenity. The two policemen on either side, with their habitual hangdog look, were simply footmen; he took their presence for granted.

The President, and despite his extraordinary clothes —all those robes and a funny hat—was even more impressive. Vera was unprejudiced, being unused to courts and to the paternalistic, slightly silly look, as of a playing-card King, of many magistrates. A noble face, which she could draw, and did; several newspapermen were doing the same. A bulky man, but not fat. A face with a great deal of bone in it. Caricaturists could seize upon the nose, which prolonged the big forehead with hardly any interval. This Greek look went round the courtroom like the beam of a lighthouse.

The assessors (noticed the experienced onlookers) were both less inconspicuous and less probably somnolent than usual. Beneath the graying curls and the roly-poly features, M. Tatin's brightness of eye belied the

"Demoiselle" nickname. Mme. Rampollion, with her celebrated elongated throat and amazingly wide mouth, was more than just stately. All the journalists wrote down "good court" in unison.

M. Mars, wrapped in the fearsome robe of the Ministère Public, and on the platform with the judges (the term "parquet" comes from the olden times when the prosecutor was on "the floor"), had a closed face giving nothing away. He looked strangely and, if it is possible, appealingly young. Certainly he was not attempting to project an artificial severity. He looked like La Touche: calm and self-confident. This resemblance—they had almost the look of twins—gave added pleasure to the gentlemen of the press.

Maître Weber—alone and the more impressive on his bench, which was usually full of black crows shaking their sleeves behind the accused and his cops—police guard—looked well up to his job. The variety of people who had muttered "looks Semitic" were now quiet—it was the same group that had muttered about the President's nose. M. Weber was a young man, and quite unknown. It didn't worry him at all to be alone where ordinarily le prime donne of the Paris bar would be sitting. He was fat, curly, comfortable, with a blue chin and library horn rims. He sat admirably still and unwound, with no nervous fidgeting, his sleeves left in peace. Vera felt obscurely comforted.

The public seemed reasonably well behaved. Vera's neighbor, who appeared to be a hardened trialgoer, smelt of peppermints and muttered wise comments to himself, but inoffensively. Like the technically minded at a football match, who count the number of touches or corners, and write it down. In technical terms, of course, as when the two teams scrimmage, and one succeeds in "hooking against the head."

The President's voice was ideal: quiet without being soft, perfectly audible over coughing.

"The court sits. Only one preliminary remark. As most but not all here present are aware, the discretionary powers given me are great. I remind you that I will rigorously enforce the rule that no signs of approbation or disapprobation will be permitted. Any person giving vent to such will simply be put outside. Furthermore, I intend that this tribunal shall proceed with sobriety and courtesy—and, where possible, brevity. May we have the jury, please? . . . I inform the public—those who are not hardened rogues—that the prosecution may without explanation challenge four members of this jury chosen by lottery from the list, and that the defense may refuse five. . . . Very good. M. Robert Abdessalem is excused. Let us please have no shuffling or muttering. Mme. Angèle Wirth is excused. . . . M. Gabriel Hautbois, we pray you to excuse us. There is absolutely no aspersion cast upon your character or judgment. . . . Admirable. We are now assembled. I ask the public to take note: there are nine members of this jury chosen from among yourselves, the public, making twelve when completed by the court. Good. Ladies, gentlemen. I ask each and every one, solemnly, whether you are in any way, even remotely, related to any party in this case? Any previous acquaintance, social, professional, or personal? Have you been in the service of the accused or any other party? . . . Admirable. The court will swear the jury. We will all stand up. We take off our hats. I remind the public that this is not superstition. This is a profoundly grave and solemn instant;

we are not just paying lip service to Armistice Day. Members of the jury, each and every one, this is an ancient and beautiful formula, nonetheless alive and vivid from being embodied in Article 304 of the Code of Criminal Procedure. You do swear and promise before God and before men to examine with the most scrupulous attention the charges that shall be preferred against the man named to you. You will betray neither the interests of this accused man nor those of society that accuses him; you shall communicate with no person until after the declaration of your judgment; you shall listen with no hatred or wickedness, with neither fear nor affection; you shall decide following the conclusions of the prosecution and from every means of defense, in obedience to your conscience and your innermost conviction, with the impartiality and the firmness belonging to free and upright men, and solemnly to keep the secret of your deliberations, even after judgment is passed and your functions have ceased. . . . This solemn oath I now administer: you will each upon the calling of your name raise your hand and repeat distinctly, 'I do swear it.' . . . I thank you."

Slipping back into his conversational manner: "M. La Touche, will you have the goodness to stand up? This, I may say, is formal. The court establishes your identity. We ask you to confirm your name, place and date of birth, your curriculum vitae, your background and circumstances, your past career. . . . Thank you, that is clear. I address a remark to the jury and the public. The accused's high place in the public administration, his eminent qualifications, his notable services rendered to the state have a place here in this trial. Under strict limitations. In the eyes of the Penal

211

Code, M. La Touche could have spent his life pushing a wheelbarrow—oh, yes, the Code has eyes." It got the first laugh, a mild one. The President let the laugh go.

"The law dictates that the judges—you, the jury—should have, and I quote, personal experience of human realities. For this reason, the debates in this court are oral. During the process of instruction, the law recognizes only the written word. Here in the Court of Assize, the opposite holds good. It is the spoken word to which you will listen. The witnesses will be asked to narrate. They may be interrupted and questioned, but it is essentially their words—their own words—to which you will pay attention. The Ministère Public, by tradition, may pose direct questions to witnesses. It is the usage that the defense puts queries through my mouth. This has been known to create an impression that the court is biased in favor of the prosecution. I wish it to be known that under my powers I give permission to counsel to question witnesses directly. With the sobriety, courtesy, and, where possible, brevity I have previously insisted upon.

"Shall we have the witnesses? . . . Have the kindness to place yourselves in line. . . . You are the witnesses. Some of you are experts, and one of you is an agent of the administration; that is to say, the police. These witnesses have previously sworn, upon their honor and conscience. There is normally no need for you to swear again. But in fact—again under my discretionary powers—I do ask you to swear again, and I hope you agree." And the formula, which has suddenly ceased to be one. Without hatred or fear . . . We've a long way to go, thought Castang. When we say it, we mean it.

"The witnesses will retire, to be called each in due turn." Vera had a mad impulse to get up and follow them.

"M. La Touche, I ask you to listen to the act of accusation, which the clerk of the court will read. In accordance with the terms of Article 327, I enjoin him to use an audible and intelligible diction." Even the two cops were infected by the ripple of laughter.

"I understand the laugh. But why did the legislator take pains to include such an injunction? So that you should all understand that the Assize Court does not try a man until every condition attaching to the pursuit of this man by society, and his examination by the instructing judge, shall have been fulfilled. We do not do this lightly."

No, thought Vera, he isn't just being theatrical. This care taken to inform the public about technicalities that easily become meaningless is good. And it is like a theatre. They have played these roles over and over. To make it come fresh each time . . .

"We are trying this man for taking away life. No man may do this in peacetime without being called to account. The law prescribes that the state may take away life, after exact and strict controlled deliberations."

There was a quiver, as of antennae, among the journalists. For the first time, something crucial had been touched upon.

"This sanction, in our time, is almost unheard of. But it exists. If the situation arises, in our deeply felt respect for life, we examine it with very great gravity. M. La Touche, I proceed now to interrogating you upon these facts, the fundamentals of the case against you."

## 29. Examination

"Would you prefer to speak from where you are?" the President asked in the easy, conversational tone. "It is the general usage, but you could come closer. The law states that you should be free from constraint."

Maître Weber, for the first time: "With respect, might that not be rather increasing the constraint? Psychologically."

"He is at liberty to say, and you to advise him."

"I'm quite happy here," said La Touche in his social-occasion voice, which Vera had never heard. Oh, I beg of you, she said silently; don't let him treat it as a joke.

"Good. Then I ask only that you pitch your voice just a little higher. I hear you very well, but I wish the members of the public sitting at the back to hear you, too. If it does not inconvenience you," courteously.

"Not at all." Very much the visiting lecturer: a slight problem with the local acoustics.

"I shall be repeating, broadly, the questions put to you by the Judge of Instruction. You are free, naturally, to add to or take away from the answers you then made. The accused," in one of his punctilious asides, "is of course not on oath, unlike the other witnesses. He may be questioned by any member of the court, as well as the advocates. If in the course of questioning a member of the jury feels he wants further enlightenment upon a point, he may ask to put a question, and I shall allow it."

"Would you like me to narrate?" asked La Touche simply. "Would it make the procedure less laborious? I mean no sarcasm there."

"By all means, narrate if you prefer. I may have to pull you up—to elucidate a detail for the court. Or possibly even to protect you from faulty interpretations."

Weber had folded his arms, and appeared made of stone. M. Mars adopted the air of the intelligent listener in the first row who will animate the lecture by asking a question.

"I will only prompt you in case of your memory lapsing," said the President, with the ghost of a smile in the voice but none on the face.

"As you have heard," said La Touche, "I am a functionary in a senior position. I keep—I am using the present tense to make this more vivid—office hours, but these are flexible. I try to keep my work as far as is possible up to the date and even the minute. This allows me occasionally to leave my office early. Such was the position on the date in question. I add that it was a very hot day—nobody felt like working much. I reached home, thus, in midafternoon. This happened, I should say, sufficiently rarely for the event to be unexpected.

"At my home—I skip the geography, which can be shown with plans and photographs—I knew that M. Davids was working. He was a painter, engaged upon a portrait of my wife. He worked there every afternoon about that time. I took an interest in this picture, and wished to take an hour to study and discuss its progress. I greatly admired and respected this painter, who was a man of the highest talent and a most interesting personality. Is it allowable and relevant to say a word about the painter?"

"It is."

"I made his acquaintance under strange circumstances. I had at that time a daughter, my elder daughter, a student in Paris. She got into bad company and was taking drugs. This circumstance was largely my fault. Suffice it that she was in circumstances of want, poverty, and misery, and that I did little to help her. There was a gap between us and a lack of communication. This is not irrelevant. The painter, M. Davids, found her vulgarly but graphically in the gutter. He took her in, sheltered her, fed, clothed, and warmed her. He also painted her, as I subsequently learned. He succeeded in stopping, or at least arresting, her dependence on drugs. When she was as he judged restored to health, some few months after, he brought her back to me, explaining what he had done and asking me to show her the affection and confidence she lacked. This act struck me very forcibly."

"We are given to understand," said the President, "that he also seduced her. Is that so, or did you so understand the situation?"

"I don't know about seduced. That he slept with her? He didn't tell me as much." A small, timid laugh amidst the public. "I suppose I am man of the world enough to realize that the probability was overwhelming."

"We cannot," said the President, colorless, "hear Mlle. La Touche as a witness, alas. She has since died. The event has nothing to do with the jurisdiction of this court."

"Nothing to do with the painter?" interjected Mars casually. His voice was light, without the resonance of

216

the President's, and more metallic than that of La Touche.

"The fact was the subject of judicial inquiry, under a commission of interrogation issued by the Judge of Instruction," making the ponderous phrase sound manageable—one of M. Ziegler's gifts. "The investigating officers were satisfied that her death had nothing to do with any party in this case—a fortuitous occurrence. She had relapsed into renewed dependence on drugs, and may have taken an overdose."

"I am satisfied," said Mars. "I beg your pardon, M. La Touche."

"I beg it of you"—Je vous en prie, that handy, untranslatable, almost meaningless French phrase used in doorways and lifts; universal expression of courtesy and consideration. "I wish only to let it be understood that M. Davids brought with him unusual recommendations to his high qualities."

"We will hear Mme. Davids as a witness to this episode. Continue," said the President.

"I asked him to stay, and to paint a portrait of my wife."

"With your permission." The soft, deep voice of Weber. Not elaborately measured—as conversational as the others.

"Maître."

"To stay—as a houseguest? So that he had your full confidence."

"Certainly."

"I need not ask whether your wife had your full confidence? It is rhetorical."

"She had—naturally. I knew, of course, that she was occasionally—sometimes habitually—unfaithful to me."

217

Two or three voices began phrases.

"Monsieur the President," boomed Weber. "Since you give me the latitude—one moment, Monsieur the Procureur. Let's get this clear. First, whatever your wife's habits or attitudes, and whatever your overt or suppressed knowledge and suspicions—this man was a houseguest. Face the fact: he abused that privilege."

"Yes, he did."

"And may I say this? As a man of the world, you may have had suspicions, or knowledge, of your wife's divagations." Wanderings from the path, thought Vera. Good word. "In the interest of family harmony and marital unity, you behaved as though they did not exist."

"That is exact."

"Until such moment as you could not avoid seeing, realizing, acting."

"We're not quite that far yet, Maître," said the President, almost apologetically.

"If the word is too harsh," said Mars softly, "correct me. You showed yourself a complaisant father, where your daughter's virtue was concerned. I think that here you showed yourself a complaisant husband."

"That is also exact."

"Do please continue."

La Touche did. He had walked in, found nobody, walked upstairs, "I have light feet," apologetically: walked into a bedroom, found—in a defensively ironic voice—"a debauch."

Clamor. The President, while as light-handed as La Touche was light-footed, wasn't having any. A debauch!

Yes, a real debauch. What else would one call it?

218

He had stood studying the situation. Thought about it. If you could call it thought. Said to himself, you know, "What does one do?" Had made up his mind. Wasn't having that. Gone to the bedside table—a small one, little drawer. Little pistol. His wife's. A toy, given by him: she'd asked for it as a present. He knew how it worked. Certainly not loaded—a dangerous toy. . . . He'd loaded it. Well, yes, they were all a bit paralyzed. Taken aback. Anyone would be. Hadn't taken this seriously? Well, he was not a melodramatic man—ordinarily. And then he'd shot all three. The little pistol held six shots. He'd fired all six. Yes, quite calmly and deliberately.

The questions came from all sides. La Touche remained calm, both unhurried and unworried.

It was the President—M. Mars, continuing colorless, was careful not to ask it—who had to put it.

"M. La Touche—are you seriously saying you gave this thought and consideration?"

"I can think of no other way of putting the truth."

"Now, think carefully—I've noticed you don't use words or legal terms loosely, and you have had, of course, legal training."

"You're asking about premeditation. Oh, yes, I thought." The antennae rippled like a cornfield.

"Why?" The word was delivered quietly, with deliberation.

"I have given that much thought. I have to admit that I still really don't know. To free myself? To simplify? To avenge? To act as a man, at last? As to that, the time has come now."

"The advocates will interpret your answers. The court will appreciate—but not prematurely. Tell me,

M. La Touche, are you aware that this answer may be damaging to you?"

"Perfectly."

Vera thought that everybody must be holding his breath. Certainly she was. The President made a slow movement, draggingly, with his hand.

He picked up a little red book, something like the "Thoughts" of some chairman or other.

"I am going to read to the court . . . Section 1 of the first chapter, of Part II of the Penal Code, concerning crimes and felonies against the person." There it is, thought Vera. Literature is full of the voice of doom. Nobody need put on any black caps. The voice was uninflected.

"Article 295. 'Homicide committed voluntarily is qualified as murder.' Article 296. 'A murder committed with premeditation or ambush is qualified as assassination.' Article 297. 'Premeditation consists in the design formed, before the action, to attack a determined person, or such person as may be found or met upon the way, even when such design may depend upon circumstances or conditions.' Article 298. 'Ambush consists in waiting for a lapse of time either great or small, in one or more places, while lying in wait for an individual with the intention either of giving death or of inflicting violence.' " A change of tone.

"Articles 299 to 301, concerning parricide, infanticide, and poisoning, do not fall within the province of this court. I pass to Article 302. 'Every person found guilty of assassination, parricide, or poisoning shall be punished with death.' You appreciate, M. La Touche, that we shall be obliged to consider narrow and exact definitions of the law."

"I appreciate," said La Touche bleakly.

"Monsieur the President . . ." said Weber, enormous in his black robe.

"You will have plenty of time, Maître, and opportunity. I think that we can now hear the witnesses."

And all of a sudden there was Castang, small, businesslike, and unemotional, standing on the parquet in front of the judges.

## 30. The Witnesses (2)

"I call you first because you were, as we understand, the first person on the scene after the event. You are an officer of Police Judiciaire. Your qualifications and experience are admitted. You will please narrate in your own words the events of that afternoon."

Castang did so. It sounded painfully curt, but he was asked to be no more than factual.

"No more than factual, Inspector," said M. Mars dryly.

"I have nothing to add."

"Maître Weber," said the President.

"While I quite agree," said Maître Weber, "that a police witness is not a technical expert on state of mind, he was the first person on the scene. His professional training and experience give weight to his personal viewpoint."

"That is reasonable," said the President.

"This collected and calm demeanor, M. Castang—it's fairly usual in such circumstances?"

"As far as my experience goes. One sees it in road accidents."

"So without diagnosing where you are not qualified, or using terminology inexactly, physiological shock or something akin? Yes? And you asked for a doctor right away, and that wasn't for the victims—they were plainly dead? Two purposes, you'd agree. Both sound —to help you know whether you could question this man, and to bring him rapid treatment in the event of his needing it. Agreed?"

"It is always desirable to have a medical opinion rapidly."

"An opinion on state of mind—he wasn't ill otherwise. My question is quite straightforward and simple —did his behavior seem natural and normal?"

"To me, no, it didn't."

"Have you experience of a cold-blooded assassination? Of a man coolly planning and carrying out a triple murder?"

"No."

"Have you ever seen behavior you would call callous or unfeeling, as opposed to this unnatural calm, in crimes of violence?"

"I've seen apparent indifference in a professional criminal after beating a man up. Some time later."

"No, your professional or hardened criminal wouldn't hang about waiting to be arrested, would he?" Both joining in the laugh.

"This occasion did not resemble that other at all?"

"No, not in any sense."

"This man expressed both pity and remorse?"

"According to my notes made an hour or so after, he felt and expressed pity, and said that he wished to feel remorse. I don't pretend to have the wording absolutely exact. That was the sense."

"And by then he was showing signs of regaining his equilibrium?"

"Yes, I think he was."

"Factual enough for you, Monsieur the Procureur?" asked the judge, smiling. "All right, M. Castang, you're excused; take a place." Vera felt quite legitimate pride.

Medical witnesses in courts are generally only too aware of the possible embarrassments inherent in giving a clear yes or no to anything much. Better to be overprudent, and the prose sound woozy, than imprudently go out on branches when there are woodcutters about. The wooziness of the prose gets worse as the technicalities designed to mask it fly thicker. As Mrs. Gradgrind, a woman who suffered all her life from ologies, remarked when dying, "There's a pain somewhere in the room, but I'm not certain I have it."

The doctor Castang had called was hopeless, but the Judge of Instruction had noticed that, too, and the President did now.

The three psychiatrists—two of them, anyhow— made efforts to be comprehensible, were patently honest, and one at least showed courage. But temporary insanity is a very thorny affair. You see, said the one who got talkative, with a man like this you must be very cautious. Highly intelligent, extremely sensitive, trained to debate abstractions. . . . . Oh, yes, most courteous; outwardly cooperative but in fact obstructive. Habits of skepticism, self-control. A whole series of public and private personages. Neuroses, undoubtedly, some crippling. But nothing psychotic, nothing disabling. Both centrifugal and centripetal patterns. My dear man, you're paranoid, I'm paranoid; everyone is, more or less. The question is, how well do we handle it? People have rigidities, hankerings for authority, reinforce their fears and uncertainties in a liking for rules and regulations. Is this psychotic? Then the whole Ministry of Finance had better get packed off to Sainte-Anne. I realize that this man sought relief from stress, and a wound, and pain. Certainly it all appeared as a betrayal. Yes, he had deep respect for his wife's family milieu and trusted her to observe forms. Yes, he was most disappointed in his daughters and blamed himself for their failings, and sought to punish himself. Yes, the painter was a man he greatly admired and respected, and this weakness—more than the betrayal of hospitality or friendship, though both these loyalties were sacred—was a fierce blow. But I'm very sorry, I'm not prepared to use the term insanity. M. La Touche, as his whole life and career shows, is powerfully structured and has unusual command. Like Mr. Kipling's shipwrecked sailor, he is a man of infinite resource and sagacity. He behaves well in tight spots. The etiology of these patterns . . . Well, etiology is the assignment of a cause; the philosophy of causation. In medicine, the science of the causes of disease . . . Now, the ethology . . . damn it, it's the science of character formation. . . . Look, this is not physics: we can't express these things as an algebraic equation.

And that awful word "para." Parapsychology, and paranormal . . .

Mme. Davids did better at first, because she was so refreshingly not paranatural. Worse as she went on, because she got angry with M. Mars. The President, hideously watchful for any accusations of anti-Semitism, began to be a little chiding. She did a lot of good, thought Castang, but she also did harm. She was too much on La Touche's side. Her simplicities, and simplifications, were too much like those paradoxical Yiddish jokes, an offense to French Cartesianism. Castang, listening, was too often reminded of the classic "If the rich could hire the poor to die for them—what a living the poor would make!" Davids in Paris had just got frustrated. Perhaps in New York a La Touche would have been simply delighted. "Those two frightful women—Lord, man, I make you a present of them." La Touche had had such peculiar notions of personal honor. And so had Davids. . . .

Once the doctors had been got rid of, it sailed ahead faster. There were few witnesses. Maître Weber had assembled a couple of distinguished gentlemen who explained the extreme integrity of La Touche's professional and personal life, and said that an assault upon this integrity would be a thing he would react against. With violence? If the threat appeared violent.

The President appeared encouraged. La Touche, re-examined after the witnesses, was brief.

"We will break for lunch. Since this trial is notably free from irrelevancies and since there is no civil pleading on behalf of injured parties, I will ask the Ministère Public to present his requisition after lunch. If the pleadings are not lengthy, there is no reason why deliberations should not take place today." This briskness startled the journalists. Good law, though, thought Castang. As long as he doesn't appear to be hurrying things unnaturally. A trial of one day only is almost unheard of in an Assize Court.

Lunch—Castang, like a good cop, had reserved a table in the local café Au Palais a day before—was mostly silent. He ferried Vera. They ate beef à la

225

mode, which was the "plat du jour"; the less prudent only got sandwiches.

"La Touche has been pretty good," Castang said. "He did one silly thing—that idiot remark about acting like a man. Self-dramatization, and self-pity."

"I don't know what to say," said Vera, "so I'm saying nothing."

"Ziegler's good. Weber's doing well."

"You did well."

"I won't get into trouble," said Castang, shrugging. In a way, he wished he had.

## 31. Pleadings

The formal phrase is "The word is with . . ."

"La parole est au Ministère Public." And this remark, brief and sober, launches the formal speech of the prosecution.

M. Mars rose to his feet, took off his glasses, arranged his robe, and placed his notes exactly where he wanted them, with no rhetorical gesture. His voice was very well pitched, his tone dry and unemotional, his command of himself and his material total. Once more, Vera was struck at the uncanny resemblance between him and La Touche; they certainly might have been twins. A very dangerous man.

He would not be lengthy. The President's appeal for brevity and sobriety was one to which he could respond with, he hoped, exactitude. Courtesy—certainly. That was an indispensable attribute of society. And so was severity. He was here to represent society. An unpopular role in certain quarters. Today, society suffered grievous and insidious attack from every quarter. And above all, its essential basic unit—the family. He would not embroider. Nothing here was on the borderline. No issue was shadowy. No trial here of abortionist or drunken driver, no homicide by imprudence or motivated by social conscience. This was basic. By admission, by legal proof, by realization and acceptance at the earliest stage, this was homicide with premeditation. No witness queried that. Everything now rested upon responsibility. That this responsibility existed was likewise admitted by all, save by Mme. Davids, whom he respected and admired, and whose ethics—he would make a brief quotation from Hannah Arendt—were based upon the necessity for total forgiveness. Society, alas, could not accept that. Charity—yes. But the notions of charity and justice cannot be confused.

A diminished responsibility? He could and did accept such a concept. In practically all cases, save hardened professional crime for venal motives. Here —he wished he could. M. La Touche had not acted basely, ignobly. But he had acted coolly, with calculation, and in full knowledge, accepting the responsibility. He had with perfect deliberation chosen to put himself outside society. He would have to accept the consequences. Not natural? Not normal? No. But deliberate. By so doing, he renounced the protection of society. He was an outlaw. No society, even in epochs when the rules for its preservation are held sacred, has ever been able to tolerate the outlaw— he who flouts the basic rule "Thou shalt not kill."

"Anarchist" is an emotional word. But it means "he who denies the existence of law."

The Prosecutor did not attack the individual. He was the defender of society. The defender of the individual, left with no defense, would launch an attack upon society. The court would hear. The court would appreciate. Society would be accused of being Fascist; he, its defender, would be painted a Hitler. The jury would decide. The jury was society.

Of guilt or innocence there was no question. Every effort had been made. The experts had strained the resources of scientific explanation. But in their conscience they could not say that responsibility was not present.

Punishment. He had given this much thought. Prisons he disliked, but until the legislator found other means of rehabilitation—and this was a most thorny subject—one would have to reckon with them. But for La Touche? In the case of a homicide with premeditation, a triple homicide, he could—the law admitted no less—ask for nothing less than criminal reclusion in perpetuity. And this was—according to his conscience—a cruel and unusual punishment. Could it help? It could not. It would be the accelerated ruin of a man who had been noble and upright. It could benefit neither society nor the individual.

Some form of rehabilitation through psychiatric treatment? A facile, seductive solution. It could and did work in numerous cases. Here it was pure hypocrisy, an evasion of responsibility. La Touche was neither insane nor even psychotic, nor likely to become so. It was excluded.

The recourse to extreme mildness, falsely equated with "comprehension." Such measures as a prison sentence suspended, the placing of the person under strict measures of surveillance and control? He was a strong believer in these. The person who has failed in an ordeal of life, which is cruel, who has fallen on stony ground—yes, wherever possible he would attempt this. The weak, the humble, the misled, the uneducated, those who have suffered long and patiently before collapse—here justice was mercy. Here in this court, a day or two previously, he had asked for such measures to be taken, and the court had agreed. To reiterate the circumstances would be emotional, rhetorical. A woman who had killed her alcoholic husband and her handicapped child, in the extremity of her despair.

Can we speak of despair here? "I would here be false to the role I have claimed were I to renounce the gravest of my responsibilities. The accused has left himself no way out, and I see no way out for him. It is for these cases that the legislator has—in wisdom— left a loophole. There is a temptation here to metaphor. The body, in its wisdom, when threatened by infection gathers its resources. Antibodies, complex immunological processes, given to the body to protect it from septicemia. These defenses cannot, upon occasion, cope with a grave infection that has been neglected. The result is gangrene—death. The only recourse left is to surgery, to amputation. Members of the court, in my soul and conscience, I do not ask you for a death penalty. I require it of you."

With nothing visible upon his large face, the President brought himself out of his attitude, the attitude of complete concentration with which the music lover listens to a very well-known piece. Even the best-known of pieces—say, the Seventh Symphony of Beethoven.

"The word is with the Advocate for the defense."

Weber, thought Vera, is not unequal. A good man comes up to scratch, like a boxer at the bell.

What, she wondered, is "scratch"?

He's equal to it, whatever it is. Massive, large, courageous.

"I will try to be even briefer than the Ministère Public. The learned and skillful, eloquent and concise Advocate-General has left me, you may think, little ground for maneuver. I do not want it. He has left me few ways out, loopholes, bolt-holes. I do not want them. I am a young and inexperienced advocate, chosen at my client's express desire from the legal-aid list, designated by the leader of this bar. That would be an excuse for my failure to rise to these heights of eloquence. I do not want it. I want nothing, members of this court and jury, and you the public, but the simplest and most obvious justice. No charity, no rehabilitation. Neither high-flown ethics concealing the most barbarous and primitive of society's sanctions, nor sobbings over our gangrenes; and abortion or alcoholism, however much the Advocate-General may pretend not to use emotional frames of reference —these are emotional, polarized, irrelevant words. The truth is that the Advocate-General does not know how to grasp what has happened here, and in his confusion grasps at the most emotional of all concepts—eye for eye, tooth for tooth. The most primitive, the least efficient, and the most senseless of all.

"You will ask me to avoid rhetoric, and you will be quite right. The death penalty is simply beneath contempt, and you will not consider it for a single instant. It is disgusting, nauseating, revolting to every honest man. The legislator has kept it among our statutes.

"You may think, as I do—as thank God an increasing number of persons do when they make the effort to think, and that is your duty—that the legislator knows very well that there is no good government without a corresponding degree of cant and hypocrisy.

"The prosecution tells you—I might be permitted to say arrogantly—that there is no question of guilt. Guilt? Who is going to judge of fire, who has not been through it? Some of you may have felt the heat of the fire in your lives, and drawn back, pretended it did not exist.

"Insanity? Do you know what insanity is? Does anyone? The three eminent specialists we have heard do not. Are you going to arrogate to yourselves a superior knowledge?

"I ask you to recall the words of the other expert witness—the experienced and honorable officer of police, who replied to questions with truth, without fear or hatred. He was guarded, and he is quite right: he is an agent of the administration, and he was seeking to insure that his professional conduct be found blameless. This cool and impartial witness to the crucial moments after the dreadful and irrevocable act did not wish to condemn, to blame, to pass judgment.

"Shall we, all these months after? The experts know nothing, and take refuge in learned jargon. We know nothing. We do not understand. We have, up till now, made little effort to understand. We might very well conclude, together with the wife of one of

231

the victims, that there is no understanding but in total forgiveness, but more is asked of us. We are asked to judge; the law insists upon it.

"Technically—technically!—guilty, no doubt of it. This alleviates and simplifies our task. There is no claim for civil redress—another blindfold the less. Nothing prevents our looking at this case with honesty and loyalty, both to ourselves and to society.

"The man is sane now; a child could see that. The man was not sane then, and a man—or woman—can see that. He acted, within the honor and integrity which nobody has questioned, for what he thought to be right. That he was mistaken, we will agree. That he acted in the grip of forces at that second stronger than his training, his skill, his intelligence, character, experience, and comprehension, I am convinced we agree. Psychiatric treatment—I am in agreement with the Ministère Public—would be futile. Prison—again —senseless, stupid, utterly negative, and cowardly; a denial of all our responsibility to society.

"I now ask you to consider. The man has already suffered. How much? A few months of prison, and is that so very terrible? These defense advocates invariably dramatize and sentimentalize. Do I do so in asking you to go just a little further? What of a man who loses everything in one blink? His family, his honor, and home. His position, livelihood, and the universal respect and esteem. He has nothing now: he is stripped naked. This is a greater punishment than any you could mete out. Greater even than the death sentence you have heard demanded by the gentleman who claims to embody all the rights and privileges of society. Those are not contained in him but in you. The man in the seat of the Ministère Public has an essential and noble function, but you must not forget that he is the prisoner of that function.

"You can do better, and you will. Since we are dealing here with a matter of technical guilt, which this man has never denied or sought to evade, the law requires of you a technical condemnation. You may pass a prison sentence, and you will suspend it. That will be one more reminder, to rest with him every day of his life, of that dreadful day.

"This will be justice. I have not asked for mercy, for that comes too late. Mercy was a thing to ask for him before it was the thing to ask of him. At the moment when he walked up the staircase of his home, unaware of the dreadful spectacle awaiting him. At the moment before, subjected to an intolerable strain, something in him snapped. At that instant, members of the jury, he had two, three seconds for deliberation. You have all the time you ask for.

"I have done."

The shuffle that fluttered through the public; the sighing, coughing, and muttering that can suddenly swell into a "mark of approbation" was quelled on the instant by the President.

"The court," he said in a loud clear voice, "is fully appreciative of and grateful for the scruple and moderation shown by these pleadings." The flutter subsided slowly to silence, subdued by the eye commanding the courtroom.

"M. La Touche. Before entering upon the final phase, that of deliberation, it is customary in our courts to ask the defendant whether he has something to add to the conclusions of the pleaders."

"Monsieur the President," slowly and uncertainly, "I—I beg your pardon."

233

"Do not hurry," kindly.

"Monsieur the President, and my judges"—his self-command was impressive—"I believe that it is customary for the defendant to say that he associates himself with the words of his defender, and to throw himself upon the mercy of the court. Yes, of course. . . . I mean I do so. But the conclusions of the Advocate-General . . ."

"M. La Touche," kindly, "the court has not yet deliberated."

"But with these conclusions I have much . . ."

Oh, sit down, Vera longed to shout. Weber's face had gone back to stone. M. Mars had an expression of serene expectance, that of a man waiting to be insulted and armed against it.

"Sympathy . . ."

"You need not say now what you feel under stress. Other opportunities will be given you."

"You are right. I am given to errors of judgment. I will say nothing."

"Very well," gathering up the courtroom between his hands, open before him on the desk; switching back, perhaps with relief, to formal language, "I now pronounce the debates closed. I order the deposit of the dossier with the clerk, who will close and seal it according to law. We will read the list of questions to which the court must answer. These concern, as the law dictates, not only the question of eventual guilt, but all the circumstances attendant upon the acts of the accused, which may be held to extenuate, or, in certain cases, to aggravate guilt if guilt be found."

We've had a few bad moments, thought Castang. What was that imbecile about to say? That he thought yes, a death sentence is a splendid idea? Clever tactics of Mars, to show "severity" by an exercise in logic that lets him pretty neatly off his hook. It might almost have been a speech for the defense! Leaves then no loophole, really, but to let the fellow go right this minute. Weber did nicely to show quickness of mind, but the Procureur had done his spadework for him!

"Before retiring," said the President, "the court has yet another vital duty. This is that I read to you Article 353 of the Code of Criminal Procedure, the text of which is also, as the law demands, exhibited in large and readable type in this place where we deliberate.

" 'The law does not demand an account from the judges of the means whereby they reach decision, and prescribes no rule wherefrom particularly depends the fullness and sufficiency of a proof. It prescribes that they should ask themselves in silence and recollection, seeking in the sincerity of their conscience, what impression has been made upon their reasoning by the proofs afforded against the accused, and by the means employed for his defense. The law asks of the judges one question and one only, summing up the full measure of their duties: "Have you an intimate conviction?" ' 

"I terminate by recalling to you Article 365, which states that the replies made by the Court of Assize to the questions posed are irrevocable.

"The accused will stand down. The doorkeeper will guard the entrance to the jury room, to which no person is granted access without my express permission.

"The hearings are provisionally suspended."

## 32. Deliberations

The public had plenty to occupy it, for some time at
least. Excited voices echoed in the corridor, on the
stairs, and in the vast hallway known as the Salle
des Pas Perdus. There was a queue for lavatories,
telephones, and to get one's word in first. The journalists milled about furiously, and the concierge collected various small bribes.

The professionals had all made their little arrangements. Castang's were to bring Vera down the stairs
and along the passage leading to the offices of the
Judges of Instruction. Not to M. Szymanowski, who,
since finishing his task, had withdrawn officially from
all outward sign of interest, wrapped in the cloud of
detachment that expresses the strict legal separation
between instruction and judgment.

They slipped into the office of the junior judge,
Colette Delavigne, who was a friend, and who had
arranged her schedule so she could spend this time
with them, in quiet and at least relative comfort. Her
clerk and her secretary made coffee in the outside
office. Colette, finger on lips, produced a brandy
bottle: needed.

"Already? . . . Ziegler was quick; is he good?"

"Very."

"Demoiselle?"

"Didn't say anything, except for associating himself with the sentiments expressed by more or less
everyone."

"Fine. And Marie-Laure?"

"Spoke briefly and well, to the effect that whatever opinion one might possess as to the role of the female sex in modern society, here the law recognized no distinctions whatever. Particularly in a sex case. Naked adulterous wives slaughtered by husbands avenging their honor were strictly for the birds."

"Marie-Laure," said Colette, who did not like the lady all that much, "is always particularly strong on everything concerning bottom-talk." The French phrase "histoires de cul" switched them all skillfully into objectivity.

"Well?" she asked.

"Well, what?" Castang said. "La Touche is a bit crazy. Provided a variety of slight but telling demonstrations. Weber succinct: suspended sentence. Mars succinct: this won't do, that won't do, so all we're left with is the death penalty. Since, plainly, that won't do, and in view of La Touche's odd behavior, Ziegler will steer them to the nervous-breakdown formula. Which is what both Mars and Weber want, and so say all of us. Excellent."

"Was that what it was?" asked innocent Vera. "I couldn't understand. Mars frightened me out of my wits."

"Just explaining that prisons are no earthly use, either forever or for a fortnight, once one has meditated upon one's sins. We're lovely and early—four-thirty." Vera wondered whether La Touche was reading Vespers.

"They won't take long in that case," said Colette.

"What happens exactly?" asked Vera timidly.

"Oh, my darling . . ."

"I spare you the section on judgments," said

Colette, grimacing at the little red book, which she, too, had on her desk. "Briefly they mayn't come out. They chat. Ziegler puts himself in the background and makes the others talk, bringing them out. They vote after a while to get the mood and general feeling. Then, bit by bit, get the voting more precise and exact. As often as they like. It's secret, of course, in writing, and the President burns the bulletins after reading them aloud. Much like electing a Pope."

"But he must have a huge influence on them," Vera said, voicing an objection often made.

"Not as much as you'd think, and even a bad judge can't budge them—they've seen how bad he is, in court."

"Have you done it?" Vera asked.

"God, no," Colette said. "I'm only allowed in felonies at the worst, with two others, and no jury. Even for children the assize is special—must be Appeal Court judges. I could be an assessor, for children's assize."

"But if he was set, say, on getting a conviction . . . he must have such overwhelming moral authority."

"It takes at least eight to four for conviction. A seven-to-five is an acquittal."

"Ziegler," said Castang positively, "isn't a convicting judge."

"What are they going to do, then?" It was a well-known trick of Vera's to get things explained three times, very simply and slowly as to a backward child. People who did not know her, watching the explanations being examined carefully for signs of speciousness, sophistry, or cant, mistook the obstinate skepticism for impenetrable stupidity.

"Jail is a good place for a nervous breakdown,"

238

Castang said. "Now we're all nicely rested, we can face the psychiatric clinic with equanimity. Suspended sentence is even better, as Mars was careful to point out, once rid of the alcoholic husband."

"But he said just the opposite."

"Oh, Vera—always takes everyone literally."

"Certainly. As he said, there's all the difference. This is a man with trained, formed decisions and judgments, not a poor wishy-wash carried helplessly along on the tide of events. With all the sophistication of several generations of leisured, cultivated upbringing."

"Which did not equip him to handle domestic crises," said Castang patiently.

"But will the jury agree with all that?"

"Hence the deliberations," remarked Colette.

"Even if there are a few fanatics on the jury," said Castang, "Ziegler will quiet them. And remember Marie-Laure. She's not going to allow sob stuff over that abominable Hélène."

"This is all very well," said Colette, "but juries are very odd. It's true that since the judges sit with them there are fewer of those idiotic sympathy votes. But it's also true—and any judge who has sat on a jury will tell you—that they're unpredictable and have the oddest fixations one can never quite get rid of."

"Certainly, if the trial's been bad. This one's been exemplary."

"Plenty of things about justice are exemplary," said Colette gloomily. "Even the Code can appear a monument of generous common sense instead of just dim-witted industry. I do agree that Ziegler is a good judge. But the rarity of that strange animal may lead one to overestimate its significance. A judge without prejudices is like an honest cop. He tends not to rise in his profession."

"What kind of prejudices?" Vera, still patiently puzzling away.

"Anything you like. Racial, political, sexual, religious. Or just plain personal. Judges being people, you see—it's the good thing and the bad about them."

"As far as that goes," said Castang, "everyone was exemplary. And we never heard a whisper about politics."

"I have never really understood why there ever should have been a whisper about politics," said Vera.

Colette chided Castang. "You're much too impatient. You live in a world where every sort of sordid little pretext is used as a possible stepping stone in the rat race. She doesn't, and you persist in being ungrateful. All those things like unselfishness and loyalty and simplicity, and you always tend to treat her as though she were divorced from reality. Whereas you know perfectly well that without her . . ."

"I'd be just another crooked cop. It's just that I detest feeling ashamed of myself. Like judges."

"You'd better keep quiet now," said Vera chillingly.

"Look," said Colette, "you are perfectly right; there isn't anything political about this and never was. But, being a senior government functionary, La Touche is judged—no, that's not the right word; opinions are formed about him—by hypocritical standards. In some way or another, he was friendly—and it doesn't bother me—with a lot of these Arabs who have so much money. It still doesn't bother me."

"It bothers me, and I think it deplorable that these people who go canting on about their oppressed brothers don't spend a penny to step in when the rice crop fails," Vera said.

"Now you are oversimplifying. La Touche may have been most concerned about the rice crop, and been working away quietly at it. These people seem always to have one thing in common and that is their morbid, pathological suspiciousness. By alleviating that, he could be doing a useful job. Meanwhile he's bound to a large extent by governmental policies. All right so far? Isn't it just the same as being a policeman? If a diplomat is not dishonest in his attitudes, how will he ever do a job?"

"Jesuitical," Castang said.

"That's the word for every one of us," said Colette, taking one of Castang's cigarettes. "Let's leave that. La Touche makes friends with a painter who happens to be Jewish. He doesn't care. What importance has it? That the man is a good painter. Just as the other man is a capitalist with money to invest, a long way before he is an Arab. But people have these facile, superficial attitudes learned from television."

"The great big lying cant machine," Vera said.

"My dear friend," said Colette. "Easy on. It's just a machine, manned if you like by bands of posturing monkeys giving a little information, and inevitably people think they get a lot. So you can't blame them, can you, when the wiseacres say that La Touche was either using or being used? Either way, because of his senior position and all his pals, he's a threat. That's all. Nobody would believe he liked Davids for picking that girl up and cherishing her, which shows he's a nice person. A nasty person, which most of us are, would have loathed Davids for just that reason."

"Maybe La Touche did loathe him," said Castang,

"and worked him deliberately into a position where he could treat him as hateful and contemptible. The psychs have been on about it no end."

"I don't care," said Colette. "I'm not judging this, thank heaven. I've only learned one thing judging children, and that is that the adults, so called, behave very much the same way. Aphorism, there are awfully few adults."

"Surely you can shut the office," said Castang. The secretary and the greffier had gone home. "Let's go have a chat, and think about supper."

"I want to hear the verdict," said Vera.

"So do I, but if we take some pizza or something we don't have to worry about the soup getting cold."

They went out to the café called À l'Écoute du Palais—the Listening Post. Most of the journalists were there. Beginning to get impatient at its taking too long, feeling hungry, worrying about where the pizza would be eatable.

"Starve those fellows into submission."

"Can't deprive a judge of dinner."

"Big chap like Ziegler, looks like a strong man with a knife and fork."

"Alsatian, isn't he? Give him a great big sandwich stuffed with sauerkraut."

"Phone's ringing."

"Bugles are sounding recall, boys," shouted the patronne. "Will everybody settle up, please? We've no shortage of change."


"Gentlemen," said the doorkeeper. "The court."

The President looked much more tired than La Touche.

"The court sits to enounce its verdict," in a dulled voice with no ring to it.

"I have here the list of questions drawn up for the consideration of the jury, with the answers duly apposed, signed, as the law requires, by myself as President and by a member of the jury designated by lot."

He's furious, thought Castang. It's gone wrong.

"I remind the assembly that a clear vote of two-thirds or over is needed to produce conviction, and that spoiled or blank votes count invariably in favor of the accused. The vote is guilty."

No reaction: none of the pundits had considered anything else.

"In the vote upon extenuating or aggravating circumstances, none have been found."

First sensation.

"Silence," said Ziegler.

Silence was restored.

"In the vote upon punishment, subsequent to consideration of the personality of the accused as the law directs, the options open to the jury depend upon extenuating circumstances having been found."

"Politics," said the peppermints man next to Vera, loudly. "Fellow too friendly to the Jews."

"Silence," said the President, departing for the very first time from his serenity.

Silence was imposed.

"In the event of extenuating circumstances not being found, the choices of the jury are restricted, exceptionally, to the fixed pains recognized by the Code."

"But they always find extenuating circumstances," said the lady on Vera's right, puzzled.

"Extenuating circumstances!" said the peppermints man with contempt. "Hypocrites!"

Silence imposed itself.

"The fixed pains recognized are criminal reclusion in perpetuity, and death. The court has refused to accept the first. The penalty has therefore been adopted in accordance with the recommendations of the Ministère Public."

"I didn't catch properly," said the lady. "What does he mean?"

"Motivations," went on Ziegler remorselessly. "The public may not be aware that contrary to the judgments of other courts, the Court of Assize is not bound to give the motives for its decision. This is because of the decision given by a jury as opposed to a bench of judges.

"The decisions of the jury," Ziegler said, plowing on, "proceed by positive and negative answers, and from their decisions there is no appeal."

"I don't understand," said Vera to the peppermints man, who seemed something of a legal expert. "There's always an appeal, surely?"

"No Appeal Court," he said angrily. "Only Supreme Court of Cassation. And they don't judge on fact. Only on law. They break the decision only if the law is bad."

"And is it?"

"Bad?" Breathing at her fiercely, "It's the best farce that ever was."

"Sorry, dear," said the lady on the right, "but I haven't quite caught on; he talks so with the points of his teeth."

"M. La Touche," said the President, now quite in

244

Vera's books; when she had first asked to be a prison visitor, she had read up on criminology and penology. Here, too, he found only laconic footnotes. The condemned is removed to the departmental prison, where he is placed in a special cell, under continuous surveillance. He may smoke, read, and write without restriction. Food is of a liberal nature. Visits are controlled in a "rather more strict" fashion: details are lacking. Such barbarous relics of medieval times as leg-irons have long been abolished. A prudish silence surrounds the subject of the guillotine—is that a medieval relic? It has no doubt benefited by all the very latest technological improvements, but there again there aren't very many. Like improving those other barbarous relics, the knife and fork. One supposes that the blade is kept sharp. Maybe they now have an instant-reaction quick-release system, though cops still talk about "pulling the string." Anyway, all that tedious muscular effort is now spared the operator, and the executioner is not overworked: he won't be going on strike or anything. Various other pruderies have been thought up by humane persons. You don't even catch a glimpse of the nasty thing till the last possible instant. The premedication department, that famous old glass of rum, seems a bit crude still, but it is hard to think of a local anesthetic that will do better. Even the pharmaceutical industry research teams, who are full of enterprise, cudgel their brains, as the saying goes, in vain on this point.

Commissaire Richard had little more to say than Colette: a mumble to the effect that juries were very odd, but if one were to make a sweep of all the medieval relics, there'd be no law left at all. What would we do then? Sociologists, Richard remarked in his occasional portentous moments, were like bad playwrights: they had no third act.

Vera knew little more. She had lunch one day with Colette (Castang, much bored, was investigating a supermarket holdup), but even inside the Palace of Justice there had not been much gossip; it had been a seven-hour wonder.

"It went nine to three, I think. Ziegler and Marie-Laure held out, and so did a juror. But that old Tatin stayed hard. And the body of the jury seem to have been resolute from the start. I don't know why. La Touche hadn't made a good impression, and then there's his background—oh, queer little things. It just added up wrong. Nobody wants to talk about it." And neither did Vera.

Time passed. The Court of Cassation, while slightly unhappy about a few of the procedural points, found nothing bad in law. So—well, it was up to the First Magistrate of the Republic. He'd commute, of course —he always did. And then one could arrange one-self comfortably. Find the fellow a nice job in the prison hospital or something. Parole him after a decent interval. People would forget about it all; they always did. Probably already had.

It came as something of a shock. The administration, like juries, was unpredictable, and the message was very curt. Telex messages often are, but Com-missaire Richard read it three times before sending for Castang.

"Don't ask me, because I don't know. Truly I don't. You are simply told to take a plane—expenses authorized—and present yourself at the Ministry— the central office in the Place Beauvau—at this time exactly, which you will observe to the minute. Slightly weird. Sorry, can't help you. Guessing is futile. Go, and doubtless you'll be told." Castang put on his best suit, to be on the safe side.

"Will you be back this evening?" asked Vera.

"I wish I knew. It's disconcerting. Perhaps I'm getting James Bond's job. We'll be moving into one of those very smart flats, the sort with closed-circuit TV in the elevator."

"I'd hate that."

"So would I. We'll cross that bridge when we come to it."

Nervousness; a rubbery condition in the thighs. Henri Castang, not being in form, is dropped from the ski team for today's slalom. Up steps. Pompous portal. Terrifying concierge person, controlling all the little pink permit slips.

"Yes?"

"Castang. I have an appointment. Don't know who with."

"I do," already bored. "Wait there." Not over five minutes passed.

"You're Castang?" said a quiet, chilly voice. He looked up. Recognizable without trouble, from press photographs and television appearances, the Minister of the Interior. Quite handsome, classical features. A slim figure, a bit round-shouldered but well tailored. Nothing much remarkable about him, except for the eyes, a blazing blue. Blue is generally considered a cold color, but these were hot, fierce, apt to strike terror. Castang wasn't impressed enough by Ministers to be terror-struck. He just wondered what the hell went on. How often did one see Ministers busying themselves with obscure provincial cops?

Not much hospitality round here. No glad-to-see-you-old-boy. The Minister just stood there with his hands in his pockets and didn't even look at him.

"Where's that wretched car?" he inquired of nobody.

"Coming up now, sir."

"About time. Else we're late. Come on," taking Castang by the upper arm, like a cop. The Cardinal's Guards will escort James Bond forthwith to the Bastille. He will remain there at His Majesty's pleasure. Signed: Richelieu. The Minister waved a cop aside, wrenched the back door of the car open, making an abrupt hand movement; Castang got into the car, and the minister jumped in beside him.

"Sorry, sir, but—"

"We're just crossing the road. Don't ask questions."

Two cops at the gate leapt to attention and saluted. A third, racing out into the road, blew a screaming whistle blast. The black DS came onto the Rue Saint-Honoré like the wrath of Jehovah, and before Castang had realized that "across the road" from the Place Beauvau means the Palace of the Élysée there were two more cops saluting, the door was being whisked open, the Minister was running athletically up another flight of steps, and Castang was stumbling incompetently under the disdainful bored look of the Paris policemen. Inside the hallway, a thin man in black clothes was inclining his head to listen attentively to the Minster talk. He beckoned to Castang with a calm, affable expression.

Double doors. Anteroom, vaguely green and gold. Style of some Louis or other, or maybe some Empire or another; he neither knew nor cared. The Minister was whisking through another pair of doors, but under Castang's nose there was suddenly a young man with a smiling, pleasant face, an open palm outspread, and unmistakable cop eyes.

"A moment. You're M. Castang, that right? Just the identity, if you don't mind. Ah, good, a policeman. I daresay you might be wearing a gun?"

"Well, I didn't know I was coming here."

"Quite all right," receiving the gun on his open palm, "no need to excuse yourself. A tiny moment." A second pair of hands slid from behind under his arms. With automatic ticklishness, Castang jerked his chest out, understood, held still while the hands slid downward and the eyes kept smiling peacefully into his. "Right. So sorry. Go ahead." The door was opened for him. The décor here was gray and gold; quiet, a little faded. Some velvet, some brocade, some white stucco, some pictures in gilded wood frames. The Minister, hands again in pockets, was talking silently to a portrait of somebody. One of his predecessors, possibly. Maybe the Duke de Choiseul?

Castang just stood there like a great clod of soil, but he didn't have time to get any duller. The third pair of double doors opened—the brocade on the far side was a dull ruby flash—and the President of the Republic walked in, shut the door quietly behind him, gave a quick sweeping look across the whole room.

"Good morning, Roger," shaking hands briefly with his Minister. "And you'll be M. Castang, correct?"

"Yes, Monsieur the P—"

"You just say 'sir.' Very good. Sit down. You don't know why I've sent for you?"

"No, sir," fighting down James Bond once and for all. Nor was it just the sack!

"No. I didn't want you to know, that's why. No previous confabulations or cooked-up stories. You're no good to me mortally embarrassed, either. Relax. Roger, just push two of the buttons, the white and the green, will you? I want to get acquainted with you, M. Castang, and it may take half an hour or more." The two sets of doors opened. Two menial persons stood obedient. The President looked at neither of them.

"The Justice dossier," to the secretary behind him. "A glass of champagne," to the footman behind Castang. The Minister, sitting with his legs stuck out, went on looking at portraits.

The service here was something like it. The President instantly had a dossier and his reading glasses. Castang, almost as instantly, had a small silver tray by his elbow, holding half a bottle of bedewed cold Krug, a little crystal jug of orange juice, two Baccarat glasses, and a saucer with six canapés.

"I want you at your ease," said the President, not looking up from his dossier. "If you smoke, there are cigarettes beside you on the little table. Take what you like and do not be intimidated."

There was a little matchbook, white and gold, saying "Élysée." Castang put it in his pocket. Nobody will believe this, otherwise. A policeman and the President: one material proof. He moistened his lips, as the saying goes, thought the hell with it, took a big swallow, instantly felt fine.

"That's exactly what I wanted," the President said, taking off his glasses. "All right, Castang; you're a state servant, you seem a good one. Forget your regulations for a few instants, and answer my questions. Be concise, yes. Be precise, yes. Be detached, yes.

251

That is all professional. The reason why you're now sitting opposite me swigging that stuff is that I want you to be personal."

The Minister didn't say anything, right to the end. He wasn't asked for any reminders, or any opinions. Castang never learned what he was there for. Presumably, they had a little chat afterward on the phone. He himself got thanked at the end, and got his hand shaken, but there are any number of obscure people in crowds who shake hands with Presidents during what the French call "crowd baths." There was a recurrence of the previous act: steps, black DS, cops, whistles, suspended traffic, salutes. And all Castang would ever be able to say was "Once, children, a very long time ago, the traffic got held up for me to cross the Rue Saint-Honoré." Even this was not the pleasure it should have been. While he was in the car with the Minister, the two piercing blue eyes were suddenly swiveled and plunged in like poniards.

"You understand the meaning of the word 'secret,' do you? I hope that for your sake you do. Because if you don't, you'll lose skin."

Decidedly, the hospitality of the President was better than the Minister's.

"I've had a very high and mighty memorandum," said Richard. "Exceedingly peremptory. So we're all going to obliterate this from our obedient and disciplined recollections. I hope, by the way, that your recollections were a bit disciplined."

"I think so. You'll never believe this, but I got a half of champagne. Krug, too."

"No!"

"Wasn't enough to get me pissed."

"How fortunate."

One could get trussed up with official secrets, singed and gutted and plucked until one was just a goose in the market. But one's wife was oneself: one was talking in one's sleep.

"Dieu," said Vera, much impressed.

"Yes, Dieu. Et encore."

"Is he bright?"

"Very. Had the dossier at the fingertips. Also knows how to use tools."

"Calling you like that proves it. In the long run, nobody knows more of it than you."

"I know very little about La Touche. I suppose nobody does. Even you. He's pretty odd, you know. Wants to die. Wrote to Pop saying so."

So had another complex character: a gangster who, condemned to life imprisonment for murder, had got hold of a gun, taken hostages in the prison pharmacy, killed a woman nurse and a prison officer before being overpowered, been tried for this new crime, been sentenced to death—hardly surprising—and caused some worry to the then President. His wish to die had, finally, been given him. One could say that the Presidential Grace had been accorded, not refused.

"Did he say anything interesting?"

"He quoted a few people. That old chestnut from Pascal about the Pyrenees and justice being contingent. Then he went over my head a little. Something from Simone Weil about nations never going to war for essentials but always for prestige. And some geezer who was a martyr in Roman times. Big shot, local Prefect, millionaire, owned half Aquitaine, offered himself as a slave to the Visigoths or some similar folk. Wrote all about it to a writer called Ausonius, who didn't understand and was most indignant about it all."

"And who did you quote?"

"Nobody much. Mme. Davids, a scrap. She has two sorts of Jewish story—besides the funny ones, I mean. One called a Haggadah, which means roughly a legend or a parable, and one called a Halakah, meaning action or law. That's this—I must say she pinned my ears back with her damned stories, but this one did stick. Apparently, it's Jewish law that a man declared unanimously guilty has to be acquitted. That is highly complex and technical, to do with there being twenty-three judges in a criminal case. But there's no Proc, and no defending counsel. So strictly only ten members of the tribunal are judges, the others being prosecution or defense, and if the whole court condemns, the argument runs that the man hasn't had a proper defense."

"None of that is the case here. And the jury wasn't unanimous."

"Doesn't matter. The modern version would be along the lines of God intervening in the debate, saying, 'You have condemned. But Me, I pardon.'"

"And did God tell you what He thought of that?"

"He didn't even tell the Minister."

"So still nobody knows."

"He reflects."

"Who was the man who wrote to Ausonius? He sounds interesting."

"I think somebody called Paulinus. But quotations made by Presidents aren't necessarily a guide to what they really think."

"No," said Vera sadly. "I learned that back in Czechoslovakia."

## 35. What Makes That Rear-Rank Breathe So Hard?

La Touche had taken up smoking, and seemed to find pleasure in it. He read a good deal, and wrote quite a lot. Most of it went into the wastepaper basket he had asked for, which the guards emptied without curiosity. Sometimes he tore a page out of his exercise book and put it in a manila envelope, whose privacy nobody peeked into.

"What do we need anyway—an art of living or an art of dying? What on earth is the use of a life one does not know how to leave?"

"Always this anxiety. A passion for 'survival' at any cost. Our admiration is reserved for those who 'fight back.' Reasonable and legitimate, as long as exaggeration does not give rise to cant. Survival can be ignoble. We admire, rightly, the Uruguyan rugby players who ate their dead companions when their plane crashed in the high mountains: that was a noble survival."

"The men who know how to die have been sentimentalized. Charles I was a despicable person, who realized some important truths about being a king. The Carmelites, who went up the steps singing, attached no importance to death. Find an example in the bourgeois class."

"Better . . . the English soldier who said, 'I am just going outside, and may be a little time.' Snow gives an easy death, it is said: one slips off comfortably to sleep. But it is the readiness which counts. There are certainly innumerable condemned criminals. I acquire no merit whatever. Less ignoble than survival, that is all."

"By all means, abolish this penalty if it can be done without cant. But a condemned man must be allowed to choose it if he wishes. As long as this hypocrite sniveling about 'respect for life' stops."

"Those who fail their tests should be given a chance to try again. And this does not mean prison, which is nothing but despair."

"I say to myself, 'I will be brave on Tuesday fortnight.' That always seems such a very long way off. But Tuesday fortnight always comes."

So it did. Commissaire Richard got an official letter.

"Well, the appeal has been refused: they're pulling the string on La Touche."

"It's what he wanted. I'm no longer surprised. Anyway, one never knows why governments do things. It's quite likely that some imbecile somewhere has quacked that firmness must be shown."

"You're being imaginative again," said Richard.

"All right, I know," answered Castang sulkily. "Bourgeois government can't be caught showing tenderness to one of their own and severity to Johnny and I'm not paid to say that. I know."

"We'll just stick to the point at issue," said Richard. "As you know, there's a long list of people obliged to attend executions and the Commissaire of Police gets his little invitation card, just like a Town Hall reception."

"I wouldn't be in your shoes."

"I've news for you: you are. La Touche has asked for you to be present. D'you want to refuse?"

"Yes. Rot the silly bastard; he's never been anything but trouble. Oh, hell, I have to say yes, don't I?"

"You do. You've never been, of course."

"Have you?"

"No," said Richard seriously. "It's the first time it's arisen. I don't like it any more than you do, and also it's not altogether bad. There are too many cops who say blithely they'd pull the string themselves. And if a cop's been killed one understands. But mostly they're desk cops. This is a lesson."

"For you?"

"Yes." Richard's moments of humanity were rare and sudden, and did not last long. "To be honest, I'll be grateful for your support."

"When?"

"Day after tomorrow." Castang did not tell Vera.

A lot of people got invitations to the government's dawn cocktail party. The President of the Tribunal, who read his with a face of stone: the Judge of Instruction, who made his worst face and was tart toward policemen. The Procureur who, to do him justice, said he'd go. M. Mars, however, said bleakly that he had forseen the event, although he had not expected it. Having taken one half of the responsibility, one could not evade the rest. I've done it before, said the Procureur, and you haven't . . . Well, I'll say no more.

The defense advocate, Maître Weber, who felt very sick.

Inside the prison, the director talked to guards, doctors, chaplains. "There's a rather horrible ritual—this stuff with a white shirt and processional solemnities. There's no use talking about being simple or human, but for the love of Christ let's make sure we're efficient."

The Protestant chaplain asked his colleagues for a whisky. "This man's officially a Huguenot, so I'm on the line. He says he doesn't belong to any church at all, and maintained that even before, but he agrees he's a believer. Well, now, we're all grown up. None of that ecumenical nonsense need apply. I'm just asking you for professional solidarity."

"Well, yes, of course," said the colleagues.

"It'll be a new story about the Protestant, the Papist, and the Yid," said the Catholic chaplain, helping himself to more whisky. "Will he take Holy Communion?"

258

"He says he will, and I'm convinced it's with a true heart. So I thought both of us—?"

"Sure, but what about old Finklestein here?"

"No bother at all," said the rabbi comfortably. "The Youps will be there. In fact, I hadn't known quite how to tell you, but he sent for me and said he'd killed a Jew and how did one go about asking forgiveness. We have edifying texts for the occasion; they'd do you both no end of good."

"And what about our esteemed Moslem brother? They're very good when it comes to capital punishment."

"And one small offense against charity, Father."

"I only confess nowadays to my analyst."

"We must certainly ask him; I know he has a special blessing. There was that Arab boy a year ago who got commuted, but it did look for a while as though. And we Semites, you know . . . I know, too, that it would please La Touche."

"Right," said the reverend gentlemen.

"I have an awful sinking feeling. I know it's only death, but they suffer, you know. That stuff about it's only knee-jerks is crap."

"So did Christ suffer," said the rabbi briskly.

"I'm certainly not saying gas is more humane. It's just that as a military man, I have a prejudice in favor of bullet wounds."

"I'm all for lung cancer, myself. An unreconstructed pacifist."

"You'll be turning vegetarian next. It's just that I'm a bit frightened about cold sweat and vertigo."

"So are we all. So is he."

"No; we can't let him be braver than we are."

## 36. What Makes That Front-Rank
Man Fall Down?

"A touch of sun," said La Touche, changing shirts.

Castang had been cowardly. He hadn't gone home at all, and told Vera he would be out all night, but nothing to worry about—nothing unsafe.

"An Englishman," said Richard unexpectedly, "called Ralee—or is it Ralay?—asked for a second shirt. I could do with one."

Stand outside it, Castang told himself. Everyone here could do with a second shirt. There is, also, a strong smell of whisky.

"I'm not very keen on the taste of rum," La Touche had said to the director. "I'd rather have a brandy if it's all the same to you."

"I put a hell of a Mickey Finn in it," admitted the doctor afterward. "Strung up like that, one can't tell how quick it will work. But some muscular relaxation anyhow."

"I'm glad I took up smoking," said La Touche.

"I never thought," said the chief guard afterward to the director, "I'd ever live to see a civil servant make like Bogart." They were both connoisseurs of last reels.

"You know what he said in reality?" the guard said, delighted. "Throat cancer, you know. Hurts to swallow."

"All right, skip that part," the director said.

" 'I know I never should have switched from Scotch to Martinis.' "

"Oh, boy."

La Touche passed in front of Castang, and his eyelids wrinkled with pleasure. "Good. By the way, there's an envelope in my cell. You'll look after that?"

"Of course."

"Kiss of peace?"

"Thank you," idiotically.

"And incidentally?"

"Yes."

"Give my love to your wife," said La Touche.

"Go in peace," said the four chaplains. "Go with God."

"Shalom," said La Touche.

That was all.


Ho! the young recruits are shaking, and they'll want their
    beer today,
After hanging Danny Deever in the morning.

—*Rudyard Kipling*

## ABOUT THE AUTHOR

NICOLAS FREELING was born in London and raised in France and England. After his military service in World War II, he traveled extensively throughout Europe, working as a professional cook in a number of hotels and restaurants. His first book, *Love in Amsterdam,* was published in 1961. Since then, he has written seventeen novels and two non-fiction works. His most recent books have been *Gadget,* a novel of suspense, and the fourth Henri Castang novel, *The Night Lords.* Mr. Freeling was awarded a golden dagger by the Crime Writers in 1963, the Grand Prix de Roman Policier in 1965, and the Edgar Allan Poe Award of the Mystery Writers Association in 1966.

Mr. Freeling lives in France with his wife and their five children.